HINDU HOLOCAUST

Camellion let the four paracommandos come halfway across the darkened room. Then he leaned around the doorframe and calmly triggered both the Detonics autoloader and the Socimi submachine gun. Two of the Indians were killed within seconds by the 9mm Parabellum slugs. The second pair of commandos cried out in shock. *"Uh-ohhh!"* jumped from one man's mouth as he started to bring up his FAL assault rifle. He fell back, blood flowing from a bullet hole just above the bridge of his nose. The other paratrooper never realized he was being changed into a corpse. A jacketed hollow point poked him in the chest and punched out his heart. He fell with his eyes wide open and his mind closed forever.

THE HINDU TRINITY CAPER

Joseph Rosenberger

A DELL BOOK

Published by
Dell Publishing Co., Inc.
1 Dag Hammarskjold Plaza
New York, New York 10017

Dell ® TM 681510, Dell Publishing Co., Inc.

ISBN: 0-440-13607-5

Printed in the United States of America

July 1987

10 9 8 7 6 5 4 3 2 1

DD

This book is dedicated to
Basappa D. Ghosh—
Thanks for the files.

Technical advice for all Death Merchant books is supplied by Colonel G. E. Ellis

of
Le Mercenaire

Chapter One

Not today, Death! Richard Camellion reasoned that it was not likely he would stop a bullet when he walked to the front door of the house. The men inside would not fire at him. Why should they? Most of the taxicab drivers in Bombay were Sikhs and his disguise as a Sikh was perfect. He was bearded, wore a yellow turban, tight blue trousers, and a long red frock coat. Should Bedsloe or any of the Indians inside be watching, they would not be suspicious. They would only think he was just another cabdriver with a stalled vehicle.

His elaborate ruse was necessary. The one-story, nine-room house could not be approached without the occupants having a clear view of the attackers. To the north and the south there were not even trees. To the west it was a hundred feet from Mookmak Road to the front of the house. To the east, several hundred feet from the house, began the sacred area of the Parsis' *Dakhma*. Not even the Bombay police would dare desecrate the sacred soil of the Parsis.

Of a Zoroastrian sect, the Parsis differed from the rest of the population in their religion, their race, and their white skins. To that could be added their high intelligence. Very influential all over India, and among the richest bankers and industrialists, the Parsis were the descendants of Persians who had settled in India in the eighth century to escape Muslim persecution.

Many of the Central Intelligence Agency's contacts in Bombay were with the Parsis, who also controlled the underworld of the city. It was from a Parsi racketeer that Barry Dillman had learned that an "Englishman" fitting the description of Edgar Bedsloe was living in a *chawl*—a kind of Indian rooming house—on Mookmak Road, just beyond the municipal city limit. Bedsloe would not be alone. There were also five men and two women in the house. The two women were prostitutes, although officially they were "cabaret dancers," the Indian term for stripteasers. Four of the men were Untouchables and *kalla-bantru*—professional criminals. They were dealers in *libli*, a narcotic similar to marijuana, only stronger. The fifth man was Ceylonese. He was a smuggler who specialized in Western-brand cigarettes and American-quality condoms.

The Death Merchant, who had just opened the hood of the Indian-built Pulga automobile, stood in front of the vehicle and stared at the engine, pretending to be searching for the source of the trouble.

The Bombay police would not have had any trouble with the house. With characteristic bluntness the police would have used armored cars to surround the house. They would have then called out for the occupants to surrender. Should the men have chosen to fight, the police would have riddled the house with machine-gun fire. Camellion, Dillman, and Hondergriff did not have the cooperation of the Bombay police. To the contrary, should the Bombay police, or the Indian DARFA, the Indian intelligence service, learn of their activities, they would promptly be arrested as foreign agents. Besides, the Death Merchant needed Bedsloe alive. Dead, Bedsloe would not be able to tell where he had hidden the PALs. As clever as Bedsloe was, he wouldn't have the PALs with him in the house.

The Death Merchant's plan was uncomplicated; yet the scheme was not simple. The house contained a telephone. Camellion, with Steve Hondergriff in the rear seat, would pretend to be a taxicab driver with a stalled car. He would walk up to the house and ask to use the telephone. The strict custom of Indian hospitality would not permit anyone inside to refuse. All the arrangements had been made. Camellion had given the real driver the equivalent of $200 American (half a year's wages) for the use of the car—"to play a joke on a friend of mine." A phone call would bring a wrecker to take the taxi (supposedly) to a garage for repairs. Everything would appear normal to the criminals inside the house. And just in case one of the men would offer to have a look at the engine, Camellion had loosened one of the wires on the distributor.

The Death Merchant wanted inside the house for only one reason: to see how the rooms were arranged. The night of that very same day, he and the two Company street men and two Indian "on-contract" agents would approach the house from the direction the criminals would least suspect an attack—from the east. This would mean that

Camellion and his group would have to pass through the holy ground surrounding the *Dakhma*. The two Indian mercs wouldn't mind; they were Hindus and belonged to the Shakta sect, which worshiped Siva and Vishnu. They hated the Parsis. All good Hindus did. The Parsi guards would be put to sleep with Mertex dart guns. The Death Merchant and his group would then move in on the house with suppressed weapons. It was a dangerous operation, but one calculated to succeed within a factor of 90 percent success against 10 percent failure.

Camellion walked around to the right side of the taxicab so that as he bent over the engine, his back would be facing the front of the house. He couldn't risk anyone inside seeing his lips move as he spoke into the TTL personal communicator resting inside one of the inner pockets of his blood-red frock coat. The TTL had a range of only 1.9 kilometers, but that distance was adequate. Hondergriff was in the rear seat of the car. Barry Dillman was in another car parked beyond some trees, a thousand feet down the road.

"Barry, I'm going in," Camellion said, knowing his words would be picked up by the ultrasensitive mike. "If I should yell 'Help,' you and Steve come in fast. You got it?"

"No sweat." Dillman's voice sounded muffled inside Camellion's coat. "Anything else?"

"I'll have the communicator on," Camellion said. "At all costs, do not speak to me until I call first. I repeat: Do not speak first."

"Yeah, I know. Watch yourself."

The Death Merchant put both hands flat on a fender.

"Steve, get out of the car and pretend to be disgusted," Camellion said. "You're in a hurry, and you're raising hell with this dumb Sikh."

A tall man with a craggy face, curly brown hair, and eyes that missed nothing, Hondergriff got out of the car and began to shake a finger at "Kimar Srinigar," making an angry face and almost shouting, "I can't sit here all day! Get this goddamn taxi moving!"

In turn, Camellion pointed to the engine, shook his head, and began moving his arms and hands a lot, in the manner of angry and frustrated Sikhs. And he whispered, "You should have been an actor."

"You have to be an actor when you're in the Company, especially when you're a street man."

"Okay. Here I go," said Camellion. "Wait in the back of the car and let's hope I learn something that can be of use to us."

"I think you'd better hope you don't get a bullet in your butt,"

Hondergriff said grimly. "Those goons in there are stone killers. Beds-loe himself doesn't have a damn thing to lose. He knows what will happen to him if the East Germans catch him."

The Death Merchant turned from the car and started toward the house. Of traditional Kashmir architecture, the wooden *chawl* looked older than Brahma, the wood, unpainted for half a century, dark and weathered. The windows were so dirty, they appeared not to have been washed since the Deluge.

In his mind, he went over the Hindi words for "Good afternoon. My name is . . . ," etc. It had not been a matter of reading the Hindi words in Latin script/English letters. Camellion was blessed with total recall. The key was pronunciation. Under the coaching of Bagdin Sattva, one of the contract agents, it had taken Camellion only several hours to get the "just right" pronunciation, and the timbre and intonation. Speaking in Hindi may not have been necessary. There were 14 major languages in India and no less than 544 dialects. Yet almost everyone spoke Hindi, and in all major cities six out of ten people spoke English and eight out of ten understood English.

The Death Merchant was armed with more than experience and instinct. He carried a .22 Magnum High Standard Sentinel revolver in a holster strapped over the shirt sleeve of his left forearm, within the wide sleeve of the frock coat. The tight trousers, especially around the ankles, excluded any weapons in ankle holsters; their outlines would have been noticed. In an Alessi belt-slide holster, on the left side of his belt, was a Steyr GB eighteen-round autopistol, each 9mm cartridge a Blockbuster bullet with the power of a mini hand-grenade.

Looking anxious and angry, Camellion hurried over the stones of the walk in the weed-littered yard. He was soon knocking on the door, on the front of which was painted, in white, an elephant-head representation of the goddess Ganesh.

The door opened a foot and a dark-skinned woman, not more than twenty years old, peered out at Camellion. There was a round red *tilak* beauty mark on her forehead.

"*Namastey.* What do you want?" she asked in Hindi.

"*Namastey!*" Camellion used the same universal greeting, accompanying it with the *anjali.* Very quickly, he joined the outstretched palms of his hands together at about the height of the lips, then bowed his head deeply. The various grades of respect or condescension were determined by the speed with which the *anjali* was performed, and the degree to which the head was bowed.

Camellion said, "My name is Kimar Srinigar. My taxi is stalled and my customer is most impatient. I am afraid I will lose my baksheesh. *Main kyaa Teleefon kar hoon kumaaree* (May I use your telephone, miss)?"

Dev Nargis thought for a moment. *"Atcha"* (okay). She opened the door. "Come into the house."

Camellion saw that she wasn't dressed in a sari or in any other traditional garb worn by Indian women. Instead, she wore very Western-type slacks and a light blue blouse to match. She was barefooted.

"Come. The phone is this way," she said—and in English.

Bagdin Sattva had said that the chawl would have a large central room because it was the custom for people to share at least one meal together, usually the midday meal.

Camellion followed Dev Nargis into the main room and did a rapid eyeball check. Three rough-looking men, dressed in Western clothes, were sitting cross-legged on cushions around a low table on which were the remains of a *bhel puri,* Bombay's usual "trash" meal, a flavorful mix of puffed rice, potatoes, and onions, garnished with chutney sauce. The men were Indian, and the Death Merchant assumed they were the dealers in *libli,* even though one of them could have been Kor Bastihouran, the smuggler from Ceylon, or more correctly, Sri Lanka, as Ceylon was now called.

In the east wall were two doors, both closed, and two doors in the west wall. They were also closed. Bedrooms, Camellion told himself. *But where is Bedsloe? Has he eaten and returned to one of the rooms? Or could it be that he was never here? Or was here and left?*

South of the men, across the room and not far from a closed door in the south wall, was a charpoy, a low bed laced with ropes. At the foot of the bed, and six feet in front of another open door—*That room must be the Hindu version of a kitchen!*—sat Roona Awardani. Not as pretty as the other cabaret dancer and ten years older, she was eating *bhel puri* with her right hand. She didn't even look up at Camellion and Dev Nargis, the latter of whom turned to the three men.

"He's a cabdriver. His taxi is stalled on the road, and he wants to use the telephone," she said in English, in a subservient voice, as if apologizing.

Hounin Chatterjee nodded. "Be quick about it," he growled to Camellion in Hindi. A big man who looked older than his thirty-four years, Chatterjee wore a ring in his left nostril. In contrast to the other two men, he was very clean and his clothes were neatly pressed.

The Death Merchant didn't understand what Chatterjee had said, but from the tone of the Indian's voice, Camellion knew that the slob had not tossed a compliment at him. Taking a chance, Camellion gave him an *anjali* and said, *"Shukriya"* (thank you).

"Here is the phone." Dev Nargis pointed to the telephone resting on a three-legged table. It wasn't an old-fashioned dial deal but a very modern push-button speaker phone with redial and automatic redial. The Death Merchant was not surprised. Drug dealers always required rapid communications; an efficient telephone service was a must.

"Shukriya," Camellion said, and reached for the phone. It was after he had pushed the buttons with the fingers of his left hand and his arm was at his side when it happened. The .22 Magnum Sentinel revolver fell from his left forearm and struck the stone floor with a resounding clang.

The odds of such a fluke happening were about the same as being struck by lightning at the bottom of a mine shaft. Camellion used only the very best in equipment. There had even been double Velcro straps over the top of the revolver. Yet the straps had somehow worked free, and the weapon had dropped from the holster.

The reaction of the three drug smugglers and the two prostitutes was predictable. Roona Awardani stopped eating and stared at the revolver on the floor. So did Dev Nargis. She quickly stepped back from Camellion.

"Get him!" Hounin Chatterjee said venomously to his companions and jumped to his feet, cold-blooded murder in his black marble eyes.

Pindim Aurobindi and Gerin Hadjibawr were on their feet with twice the speed it takes to say "Oh, my God," the cunning-looking Aurobindi reaching inside his shirt.

The Death Merchant felt more stupid than afraid. It was as if he had gone to a banquet in his honor, had forgotten to put on his pants, and everyone was staring and laughing at him.

Dev Nargis didn't attempt to pick up the .22 revolver. Neither did Camellion. He didn't have time. He dropped the phone, reached for the 9mm Steyr GB under his frock coat, and then had to duck a square brass plate that Hadjibawr had thrown at him. He had the Steyr pistol half pulled from its holster by the time Chatterjee—very fast for a big man—reached him.

His breath a hot exhaust of garlic and onions, Chatterjee tried to polish Camellion's jaw with a left uppercut as his right hand streaked out and fastened itself around the Death Merchant's right wrist, preventing Camellion from freeing the pistol from underneath the coat. In sheer brute strength, the Hindu half-wit was almost twice as strong as Camellion. Fortunately, in hand-to-hand combat he was twice as dumb. Chatterjee always telegraphed his moves and depended solely on strength. Both are always fatal—except to another dunce. . . .

The Death Merchant stamped his left heel on Chatterjee's right instep, his target at the base of the first and second metatarsals, where the shin meets the foot. Chatterjee howled like a woman whose nipples had been kissed by the tip of a red-hot poker. He had good reason to scream. Not only had the Death Merchant's pile driver foot-stomp broken the main tarsus bone, it had also injured a large portion of the medial plantar nerve, as well as smaller portions of the deep peroneal nerve and the superficial peroneal nerve. In agony, Chatterjee had lost coordination of his entire right leg, which was now paralyzed, the pain so intense that it even throbbed in his groin. During that split second, a man of iron had been turned into a mass of quivering jelly. Chatterjee was helpless. Automatically he released Camellion's wrist and stood there swaying, looking astonished and stupid.

It was also during that twinkling of a bat blink that the Death Merchant stepped back, finished pulling the Steyr pistol from underneath his frock coat, and let Chatterjee have a front snap kick, the slam of such power that it could be compared to an irresistible force meeting an immovable object.

A quick, agonized scream jumped from Chatterjee. Again he had a very good reason to howl. The Death Merchant's power kick to his scrotum and testes had crushed the organs against the pubic bones and had half castrated him. Dropping into a black pit of unconsciousness from shock, Chatterjee didn't fall, not then. Just as Pindim Aurobindi threw an Indian *Kall,* Camellion grabbed Chatterjee by the shirtfront with his left hand and jerked the man to his left—and just in time! The razor-sharp nine-inch blade of the *Kall* buried itself in the right side of Chatterjee's back, the heavy weight of the blade forcing several inches of the bloody tip to protrude from the dying man's upper chest.

No fool, Aurobindi had no intention of physically fighting any man who could demolish Chatterjee. He spun around and headed toward the closed door directly behind him. He had only one goal: to reach his fully loaded 9mm Browning pistol in the bedroom.

By this time Gerin Hadjibawr, who had grabbed an ornamental twenty-four-inch *Bundi* dagger from the east wall, was charging the Death Merchant and was only six feet away, the fearsome double-edged grooved blade pointed at Camellion's stomach. Hadjibawr's rage turned to stark fear when he saw the Death Merchant release the near-dead Chatterjee and swing the Steyr autoloader in his direction. He didn't hear the weapon fire. The 9mm Blockbuster bullet traveled too fast, at a speed of 1,750 feet per second, far faster than human thought can form. He didn't feel any pain, either. The 9mm quick-kill bullet turned off his brain too fast; it had also exploded his forehead!

The Death Merchant hadn't failed to see Pindim Aurobindi race toward one of the bedrooms. The terrified Aurobindi had jerked open the door and was half inside when Camellion again pulled the trigger. The slug caught Aurobindi in the small of the back, only five inches above the coccyx or tailbone. The projectiles exploded vertebrae in the fifth-lumbar and sacrum regions, and pitched him forward as though he had been shot from a cannon. He was a corpse even before his body began to fall.

Backing toward the front door, Dev Nargis screamed shrilly when she saw how Camellion's bullet had torn off half of Hadjibawr's skull. She didn't know that the terrible damage was due to the way a Blockbuster bullet was put together. The slug was a normal copper-jacketed bullet with a lead core and a large BB in the nose of the bullet. On contact the BB was forced rearward, mechanically opening the bullet to a diameter three times the original jacket size.

While Dev Nargis was horrified, Roona Awardani was made of sterner stuff, so much so that she was on her hands and knees, crawling toward Camellion in an attempt to pick up the .22 Magnum revolver that lay on the floor a foot to his right. She should have known better. Camellion kicked her full in the face, his foot breaking her lower jaw and knocking out most of her upper and lower front teeth. A lot of things happened simultaneously as she collapsed and fell flat on her face amid blood and broken teeth. Dev Nargis turned, jerked open the front door, and darted outside. Camellion stooped and reached for the .22 Sentinel revolver. At the same time, the bedroom door in the southeast corner of the room was flung open and Kor Bastihouran rushed out. In his left hand was a 7.63mm Broomhandle Mauser.

A short, rotund man with a head as devoid of hair as a doorknob, the Ceylonese smuggler couldn't leave by way of the bedroom window. All the windows were covered on the outside with protective bars. All Bastihouran wanted was *out*. He didn't want to shoot anyone. The Mauser machine pistol was only for protection.

No sooner had Bastihouran stepped from the bedroom when another door opened slowly and without any noise, this bedroom door in the southwest corner of the large central room. Another man, dressed in a smudged eggshell suit, stepped out, a Walther P-5 autopistol in his right hand.

Indirectly, it was the pudgy Bastihouran who saved the Death Merchant's life. Richard Camellion had many talents, but none of them involved instant mind-reading. Seeing the Broomhandle Mauser in Bastihouran's hand, the Death Merchant automatically assumed he was a potential target and reacted at the same time that the other man in the eggshell suit drew down on him with the P-5 pistol.

Camellion jerked to his left, snap-aimed and fired as he headed toward the dirty stone floor, the loud crack of the Steyr mingling with the sound of the exploding cartridge in the Walther P-5. The Death Merchant's 9mm Blockbuster bullet bored into Bastihouran's chest and killed him instantly. Eggshell suit's 9mm projectile missed Camellion by a foot and a half; it zipped through the wooden front door and continued on its way. If Camellion hadn't spotted Kor Bastihouran and jerked his body to the left, Eggshell suit's bullet would have caught him in the right side of the neck. Again the Pale Priest of the Mute People had passed him by.

Just before Camellion's body hit the floor, he twisted and got off another round at the man who had stepped out of the bedroom in the southwest corner. He missed, the bullet cutting air only inches from the would-be assassin's left shoulder. The bearded man spun, ducked, and darted through the doorway into the kitchen. The Death Merchant had only gotten a brief glimpse of the man, but that one second look had been enough.

The man was Edgar Martin Bedsloe.

Camellion rolled over, jumped up, and sprinted southeast. He jumped across the corpse of Kor Bastihouran, leaped over the charpoy, and took a flat-against-the-south-wall position. For a moment, he glanced down at the Broomhandle Mauser, thinking of another time and of another place:* He then said in a low voice, directing his words to the TTL personal communicator.

"Barry, Steve! You heard the shots. I've scratched four of them. Bedsloe was here, but he's escaped. He's in the—"

The outside door of the kitchen slammed. It could be a trick. Bedsloe, a trained intelligence officer in East German intelligence, could have opened the door and then slammed it shut, yet still be waiting in the kitchen.

Bamm! Bamm! Camellion heard two shots from the front of the house, estimating they had been fired halfway between the house and the taxi.

"I just fired at him!" Steve Hondergriff's excited voice floated out of the TTL-P.C. "I think I winged him; I can't be sure. The son of a bitch is running east. He's headed straight toward the dakhma area, the damn fool! The girl that ran out of the house is headed down the road."

Barry Dillman cut in. "What do you want me to do?"

"Remain in the car and wait," Camellion told him. "Steve, you get back to the taxi. Stick the wire back in the distributor and get out of here. Barry and I will meet you at the S-house. I'm going after Bedsloe. There's a slim chance I might be able to grab him."

"You'll make the Parsi Guardians angry!" warned Steve Hondergriff.

"Then I'll have to change their attitude, won't I? That's it! Get moving. Out."

The Death Merchant tore through the kitchen, kicked open the outside door, and began running east. Not for a moment did he believe that Bedsloe wasn't aware of the danger of moving through the sacred area of the Parsis. Bedsloe had to know that the Parsis would consider it the worst kind of sacrilege for a nonbeliever—and an Occidental at that!—to place even one foot on the ground surrounding a *Dakhma*. It would be on par with an atheist's storming up to the high altar in St. Peter's in Rome, during Christmas midnight mass, and shouting for the Pope to perform a sexual impossibility upon himself.

He darted across the yard toward the east end of the Parsis grove. Very soon he had reached the woodlet in which were mixed cinchona trees and could see Bedsloe tearing through the dense vegetation,

* See Death Merchant #66, *The Cobra Chase,* also published by Dell.

running in a southeast direction. Only 150 feet in front of Bedsloe were the *Dakhma* and the ruins of a Parsi fire temple.

In far better physical condition than Bedsloe, Camellion began to close in on the elusive East German agent, who, several times, turned and snapped off quick shots. Soon, both men—the Death Merchant gaining steadily—were close to the *Dakhma,* and the stone floor and toppled pillars of the fire temple.

Also called a Tower of Silence, the *Dakhma* was a round enclosure 160 feet in diameter and surrounded by a 20-foot stone wall. It was to the inside of the *Dakhma* that the Parsis took the cadavers of their people, not to be buried but to be devoured by vultures. Once the corpse was picked clean by the big birds, the bones were tossed into a central pit lined with charcoal to filter the rainwater and avoid polluting the earth.

The enraged white-robed Parsi Guardians soon put in an appearance. Four, carrying *Vitas,* rushed Bedsloe, who promptly stopped, calmly took aim, and fired, his 9mm Walther slugs knocking two of the Guardians to the ground. The other two Parsis pulled up short and ducked behind trees. Bedsloe kept right on going.

The Death Merchant would have eventually caught up with Bedsloe if it had not been for the other Guardians. Screaming curses, five rushed toward Camellion as he was passing the *Dakhma,* two from the front, three coming at him from around the north side of the Tower of Silence. Two of the Guardians were carrying *Vitas,* five-foot-long spears with a strong cord of equal length attached to the butt and secured at the wrist of the hurler. The three other Guardians were armed with *Lathis,* six-foot-long hardwood staffs.

The Death Merchant had no desire to hurt the Parsi Guardians. At the same time, he did not intend to let them use him for a pincushion, or bash in his brains with their hardwood staffs.

He took out one Guardian in front of him by putting a 9mm Blockbuster slug into the man's chest. He whacked out a second Guardian by blowing out his stomach. Turning, Camellion saw that the other three Parsis were closing in fast. He could have killed all three in a matter of seconds, but he disliked having to put to sleep forever any person because of his religious belief, even though the man might be an uneducated crackpot.

Instead of firing, the Death Merchant ran toward the entrance of the Tower of Silence. The opening was only ten feet away. As he saw it, he would go into the enclosure through one entrance and leave by way of another. In their long white cotton robes, the Guardians would not be able to outrun him.

He raced to the inside of the *Dakhma* and at once saw that he had made a serious miscalculation. There was only one entrance, and he had just rushed through it. He had only succeeded in trapping himself. He had jumped into quicksand in another way. There were three more Guardians inside the enclosure. Two were standing on the north side of the bone pit. The third was toward the rounded wall on the west side. He had been repairing one of the six raised platforms on which the Parsis placed their dead. The two other Parsis had been taking dry white bones from platforms and tossing them into the rectangular pit.

The Death Merchant saw why the three Guardians were unharmed. They had leaned their two *Lathis* and one *Vita* against the wall, inside the tower, to the left of the entrance. The Death Merchant knew he had still another problem if any of the Guardians reached him. They were trained in the Indian martial locking technique of *Bandesh,* which permitted an expert to defeat an opponent without killing him. Camellion did not intend for the Guardians to deliver him to a police station with both his arms and legs broken.

As the three Guardians inside the tower rushed toward him, Camellion holstered the Steyr and grabbed the two *Lathis.* He was just in time to drop down and hold the two hardwood staffs horizontal across the narrow entrance, one a foot above the ground, the other six inches above the ground.

The first two Guardians, coming in from the outside, didn't have time to stop. They tripped and fell flat. The third didn't have time to stop either. He fell almost on top of the other two Guardians, his white robes twisting around his legs.

Camellion instantly went to work on the three Guardians with the two *Lathis.* He slammed the last man to go down in the side of the neck with the end of one staff, and cracked the skull of another Guardian with the second *Lathi.* The third Guardian frantically tried to roll away, but Camellion caught him with the end of a staff in the collarbone. The man screamed as the bone snapped, one jagged end penetrating the subclavian artery that lay just behind the bone.

The Death Merchant would just as soon have taken his leave through the single entrance. He couldn't. The three other Guardians were closing in, one coming straight at him, the other two from either side. At such close range the staffs would be a disadvantage, especially with three opponents. He tossed both *Lathis* through the entrance, throwing them like spears. He then spun around and did what the three Guardians least expected him to do, timing the maneuver expertly. Just before the Guardian in the center reached him, Camellion did a forward handstand and kicked upward with both feet, the double upside-down slam catching the man under the chin and breaking his lower jaw. With quite a few of his upper and lower teeth knocked out and his tongue almost cut in two, the man gurgled a scream that was lost in blood and fell back. Camellion jerked his legs back for leverage, uprighted himself, and prepared to meet the other two men, both of whom now had the advantage of not being clothed in long robes. They had removed their robes and were wearing only loincloths. And they were young, only in their middle twenties. Which meant they didn't have much experience.

Screaming "Filthy infidel!" in Pernui, Babur Sadika attacked with a rapid front-thrust kick aimed at Camellion's face while Ghulam Kolhapur used a sword-ridge hand-strike aimed at the Death Merchant's right temple. Camellion quickly demolished the kick by stepping to his right, and he wrecked Kolhapur's attempted blow with a right-forearm block.

Camellion feigned with a left *Seiken* forefist and followed with a four-finger *Nukite* spear stab aimed at Sadika's solar plexus, and a right fist directed at Kolhapur's throat. Both Guardians were very fast. Sadika blocked with crossed-X forearms. Kolhapur jerked back and countered with a two-handed knife-hand strike intended for the sides of Camellion's neck. Simultaneously, Babur Sadika attempted a left knee slam to Camellion's groin, and combined it with a sword-ridge hand and a right spear-thrust, the former aimed at the right side of Camellion's neck, the latter sighting in on his throat.

Walk them into it! Make them overconfident!

It was not difficult for the Death Merchant to counteract Kolhapur's intended strikes. Camellion used a left block at the same time he utilized a right arm block and a right leg knee-lift to prevent success of Sadika's groin and neck attacks.

Camellion only partially wanted to wreck Sadika's hand strikes, in particular the left sword-ridge hand. He succeeded, the edge of Sadika's hand barely touching his neck. It was a calculated gamble because an experienced fighter would realize instantly that he had inflicted what amounted to only little more than a hard tap. Camellion was hoping that in the excitement of the moment, Sadika would let enthusiasm overpower training. The Parsi Guardian did just that. As Camellion let out a fake cry of pain, a triumphant Babur Sadika and Ghulam Kolhapur rushed in for what they assumed would be the "kill." Sadika's tactic was a left flare punch and a right-handed one-finger spear stab at the hollow of the Death Merchant's throat—the soft jugular notch.

Not so overcome with eagerness, Kolhapur used a short snap-kick directed at Camellion's scrotum and a right palm edge and a left knuckle-fingertip strike. In his mind Kolhapur was positive that soon this damned infidel with his white skin would be dead. Why only disable him? Why bother to take him to the police? He had actually entered the tower. Such a horrible sacrilege deserved death.

For only the barest fraction of a second did Babur Sadika let his guard down. But that shave of a second was all the time the Death Merchant needed. His left arm streaked out, the fingers bunched in a deadly *Yon Hon Nukite* four-finger spear stab. He hit the target, his fingers crashing in just below Sadika's Adam's apple and crushing the thyroid cartilage. The result was instant hemorrhage, instant swelling of the windpipe, and almost instant suffocation.

Sadika's eyes went as wide as possible, in horror and in shock. And in disbelief. Sounding as though the entire Indian Ocean were trying to gurgle in his throat, Sadika fell back on rubber legs turning to water. His mouth was open, his nostrils working overtime in a vain effort to draw in lifesaving air.

The Death Merchant didn't have any trouble blocking Ghulam Kolhapur's right- and left-hand strikes with his right arm. He made a poor joke of the snap kick by twisting slightly and moving to his right. Even so, he made a slight miscalculation—by 4.11 inches. Instead of Kolhapur's foot connecting with Camellion's testicles, it slammed into the top thigh of his left leg, ten inches above the knee. The Death Merchant yelled in pain, and this time the cry was genuine. The pain was intense, the blow having temporarily paralyzed the rectus femoris muscle. Unable to stand, Camellion went down hard, his right buttocks hitting the stones.

At once, with a wild cry, Kolhapur leaped forward and attempted a right-foot stamp to Camellion's abdomen. Camellion didn't have time to roll away; yet he was far from helpless. He grabbed Kolhapur's right foot with both hands and twisted with all his strength, throwing the man completely off-balance. Kolhapur screamed in rage and agony and fell heavily to the side, landing hard on his back.

Getting to his feet on his good right leg, the Death Merchant propelled himself like a rocket toward Ghulam Kolhapur. He reached the rear of the doomed man as the Guardian—now having second thoughts about his own survival—tried to get to his feet. Camellion, supporting himself on his right knee, slammed a hard *Seiken* forefist into the back of Kolhapur's neck, the terrific blow stunning the Indian and forcing him to give up the attempt to get to his feet.

Camellion had him! His left arm shot out in front of Ghulam Kolhapur's head, his forearm pressing against the man's throat . . . pressing inward and upward, tilting the head back. In concert with this move, the Death Merchant rammed the heel of his right palm savagely against the back of the Parsi's head.

Snap, crackle, pop! The vertebrae parted and the vital cord separated. Ghulam Kolhapur went limp, his life rushing from him. Camellion released the corpse, watched it sag sideways, got to his feet, and shook his left leg. The muscle was still sore and very tender, but feeling was rapidly returning to the nerve endings.

He glanced around the interior of the *Dakhrna* and listened to the wind rustle through the six raised burial platforms. A weird custom, exposing naked corpses on platforms to be picked clean by vultures! Not at all. It was all relative. The Parsis way of disposing of their dead made as much sense as spending two or three grand on a casket in which to put a body, and then burying it all nine yards underground. Not to mention spending another thousand dollars on a headstone. At least the Parsis proved they believed in dust-to-dust.

Six vultures resting on a platform looked balefully at him, several fluttering their wings as if in anticipation.

"Not this day, little brothers . . . not I," muttered Camellion softly. "Your dinners are lying on the ground."

He spoke into the TTL personal communicator. "Barry, are you still there? Come in." There was no answer. "Dillman, answer! Do you hear me?" No answer. *A dumb question! If he had heard me, he would have answered!*

Camellion reached into his frock coat and pulled the TTL-P.C. from an inside pocket. Slightly larger than a pack of cigarettes, of Lights 100 size, the small transmitter had a built-in antenna and a small green light that glowed when the set was operating. The green light was out. Either the Selene cell was dead or something had been dislodged during his violent struggle with the Guardians.

He pulled the Steyr GB pistol and walked toward the entrance of the *Dakhma*. He wouldn't have put it past Edgar Bedsloe to have slipped back in an attempt to ambush him. The East German agent was very intelligent and had more than his share of gut nerve.

Limping slightly, Camellion moved through the entrance, his every cell ready for action. There was only silence and the breeze, and the sweet stink of Death. . . .

Chapter Two

East Berlin:
German Democratic Republic.
15.00 hours.

Karl Gunther Hossinger and Friedrich Seckendorff were in awe of Markus "Mischa" Wolf, the director of the Ministerium für Staatssicherheit of the Deutsche Demokratische Republik—the Ministry for State Security of the German Democratic Republic.

Wolf was an enigma. If any man on earth was a survivor, it was Mischa Wolf. He had become head of East German Intelligence at the age of twenty-eight. Now, thirty-five years later, he was still firmly in control of one of the world's best intelligence-gathering agencies. No other spy chief had survived for such an incredibly long period of time, in neither the East nor the West.

Sitting in Wolf's private office, Hossinger and Seckendorff were edgy and uncomfortable. Their boss was in a foul mood and made no secret of it.

"At least, Karl, you and the other agents managed to get to the Amarillo library before the American FBI and the CIA made a check and learned of the books Holtz removed," Wolf said in a voice that was one long sneer. Then, in a more calculating tone, "We don't have any hard evidence that the Americans even went to the library, or suspect that Holtz is in India. However, we must assume that they do have the true facts and proceed accordingly."

"Herr Direktor, this is a very complex operation," pointed out Friedrich Seckendorff, who was thirty-four years old and unnaturally slender for a tall man with large bones. "Holtz is aware that we've traced

him to India. He's already killed two of our people when he tried to reach the Soviet embassy in New Delhi. As it was, he came very close to getting past the gates. There's the KGB. We have no way of knowing what the damned Russians are doing."

Hossinger betrayed his nervousness by shifting his weight in the leather chair to the left, then back again to the right. He cleared his throat. "Sir, how far will the Russians permit us to go before they oruer hands off? Holtz does belong to us. He is MfS."

"Das ist richtig; Holtz is our agent," Wolf said firmly. "It would be against all protocol for the KGB to request that we stop pursuing one of our own who has betrayed his nation, a man who is a traitor."

"Then the KGB will only fight us 'in the dark,' " Hossinger said.

"Exactly, and the KGB will expect us to do the same," Wolf said, slight amusement in his voice. "Let's face facts—grim facts for the KGB, hard facts that General Chebrikov will have to swallow and hopefully choke on. We're not Poland, and even those religious swine are right up to the edge of open revolt. We're not weak like the Czechs and stupid like those idiots in the Balkans."

"Those damn-fool Bulgarians couldn't even shoot the Pope without making a mess of it," interjected Seckendorff. "Those Bulgarian *arschkriecherei!* The KGB wasn't too bright, either, in the matter, or they would not have turned the action regarding the Pope over to the damned Bulgars."

"There are no Russian 'uncles' in the MfS, and we know all the doubles the KGB thinks are safe," continued Wolf thoughtfully. "The Soviets also know that it's we—the MfS—who are keeping peace and order in the GDR. Without us the people might start demanding unification with West Germany. The entire world knows how the Soviet Union is terrified of a united Germany."

Hossinger, a florid man with thin, wheat-colored hair, twisted his mouth into an ironic smile. "We can't blame the Russians. We'd also be afraid of a nation that killed twenty million of our people in a war."

Wolf turned a dismal glance on his, his frigid expression remaining unthawed. "It's Soviet fear of German unification that keeps us in business. In a sense, it is part of the same fear that will prevent the KGB from even discussing Holtz with us. The Russians know how far they can go with us. The KGB will pretend that Holtz doesn't exist. But all the while the KGB will do its best to find him. Should we grab him before the Russians do, they will say nothing, just as we will pretend all is normal if the KGB reaches him first."

Friedrich Seckendorff murmured, "We also have to contend with those stupid Americans." He shook his head back and forth in disgust. "The Americans and their unrealistic morality are always stirring up trouble. And they are so naive! Think of it! Their security was so lax that we were able to plant an agent in the very factory where nuclear warheads are assembled. It's unbelievable!"

"The Americans are on a self-destruct course. It's their own 'freedoms' that will eventually make the United States go the way of the Roman Empire." Wolf permitted himself one of his very rare smiles. "Recently I was looking through some American newspapers brought in by our Foreign Department. I saw in one paper that American schools can't use metal detectors to look for knives and other weapons on the blacks who attend because it was against the law. A search would interfere with their 'civil rights'! Such nonsense."

"Since when do monkeys have 'rights'?" laughed Seckendorff, feeling more relaxed.

"It's to be expected in any government so foolish that it refuses to protect its own borders," commented Karl Hossinger. "A Mexican is only a brown *schwarz affe* and millions of them are pouring into the United States each year."

"Let's hope the flood of Mexican trash continues," Wolf said, sounding satisfied with himself. "Even the Mexican police can cross the southern U.S. border with impunity. When I was looking through the U.S. newspapers, I saw an article in *The New York Times.* The piece stated that during September 1985, Mexican law-enforcement officers, armed with machine pistols, accompanied drug traffickers across the border in Starr County, in the state of Texas. According to *The New York Times,* these allegations were contained in a letter written to President Reagan and thirteen members of the U.S. Congress. The letter was sent by the Fraternal Order of Border Agents, an organization of the United States Customs Service and the American Drug Enforcement Agency. What did that fool in the White House do about it? Nothing. I would assume he was afraid he might make those half-Indian apes 'angry'!"

Anxious to please their chief, Hossinger and Seckendorff laughed extra hard. At length, Seckendorff said, "What I can't understand is why some Americans actually try to help the aliens with various 'sanctuary movements'! Don't those fools know that by bringing such backward scum into their nation they are only weakening their own society and taking the future from their own children?"

"Religious and idealistic people can't think logically," Wolf said crossly. "They are too much in love with their own self-righteousness. They are always more concerned with what 'God wants' than with common sense. That ridiculous Pope is a good example of unreality in action. He is constantly visiting Africa and South America and urging all those stupid bastards to have all the children 'God sends.' He forgets to tell them that 'God' isn't going to feed them, and he conveniently ignores the fact that the blacks and Latin Americans can't even feed the brats they already have."

"And to think that the Americans worry about Communism!" snickered Hossinger. "Their country is being invaded every day, and they haven't the sense to know it. Their government knows it and doesn't give a damn!" Hossinger laughed again. "Maybe we should ask some of those idiot Americans who protect aliens to help us find Holtz—as a 'humanitarian' gesture!"

Wolf was not amused. "Don't confuse the issue," he warned, his eyes swinging toward Hossinger. "We're not dealing with the hypocrites in the American government. We're crossing swords with the CIA. The danger is that we won't be able to find and intercept Holtz before the Americans find him, or before he can reach the KGB. For those reasons, I must insist on speed after the two of you arrive in India."

Seckendorff uncrossed his legs, leaned forward, and thrust out his head toward Wolf, who was behind his desk. "From the passages and maps that Holtz marked in the library books, we know he could be hiding in New Delhi, Bombay, or Calcutta. To be on the safe side, we must also consider the possibility of his changing plans at the last minute."

"If he ever manages to get into Pakistan, we will have lost him," Wolf said, a dark note of finality in his voice. "I don't think he'll attempt that route. Holtz has to realize that his chances of going through Pakistan, and then on to Afghanistan and making contact with the Soviet forces there are almost nil. More likely than not, he'd have his throat cut by bandits, and he knows it."

"The Soviet Union has consulates in Bombay and Calcutta," offered Hossinger, making a disparaging noise with his lips. "He'll have no choice but to try to reach one of the USSR's consulates. Then again, he could return to New Delhi and make another try to reach the Soviet embassy."

"If he ever left New Delhi!" jumped in Seckendorff. He sat up straighter. "We can be positive that he won't have the PALs with him. The four of them are small enough to be carried in a suitcase, but to carry them around in India would be insanity."

"Holtz could have disguised the devices as pocket radios," Wolf said. "He would have to in order to get them aboard an aircraft."

"Or the PALs could still be in the United States," Seckendorff said. "He could have hidden them in Chicago."

"We can't be positive that he took an international flight from Chicago," Hossinger said. "We're faced with any number of uncertainties. Did he or did he not run out on Cora Bedsloe, or Erika Hoffman, if one prefers to use her real name? Was she or was she not planning to defect to the Soviet Union with Bedsloe?"

"We do know that Hoffman was arrested by the American FBI," Seckendorff said. "Either the FBI or the CIA forced her to confess. We can be positive of that. For that reason alone, I can't understand why Holtz would flee to India. Surely he realized that she would confess the escape route—wouldn't you think?"

"Which one? Which escape route?" Wolf demanded harshly, his intense stare making Seckendorff uncomfortable. "If she was not a part of Holtz's plan to defect from us and go over to the Russians, she could only confess the escape route we had established for them in case of an emergency—to New York from Texas, from New York to Europe. But if she also intended to defect, she would confess their own private route—from Chicago to San Francisco, then a flight to India. Keep in mind, all of that is based on our assuming as fact what our agents in Washington, D.C., heard during that single telephone conversation. The tap only lasted a few minutes; then someone in the U.S. Justice Department remembered to turn on the scrambler. The Chicago route had to have come from Hoffman."

"In that case that would be proof that she intended to defect with him," Karl Hossinger remarked thoughtfully. "Holtz not only double-crossed us but betrayed her as well."

"Unless all of it is disinformation distributed by the Americans!" suggested Seckendorff.

Wolf and Hossinger did not have time to comment. The interoffice communicator buzzed. Wolf reached out and pressed a button.

"Ja?"

"Herr Direktor, we have received a special report from the Center at our embassy in New Delhi. The report had just been decoded."

The voice belonged to Heinz Hafner, one of Wolf's five assistants.

"Danke schön, Heinz. Bring it in." Wolf shut off the box.

Wolf read the two-page report as soon as Hafner handed it to him. He placed the report on his desk, then looked over at Karl Hossinger and Friedrich Seckendorff, his expression intense.

"Holtz is in Bombay," he announced in a pleasant voice. "Read the report for yourselves."

The spymaster did not get up, lean across the desk, and hand the report to either of the men. He merely picked up the sheets and reached out with his arm. In his youth, Mischa Wolf had been dapper and athletic. Now, at the age of sixty-three, he was still jaunty and well groomed. But arthritis had attacked his legs, and there were times when he had to walk with the aid of two canes.

Seckendorff stood up, took the report from Wolf's hand, read it, smiled, handed the sheets to Hossinger, and sat down.

The special report had been sent by Gerhard Bohm, the chief of the MfS station at the East German embassy in New Delhi. The report was direct: During the previous afternoon there had been a gun battle in a house on the outskirts of Bombay. At the time, everyone in the house had been killed by a Sikh cabdriver, with the exception of one man and one woman. Dev Nargis, the woman who had escaped with her life, had told police that only she and Edward Smythe, an Englishman, had escaped. The Indian police did have evidence that the murderer was not a Sikh. Another cabdriver had come forward and had told Indian authorities that a white man had given him a large sum of money to borrow his vehicle for a few hours, to play a joke on a friend. The police were now looking for a tall red-headed man with a thick mustache and a short beard. The man had walked with a limp, the cabdriver said, and he also had a blue-black birthmark on the left side of his chin.

Others had been killed. A group of Parsis, Guardians of a Tower of Silence, had also been murdered. The Indian police were theorizing that either Smythe or the other Occidental had killed them. The odd part was that most of the Parsis had not been shot. Whoever had killed the Guardians had either used his bare hands or a wooden staff. The police were puzzled why the killer had not used a gun to shoot all of the Parsis. Nor did they know why he—or could it have been two persons?—was able to kill so many Parsi Guardians with only his bare hands! It was well known that all Guardians were masters of *Bandesh,* a martial-arts technique that was deadly.

Hossinger got up and handed the report back to Wolf, saying, "I don't see how the report is proof that Holtz is in Bombay. Just because someone posing as a taxi driver and another man, who was an Englishman, were involved—"

"Proof is not needed," Wolf said, cutting him off. "In this case, intuition alone is enough. Edward Smythe was no doubt Holtz. He once spent three years in London before going to the United States as an illegal. It's only logical on his part that he should choose to pose as an Englishman. It's logical but stupid. But then, he didn't count on being discovered."

If any other man had mentioned "intuition," he would have sounded ridiculous and Hossinger and Seckendorff would have considered him a fool. It was very different with Mischa Wolf. His uncanny sense of insight and perceptivity had been proved accurate all too often in the past for Seckendorff and Hossinger not to take him seriously.

"There wasn't any indication in the report who the cabdriver really was," Hossinger said, sitting back down. "He had to be a wet-work man from either the KGB or the CIA. Yet we can't discount Indian Intelligence. But why would the KGB want to kill Holtz?"

"Exactly," intoned Seckendorff. "Whoever the cabdriver was, he wasn't working for the Russians. I think—"

"I'm not interested in discussing the merits of an agent of the Other Side," Wolf said high-handedly. "My only concern is that we take Franz Holtz into custody."

"There could be a problem, sir," Hossinger said casually. "We may not be able to take him alive. *Herr Direktor,* I should like you to make it clear what our course of action should be if we have a choice between killing him or allowing him to escape."

"Kill him, of course," Wolf said promptly. "I would prefer that he be brought back for trial and then shot. But kill him if there is no other way. The American PAL devices are useful only to the Americans and to the Soviet Union. Now get out of here. You have only three hours before your flight takes off for New Delhi. . . ."

Chapter Three

The statue was damned ugly, thought Boris Bukashev. Well, that was Konstantin's business.

"So far, all we've been able to find out is that DARFA is now taking an active part in the investigation," commented Bukashev. He sat down on the chair in such a way that he was facing the short wooden back. "Our informant said that Indian Intelligence suspects that the Pakistanis were responsible for the shoot-out. It only goes to show how stupid the people in DARFA are."

Standing by the side of the table, Shatalin continued to polish the face of the bronze statue. "Did the contact say why the Indians suspect the Paks?"

"They believe that the shooting inside the house was only a smoke-screen," explained Bukashev. "DARFA thinks that the real targets were the Parsi Guardians. The Indians think that the Paks want to cause friction and social unrest between the Parsis and the Hindus and the Moslems. And we can add the Jains, the Christians, and all the other religious sects in this backward land. Have you heard yet from the Center back home?"

Finished with the face, Shatalin put more polish on the cloth.

"We received a message a few hours ago from Moskva. The East Germans are sending two of their best to India. They will arrive late this afternoon." He glanced briefly at Bukashev and resumed work, this time polishing one of the four thin arms of the statue. "Our analysts have also narrowed down the possibilities of American tourists and businessmen who might be working for the Central Intelligence Agency."

"The East Germans could have been responsible," said Bukashev, frowning as he studied the twenty-five-inch-high statue of Kali the Black. "Wolf's boys can be barbarians when they want to be."

"It might very well have been MfS, Boris, but Moskva is convinced it was CIA specialists. An analysis indicates the probability that a Mr. and Mrs. Bruce Canover are working for the CIA. The Canovers came to India several weeks ago with their son. Bruce Canover is a professor of ancient history and culture, and he specializes in India. He's on leave from the Briswinn Institute of Social Studies in Maryland."

Bukashev nodded his small head. "And the Home Office knows that the Briswinn Institute is not a CIA front and that there is a genuine Professor Canover on leave from that institution."

"Who also matches the description of Bruce Canover in Bombay," finished Shatalin. "The wife's description also fits and they do have their twelve-year-old son with them."

"They could be the real Canovers. The Center has to have considered that possibility. Or else the Center has information we don't have."

"I think that's the answer." Shatalin paused and looked at the arm of the statue, which was beginning to shine.

"You're going to have the Canovers tailed," Bukashev said as fact.

"*Nyet.* CIA specialists are very good at spotting shadows. They're also very good at finding any hidden transmitters that might be placed in their rooms. But I might order a bug placed in their suite—that is if you approve!"

"I don't mind, Konstantin. You have my permission," Bukashev said with a hearty belly laugh. "Just as soon as I check with Moskva!"

In spite of Konstantin Shatalin's being the *Rezident,* or station chief, at the Soviet embassy in New Delhi and the boss of the entire *Rezidentura* in India, it was normal for him and Boris Bukashev to joke back and forth and poke fun at each other when no one else was present. The two men had grown up together in the Ukrainian SSR and had been boyhood friends in Berdyansk. They often reminisced about swimming in the Azovskoye More—the Sea of Azov—and often talked about the "good old days," which had not been good at all. But with age, nostalgia often replaces reality.

In appearance, Shatalin and Bukashev were as different as an Arab is from a Jivaro headhunter. At thirty-seven, Shatalin was an even two hundred pounds, all of it muscle without a gram of fat. Aristocratic-looking and with easy manners and an affable personality, he was even well liked by personnel of the Western embassies, although at diplomatic functions they were careful what they said around the Soviet attaché of agronomy. After all, he was *Soviet,* which made him The Enemy.

Half a head shorter than Shatalin, Bukashev was partially bald and looked ten years older than his thirty-seven and a half years. Weighing only 164 pounds, he had a plain face and could easily have been cast in any movie as an ordinary clerk. He was the kind of man one could stare at for thirty minutes but ten minutes later not remember what he looked like. It was his deadliness, however, that had made him a major in the KGB and the leader of a six-man, two-woman Mokryye Dela assassination squad. He knew a hundred ways to kill an individual, whether face-to-face or at a distance.

"What do you think of it, Boris?" Shatalin stepped back from the statue and admired it.

Bukashev took out a pack of American True Gold cigarettes and looked at the statue of Kali, the Hindu goddess of destruction. Her face had bulging bloodshot eyes and her hair was matted. Between her fangs her pendulous tongue was covered (painted) with blood and gore. Around her neck was a necklace of skulls; a girdle of teeth circled her waist.

"That goddamn thing is the ugliest monstrosity yet, the worst you've ever collected," opined Bukashev. He lit the cigarette and dropped the lighter into his coat pocket. He did respect all the effort Shatalin had put into removing the black lacquer, then laboriously polishing the naked bronze. It had taken him weeks, working in his spare time. He had not, however, removed the paint from her eyes and tongue.

Shatalin chuckled. *"Da,* she is an ugly bitch. I guess that's why I like her," he said proudly. "I suppose you know that Kali is minor compared to Brahma, Vishnu, and Siva. Those three are the Hindu trinity—the Creator, the Preserver, and the Destroyer. In Christianity, it would be God, Christ, and Satan."

"Uh-huh," sighed Bukashev. "So who really cares—except a Hindu or a Christian. It's all superstitious crap."

Shatalin smiled. "The Hindus believe that Kali's presence not only shapes reality but also gives vital energy to all things that exist. They consider Kali to be the dynamism of the universe. I'd like to know why the poor fools don't wonder why Kali doesn't feed them."

Bukashev got to his feet, walked over to the desk, and dropped ashes into an ashtray. "I suppose all of it makes as much sense to the Hindus as a resurrected god makes to the Christians—and to the Jews, who are convinced they are the Chosen People."

"Nine-tenths of the world is composed of superstitious sheep," Shatalin said, his tone suddenly serious. "It's to our advantage. Think of all the religious 'peace' groups in the United States we've infiltrated. It's nice to have such naive fools doing our work for us."

"None of them are going to help us find Franz Holtz. All we have are a lot of suppositions built around conclusions that might very well be false."

"Such as?" asked Shatalin, screwing the top onto the can of polish.

"Such as our concluding that Edward Smythe is Franz Holtz," said Bukashev. "We're going forward on a premise we assume is valid. There are any number of Englishmen in Bombay. Why, I don't know. They must be crazy. But where's the evidence that Smythe is Holtz?"

He sat down on the edge of the desk and watched Konstantin Shatalin drop into a leather chair.

"Ah, Boris, you're a good hunter, but a terrible detective," Shatalin said, his eyes taking on a rare warmth reserved for mischief.

Bukashev looked irritated. "Konnie, you've been watching too many American television programs."

"When detectives—and in any nation—are stumped and without clues, they proceed on theory. They develop their own clues. It's the same in the intelligence game. We're going to move on the theory that Smythe is Holtz, and that Bruce and Ethel Canover are working for the CIA."

Bukashev put his hands on top of his head, locking his fingers together. "Uh-huh. And on the theory that Holtz wants to betray his own service and come over to our side, dangling those nuclear safety circuits in front of us as a prize."

"The Center wants those four devices—'PALs,' as the Americans refer to them," Colonel Shatalin pointed out. "The Center is also convinced that Smythe is Holtz, and I do mean convinced." He paused and added, "We know the Center is never wrong, don't we?"

"Then Smythe must be Holtz," Bukashev said, stubbing out his cigarette. "What's the next step?"

Regardless of their long friendship and fondness for each other, Shatalin and Bukashev never made jokes about, or cast aspersions on, the Center, KGB headquarters outside of Moskva. Both men were members of the Communist Party. Both had excellent records, not only in the party, but also in the KGB. Yet both knew that as a socioeconomic system, communism was one of history's biggest jokes. The two men did have a single goal in life, as did all KGB officers and/or other Soviet government officials: to protect their *vysshy svet,* their upper-class status. Another part of the survival game was to pretend, even to each other, that the Soviet Union was the best nation on the face of the earth, that the Soviet Union was "fair" and "just" and "seeking freedom" for all the peoples of the world.

We know the Center is never wrong, don't we? There was nothing wrong with the remark—on the surface. Colonel Shatalin was only saying that the Center seldom, if ever, made mistakes. But Bukashev had not missed Shatalin's real meaning: that wise KGB officers do not disagree with higher authorities. One does not get promoted by rocking the boat from side to side in red waters.

Accordingly, Major Bukashev had agreed with his old friend, who was also his superior. It was his way of saying *I understand perfectly.*

"It will take several days to dig up more information about Professor Canover and his wife. Our people in the United States are working on that aspect right now. Depending on what they learn, you and your squad will then take over."

"Does the Home Office think that Canover himself had a hand in the shooting in Bombay?" queried Bukashev.

"The First Directorate has considered the possibility," replied Shatalin. "The whore that escaped from the house told police she saw the passenger in the taxi, and that he had a gun in his hand. So we know that two men were involved in the operation; and it's almost a certainty that the cabdriver was an Occidental."

"He was supposed to be a Sikh!"

"He was a CIA specialist in disguise; I'm certain. It's just a hunch but I'm certain."

Boris Bukashev nodded. The Home Office might very well be correct about everything. Smythe could be Holtz. Bruce Canover could have been in the shoot-out. But who was the "Sikh"? Bukashev was positive of only two things, two truths: Konstantin was right about the Center. To disagree with the bosses would be a definite mistake. The second was that there is always a bigger fool than the fellow who knows it all. It's the damn fool who will argue with him.

Chapter Four

The Death Merchant felt half safe in this northwest section of Bombay. The large two-story hermitage, its white walls glistening in the bright sunshine, had been built by a wealthy Punjabi who had made his fortune in the clothing industry. As his wealth had increased the house had become too small for his entertainment needs, and he had sold it. Over the years the house had passed to various owners. For the past four years the eighteen-room mini-mansion had been owned by Union-Indian Petroleum, an American and Indian oil company that was a subsidiary of Credhoodt & van Oordt Metals, a mining corporation in South Africa. Credhoodt & van Oordt was controlled solely by Exchaquet, Dietschi & Schnyder (diamonds and other precious stones) of Zurich, Switzerland.

Exchaquet, Dietschi & Schnyder was a proprietary company of the Central Intelligence Agency.

From Poon-Pon Fond Road, on which the house was located, one could look west and see the vast expanse of Arabian Sea, whose tall waves shattered themselves on the sea wall when the monsoons thundered up behind them. Water entirely surrounded Bombay, which appeared like a clawlike promontory, some twelve miles long, then hung, pointing south, from the west coast of India.

Standing in the wide doorway and watching the *Kilis* fishing boat in the distance, Richard Camellion reflected that Bombay was a freak city, possessing a culture all its own, one apart from any in India proper, a very live thing that drew people from all over the vast nation and kept them there. Gujaratis, Maharashtrians, South Indians, Goans, people from North India, were joined together in a mass of over seven million and would never return to their *muluk*, or home region.

Dressed casually in a light tan Altese silk shirt, linen slacks with tan and cream stripes, and tan and white wing tips, Richard Camellion turned and walked back into the room as Barry Dillman turned off the television set, which had shown Indian police dispersing rioting Parsis.

"We sure stirred up a hornet's nest, didn't we?" Dillman said rhetorically, looking around at the others. His gaze finally settled on the Death Merchant, who was sitting down. "The Parsis are rioting all over the city. The poor bastards think the Hindus killed those Tower of Silence guards."

"The worst rioting is going on in Horimar Circle, close to Town Hall," agreed Stephen Hondergriff, who was an old India hand. "If the Parsis don't slow down, the authorities will call in the army, and then the head-bashing will begin in earnest."

"The Parsis certainly take their religious beliefs seriously," said Lana Stanley, brushing hair from her forehead.

"All Indians are religious-oriented," Hondergriff informed her in a bored voice. "Religion is the central part of their lives. That's the main reason why they'll always be at the bottom of the totem pole of life. No matter what happens, they think it's the result of karma, or else it's the will of the gods. If you're sick, what the hell—it's your karma. If you're rich or poor, it's karma. It's their wacky religious beliefs that kill their initiative to better themselves in life. Add to that a runaway population explosion and you have misery growing like a pyramid."

"What bothers me are the people in general," said Lana Stanley. "How do you tell a Punjabi from a Bengali, a Brahmin from a lower-caste person, or a Hindu from a Moslem?"

"You don't, kid," piped up Wilbur "Weejee" Theimer in his high and small voice. "Remember what they told us during the briefing in D.C.—not to expect to identify anyone immediately, but to look for the most obvious characteristics of some kinds of Indians."

The Death Merchant joined the conversation. "I think all of you are missing the basic reality. India is such a diverse mixture of ethnic groups and religions that the name is only a geographical expression, like 'Europe' or 'Asia.' The truth is that there never was an 'India' until British mapmakers put a dark line around the whole mess and painted the inside pink!"

"Maybe so, but we still stand out like members of the Tall Society at a convention of midgets," said Barry Dillman. He added for Wilbur Theimer's edification, "No insult intended, Weejee."

Theimer, who was only forty inches tall, grinned. "You're forgiven. But you've made one hell of a comparison."

Steve Hondergriff was cleaning the lens of his sunglasses with a tissue. "The plan was basically sound," he said, grimacing. "We found Bedsloe, and then the unexpected happened." He uttered a half laugh and his alert brown eyes darted to Camellion. "You have a bad karma Camellion. That's why the gun fell out of the holster. Your bad karma made it happen!"

Even Camellion laughed. "Like the lyrics of the song go—'It was just one of those things.' The odds are that the Velcro straps wouldn't come loose again in twenty years, if ever. But they did several days ago. The mag revolver slipped out and fell to the floor. We have to live with it."

"So now we light a black candle. A get-well card won't do," grunted Dillman. Loose-limbed, he had a mournful face that was decorated with a long, thin mustache and a shadowed jaw, unless he shaved twice a day.

"I didn't say we should carry a coffin of defeat," the Death Merchant said in a soft voice. "We're going to sit tight for a week, and hope that Mr. G. can develop a lead for us."

"He didn't sound very optimistic yesterday when we contacted him on the shortwave," objected Dillman, his expression uncertain. "He hasn't the first clue where Bedsloe might run to, and neither do we."

"Bedsloe is in a worse fix than we are," Camellion said calmly. "He's white and stands out the same way we do. He's also limited in where he can hide. At least we have this safe house and two others in Bombay."

Wilbur Theimer rolled his eyes upward and made a snickering sound.

"All Bedsloe has is his own wits, and maybe the underworld contacts he has made since he landed in India. He will lose even those contacts should they learn he was the 'Englishman' living in the *chawl* on Mookmak Road. They will consider him too hot to fool with."

Twenty-nine years old, Theimer was a perfectly developed male of the species, but in miniature. He was a midget. He also looked many years younger than his chronological age. He didn't mind the word *midget*, although he always referred to himself as one of the "little people." He was an expert cryptographer, an authority on the writings of Pindar, the Greek lyric poet who had died in 438 B.C., and knew almost as much about poisons as the Death Merchant. He did have the odd habit of almost never using contractions in his speech.

"Camellion, are you sure that the Indian authorities will not be able to identify you as the man who 'rented' the taxi, with the excuse that he wanted to play a joke on his friend?" asked Lana Stanley, putting out her cigarette. "We know they'll be checking the hotels where Occidentals stay, including the Shalimar."

"Not to worry. I don't have red hair and a red mustache and a red beard," Camellion reassured her. "I don't have a noticeable birthmark on my chin. I don't have a limp. And a good many white men in Bombay have my height and build. Besides"—a thin smile curled on his lips—"I was born under a lucky star."

He gazed steadily at Lana Stanley, who was posing as Ethel Canover, his "wife." She wore a grass-green *cholis*—a sari blouse—and an emerald-green skirt, the latter short enough to reveal nicely shaped legs with smooth, rounded knees. She was thirty three years old, and while she was not a beautiful woman (which would have been a disadvantage for the purposes at hand), her long blond hair and even features did give her a certain attractiveness. She possessed a blasé, cool worldliness and in her private life lived without apologies or pretexts of any kind.

The Death Merchant continued in a quiet voice, "The flaw in our security is Dev Nargis, the prostitute. We hadn't counted on her escaping. She could identify you, Steve. For that reason, you'll have to remain here out of sight until this mess is over."

His face set in granite, Hondergriff agreed with a quick nod of his head. "It's my fault," he was quick to admit. "I should have blown her head off. At the time, I just couldn't pull the trigger and snuff her."

"Don't apologize for being human," Camellion said sympathetically. "What's done is done. All God's children have feet of clay."

The real blame can be placed on Edgar Bedsloe—Franz Holtz, he thought. *He's the reason we're here in India.*

It was several months earlier that Bedsloe had stolen four PAL devices from the Pantex laboratory where he was an assembly technician. All of it had to do with nuclear warfare.

The United States is constructing five nuclear devices a day, the final process taking place at the Pantex laboratory, fifteen miles from

Amarillo, Texas. Part of any nuclear warhead is a small but extremely sophisticated electronic system known colloquially as PAL—from "permissive action link." About three times the size of a box of pocket matches, PAL is used to foil anyone who might try an unauthorized detonation. The sole purpose of PAL is to prevent the warhead from exploding unless the authorized codes from the President of the United States are punched in on the general control equipment outside of the warhead.

The story had really begun almost eight years earlier. It was in late 1980 that MfS, East German Intelligence, sent two illegals into the United States, two highly trained deep-cover agents: Franz Joseph Holtz, and Erika Ermatrude Hoffman. Under a man-and-wife cover of "Edgar and Cora Bedsloe," the couple settled in Amarillo, Texas, supposedly moving from Du Quoin, Illinois.

Their target was the Pantex nuclear warhead assembly plant.

In 1983, Edgar Bedsloe obtained employment at the Pantex facility. A conscientious worker, he was promoted in 1983 to a position that gave him access to the section where the permissive action links were kept.

Bedsloe (or Holtz) was very cautious and bided his time. It wasn't until October 1986 that he stole four PALs—and vanished.

The FBI and the CIA had not been taken by complete surprise. The FBI had been quietly watching Edgar and Cora Bedsloe for six months. The FBI had been tipped off by the CIA, which had discovered that the Bedsloes were agents of East German Intelligence. The CIA did not reveal its source to the Federal Bureau of Investigation.

But why had Bedsloe left his wife behind? The FBI could only surmise that something had gone wrong and that "Cora Bedsloe" had failed, for some reason, to flee in time. Or had Bedsloe deliberately left her behind. If he had done so deliberately, then he had betrayed her. If so, why?

Cora Bedsloe—Erika Hoffman—had refused to talk, neither confirming nor denying the accusation that she was an agent of a foreign power. In the meanwhile, the CIA quietly entered the case. Courtland Grojean, the director of the covert division, sensing that something very big was developing, called in Richard Camellion. He had managed to contact the Death Merchant at his Memento Mori ranch outside of Votaw in the Big Thicket region of southeast Texas.

Using the name of Paul Glenn Newmone and armed with credentials that stated he was an agent in the CIA's counterintelligence division, Camellion had decided to make his own clues. With a real FBI agent and a genuine CIA operative (ordered by Grojean to cooperate with "Mr. Newmone"), Camellion had gone to the main library in Amarillo, Texas, and checked on any books the Bedsloes might have checked out during the past year.

He and the two other men had received two surprises. The first had been pleasant. During the past fourteen months, Edgar Bedsloe/Franz Joseph Holtz had taken out fourteen volumes—seven on India, five on Pakistan, and two dealing with Afghanistan. He still had two books out, both on India. Both books were overdue.

The Death Merchant had made a check of the books. Nine books were still in the library. Three had been taken out by other people. Six of the books, dealing with India, had been extensively marked by transparent fluorescent marking pens. In one book, foldout maps of New Delhi, Bombay, and Calcutta were missing. But . . . had Bedsloe made the markings and taken the maps? He had not been the only one with a library card to take out the books.

The second surprise had not been pleasant. The librarian could not understand why the FBI should "come back today and ask what you asked yesterday." She then explained that two FBI agents had come to the library the previous day and requested a list of any books the Bedsloes might have taken out during the past two years.

Richard Camellion and the two agents had known at once that either the Soviet KGB or the East German MfS was a giant step ahead of them.

Now, their only hope was Cora Bedsloe—Erika Hoffman. Kept incommunicado for reasons of national security, and her mental resistance weakened by lorazepam, Erika Hoffman broke down when confronted with the evidence that Camellion had found in the main library in Amarillo. She readily admitted that she and Holtz were professional agents of the East German intelligence machine. She confessed that she was to have met Holtz in New York City, where the two of them would have taken a flight to Paris. From Paris, they would have made their way to the German Democratic Republic—East Germany.

Uh-huh . . . so what had gone wrong?

Erika Hoffman said that the FBI had become suspicious, and Holtz had fled ahead of schedule. She had not had time to pack. The PALs? She didn't know anything about them.

How had Holtz known that the FBI was watching him and Erika?

She said she didn't know. Holtz had not told her.

Crocodile crap!

The Death Merchant had flatly told Erika Hoffman she was a liar. He had then ordered a CIA technician to "give the bitch a shot of 16-F." The CIA did not have a drug known as "16-F." The technician did, however, give her an injection of twenty milligrams of cinchonine, a drug that causes severe nausea, vomiting, rapid heartbeat, and, in an overdose, death.

"You'll be dead within ten hours," Camellion had told her, "unless you tell the truth. Only then will we administer the antidote."

Within an hour, Hoffman had developed all the garrulousness of a parrot. She confessed that East German Intelligence had sent her and Franz Joseph Holtz to the United States to steal one of the permissive action links. Then she and Holtz had come up with a scheme of their own. They would indeed steal a PAL, but would defect from the MfS, turn the device over to the KGB, and become citizens of the Soviet Union. The Russians would treat them as heroes and give them good jobs in Soviet Intelligence.

She and Holtz were to leave Texas together and take an Indian Airlines flight from O'Hare International Airport in Chicago. Destination: *India*.

Why had Holtz left her behind? Had someone tipped him off that the FBI was closing in?

Hoffman confessed that neither she nor Holtz had even suspected that the FBI had them under surveillance. She had no idea why Holtz had suddenly vanished, leaving her behind in Amarillo to dance to U.S. Government music.

Unless it was because she was six weeks pregnant!

She did have a question. *I'll be in jail when my baby is born. Will my baby automatically become a citizen of the United States?*

The Death Merchant had a question. Why did the East German Ministry for State Security want a PAL device? All the missiles in East Germany had been made in, and were possessed and controlled by, the Soviet Union. Had the KGB or the GRU ordered MfS to steal the PALs?

Hoffman didn't know. She had only followed orders. So had Holtz.

Courtland Grojean had insisted that this time Camellion had been suckered. This CI chief had pointed out that it was too easy, too convenient. It wasn't that Grojean didn't believe Hoffman's story in regard to her and Holtz defecting to the pig farmers in Red-Slop Land. But Grojean did not believe that Holtz ever intended to fly to India, insisting that a trained intelligence agent would never go to a public library and request books on the very nations in which he intended to hide. At least he would use an alias to acquire a library card, and he would not underline and mark passages in the volumes.

Well, Camellion. How about it? The Death Merchant had replied that Holtz had not been cautious enough, and he reminded the CIA boss that two hypnosis sessions and three different polygraph sessions with Erika Hoffman had indicated that she was telling the truth.

Camellion pointed out it was only another inconsistency that often popped up in life—Holtz's lack of proper security methods. After all, there were thousands of incongruities in operation in the world. For example, would you believe that the people of India eat more nutritious bread than do Americans? They do because they bake their bread with the whole grain. Or again, many backward nations, whose greatest need is to feed their people, sell their crops and bankrupt themselves to buy not food but advanced military hardware for the purpose of defending themselves against their equally backward neighbors, who are doing the very same thing.

"Or take the search for a cure to cancer," Camellion had said. "The search is costing a terrible amount of money for the limited progress that has been made. Yet almost certainly any cure will come not from a direct investigation of the disease, but rather through an advance in fundamental biochemistry. And the greatest contribution to solving the world's food shortage lies not in finding ways to grow more food, but in efficient birth control, efficient contraceptives."

The Death Merchant had made it clear he was convinced that Holtz had fled to India to make contact with the KGB at the Soviet embassy in New Delhi. Should he fail in New Delhi, he would try at the Soviet consulate in Bombay.

You're going on that intuition of yours, aren't you, Camellion? You got it!

Richard Camellion had flown to India as Bruce Canover, a professor of ancient history at the Briswinn Institute of Social Studies in Maryland. Bruce Canover was a flesh-and-blood human being. He was also a doppelganger, a double, that the CIA could use. Grojean had assured Camellion that there would not be a problem with the Canover cover.

With the Death Merchant had gone his "family"—his wife, "Ethel

Canover," who was Lana Stanley, a career employee of the CIA, and his "twelve-year-old son William," who was Wilbur Theimer, an agent on contract.

The mission was code-named Brahma-Vishnu-Siva, after the three gods of the Hindu trinity.

Camellion and his family had been in New Delhi only three days when Grojean tipped him off that the CIA had learned that Holtz had tried to reach the Soviet embassy and had failed. Avenging MfS agents, expecting such a move on his part, had been waiting. They had prevented Holtz from getting to the Soviet embassy but had not been able to capture or kill him. Instead, he had shot and killed two of them and escaped.

The Death Merchant had been faced with another problem, and another question. Would Holtz now head for Pakistan, or make his way to Calcutta or Bombay? The Pakistan route would be dangerous. Holtz would choose that route only as a last resort. That left Bombay and Calcutta. The Soviet consulate in Bombay was larger and more approachable by anyone on the run than the Soviet consulate in Calcutta.

The Death Merchant and his family had proceeded to Bombay. With the help of the CIA network in India, he had put into operation a plan he had concocted, one that would help him find out where Holtz-Bedsloe was hiding. The CIA had numerous contacts with gangsters in Bombay. For a price they would help. There was a flaw: Could the same mobsters be taking money from the KGB or the MfS?

Via the Bombay underworld the word was spread that certain people would pay fifteen million rupees to anyone who might give information about Franz Holtz . . . where he was hiding. Three hundred small photographs of the East German agent were also distributed.

The plan had worked!

And had blown up in their faces. . . .

"Camellion, I don't see any need for us to remain in Bombay," Dillman said. "In view of what's happened, it isn't likely that Holtz will try to get to the Soviet consulate. He would have to be crazy. He's not stupid. He knows he's been spotted."

Attached to the CIA station at the United States Embassy in New Delhi, Dillman had followed Camellion, Stanley, and Theimer to Bombay.

"All he can do is go underground, or else leave Bombay," concurred Lana Stanley. "He realizes that the MfS is out to kill him, and he has to suspect that the CIA is after him. As things stand, Holtz doesn't know whether it was the CIA or the MfS who found him on Mookmak Road."

"I will tell you my opinion," Theimer said brusquely. "We know that Holtz has read extensively about Pakistan and Afghanistan. How do we know that he will not try to reach Pakistan? Many of the ships that put in at the Bombay docks also sail to Karachi."

Camellion looked at Theimer. Sitting with his back against the bottom front of the sofa, the "Little Person" seemed comical, even more so when he spoke imperiously in his normal voice, which was only a few octaves higher than the voice of a normally developed man.

"Holtz won't risk the docks," Camellion said. "He assumes that we and the Russians and the MfS will be watching the docks. If he knew he could bump into the KGB first, he might risk it. The Russians would protect him. They take very good care of the people who work for them or who come over to their side."

"But we are not watching the docks!" protested Theimer.

"Holtz doesn't know that," Camellion replied. "We're in the dark, but so is he. His only hope is to find the KGB."

Hondergriff snorted. "The only reason the Russians protect traitors who go over for them is that they use them for propaganda purposes."

"Naturally, and it works," Camellion said. "I didn't say that the Russians respected traitors. But they do give traitors the 'good life' once they're in the Soviet Union. So do the East Germans. It's the East Germans and the Russians who represent the second greatest flaw in our overall security."

"I think the KGB and the MfS are long-distance threats," said Dillman. "No one knows who we are. But . . . we are Occidentals . . . That means . . ."

"Exactly. The KGB and the MfS can narrow down possibilities the same way we did. Then it becomes a matter of clever guessing." There was a smile in Camellion's strange blue eyes. "The KGB and the MfS must have heard about the reward we offered for information about Holtz. This means that the KGB thinks the money was offered by either the MfS or the CIA. MfS doesn't know whether it was CIA or KGB. All three services are right smack in the middle of a pond of uncertainty. Holtz is in the same pond."

"Nonetheless, we still don't have a clue as to where Holtz might go or what he might try to do," Hondergriff said, his clipped accent giving the words added impact.

Barry Dillman almost glared at the Death Merchant. "I sense you're more concerned with the East Germans than with the Russians. The East Germans don't have anything special going for them."

"There's a difference between being worried and being practical," Camellion said coolly. "Don't underestimate East German Intelligence. Where Mischa Wolf's boys specialize, they do so with a meticulousness that impresses others in the intelligence game. MfS is the end product of German thoroughness combined with centralization and discipline that would be unthinkable in West Germany—and you had damn well better remember it!"

"He's right, Barry," Hondergriff said. He watched the Death Merchant get to his feet and walk to a large thermos pitcher on a side table. "Old Mischa Wolf commands an estimated twenty-five hundred intelligence officers. The general consensus is that the quality of these officers has improved markedly over the past ten years. I was at the Pickle Factory station at our embassy in East Berlin for several years. I've had first hand experience with MfS."

Knowing he had said too much without giving facts, Dillman toyed with a button on his blue Brisbane shirt.

Hondergriff continued matter of factly. "I've seen the East Germans use as many as ten to fifteen men to tail one subject. It's all done very smoothly. They're good, those krauts—and they're neat.

"In Moscow or Leningrad, the Soviets will leave your room in a mess after they search it, partly because they're pigs and partly to advertise their power over you and to let you know what they can do. The East Germans would never do that. They're compulsively neat."

"You make them sound almost like gentlemen!" piped up Wilbur Theimer.

"The MfS has its bullyboys, the men in polyester slacks. You can always spot them. But they never physically abuse you the way the Russians sometimes do. You see, with the East Germans you're dealing with a more subtle, more sophisticated, more refined secret police."

The Death Merchant had poured a tall glass of cold *falooda* from the pitcher. *Falooda* was a drink—more of a soup—based on cream, flavored with rose syrup, shredded pistachios, and almonds, and filled with fragments of transparent vermicelli. He turned and headed back toward the chair, glancing at Steve Hondergriff.

"You forgot to mention the more significant ability of the East

German intelligence service," Camellion said. "The East Krauts are masters in the art of training foreign intelligence officers and secret police forces."

"The CIA hasn't done too bad in that direction," spoke up Dillman, defending the Agency. Camellion didn't fail to detect the hardness in his voice and knew that he was all Mom, apple pie, and God Bless America—*Another goof! The CIA can do no wrong! And the President is "sacred" and akin to the Pope!*

Camellion sat down, the glass of *falooda* in his right hand. "The CIA isn't as effective as the MfS in training foreigners because it's chained by a lot of moral restrictions and doesn't build its training methods around a central core of brutality."

"What's so terrible about our not being as sadistic as the East Germans or the Russians?" Dillman fired back.

"Plenty, when it comes to our losing," Camellion replied. "You're making a moral value judgment, and value judgments have nothing to do with effectiveness, with getting the job done, with winning. If they did, the Pope could wave his hands and give his 'blessing,' and we'd have instant world peace."

"Heh, heh, heh," laughed Theimer. "That is a good one! The Pope keeps giving his blessing, but the world keeps right on having wars."

"We'd have 'peace' all right!" grumbled Hondergriff. "If the Pope had his way, world society would move rapidly backward, and we'd have another Dark Age with all the repression that goes with ignorance and superstition."

"We already have a taste of the Great Step Backward—and not from the Pope, either!" spoke up Lana Stanley. "But from our very own President Reagan, who's trying to impose censorship on the American people under the guise of fighting pornography."

"One has to look at facts," Camellion pointed out. "We have proof of the East Germans and their effectiveness by their activities in Angola, Mozambique, Ethiopia, South Yemen, and Nicaragua."

"Well"—Stanley gave a long sigh and looked thoughtfully at Dillman—"I think we can agree that the East German Ministry for State Security is a hundred times more effective than the West German BND, which most experts consider a joke. It wouldn't surprise me if the head of the Bundesnachrichtendienst wasn't an MfS mole! Or a KGB agent-in-place!"

"Mischa Wolf's boys can be found at all levels of West German industry," Camellion said, giving Dillman the eye and seeing him meet his penetrating appraisal. "The majority of them are 'business suit' agents whose job is to steal high-level technology secrets."

"Hold on," Dillman said, annoyed. "The successes of the MfS in West Germany isn't due entirely to the tradecraft brilliance of the East Germans. A lot of it is due to the laziness and the stupidity of the BND."

Camellion finished taking a drink of *falooda* and nodded.

"That's true. It's the inefficiency of the West German BND that makes it so easy for Wolf to send his agents into West Germany. All an MfS agent has to do is get on an S-bahn train at East Berlin's Friedrichstrasse station. Within ten minutes he's in West Berlin. He can be sure that no questions will be asked upon his arrival. A West German spy who might try to make the reverse trip would have to face a phalanx of police."

"It is too bad that we are not looking for Bedsloe in West Germany," offered Wilbur Theimer.

"The only difference would be that we'd be in a white man's country," Camellion said. "We'd still have the KGB and the MfS against us. We know the KGB and its wet-work boys. In case any of you are wondering, the MfS hit boys are just as good, and we can be sure that Wolf will send the best agents he has to find Holtz."

"And to snuff any opposition, which means us!" Hondergriff said. He gave a little laugh. "But I should worry! I have to remain here. For all practical purposes, I'm out of the operation."

"I was thinking that your remaining under cover might not be necessary," Camellion said. "Holtz is going to 'bury' himself, if he hasn't already fled Bombay. Then we have to consider the Indian intelligence service. Sooner or later, DARFA is going to realize that what happened involves international intelligence."

Hondergriff blinked rapidly and moved a hand through his curly brown hair. "What does that have to do with me?"

Lana Stanley said, "DARFA would suspect that Smythe was Holtz? Is that what you're saying, Richard?"

"Steve, you could go to New Delhi with Barry," Camellion said. "You'll both use the underground route and there won't be any danger of DARFA agents or regular Indian police spotting you from an identification sketch based on any description Dev Nargis might have given the Indian authorities."

Steve Hondergriff's face screwed up in thought. "If something broke here in our favor, then you could use agents from the station here in Bombay?"

"Something like that. They can't all be paper pushers."

"Most of them are radio-intercept personnel. There may be a street operative or two among them. I don't know how much experience they've had."

"Richard, you never did answer me," Lana Stanley said in a louder voice, getting to her feet.

"The Indians would suspect that Smythe is Bedsloe, once they get wind of what's going on," Camellion said. "They aren't stupid, even if they do believe in any number of gods."

She made a face and shrugged her slim shoulders. "Personally, I think we've scored a big fat zero. We had our chance at Holtz and blew it." She tacked on quickly. "It wasn't your fault, Richard. But I think it's over." She continued to talk as she walked toward the side table. "I also think that Holtz is rather stupid. Why does he have to go in person to the Soviet embassy or to one of their consulates? All he would have to do is telephone and have the KGB come and get him."

Camellion followed the curve of her hips and watched her pick up the pitcher of *falooda*. "It wouldn't do Holtz any good if he did phone. The KGB isn't about to go out and meet anyone who says he's so and so. The KGB is always very cautious. So is Holtz. He's not about to turn over the four PALs until he's positive the Soviets will grant him asylum."

"I can't feature Holtz trying to reach the Soviet consulate here in Bombay," Hondergriff said ominously, "not after what happened at the house on Mookmak Road. There's a Soviet consulate in Calcutta. That's his best bet."

"But from here, Calcutta is twice as far as New Delhi," Camellion said. "When he leaves Bombay, he'll return to New Delhi. He almost has to. He's a white face in a sea of brown."

"Then what?" A tall glass in her hand, Stanley walked back to the sofa. "Not that it makes any difference, Mr. G. is at a deadend, and our station here in Bombay hasn't even heard a worthwhile rumor."

"A lot can happen in a week," the Death Merchant reminded her. "Meanwhile, we have to keep up the pretense that we're the Canover family. I'm on leave from Briswinn Institute and doing research for a book—remember?"

Stanley's expression changed to one of dismay. "I suppose that means we'll visit the Elephanta Caves in a few days. They were next on the schedule."

"We'll take a lot of photographs and make notes," Camellion said. "Everything has to appear normal."

"Yeah, well do not count on taking your 'son' with you to those stupid caves!" protested Theimer. "I'll remain at the hotel where it's cool."

Once more a mental picture of Professor Canover rose in the Death Merchant's mind. *He's on vacation in Colorado,* Grojean had said. *He'll be in the mountains, not far from Boulder, for six weeks.*

Even so, the feeling of uneasiness persisted. . . .

Chapter Five

Richard Camellion and Lana Stanley did not go to the Elephanta Caves with only hope and a trust in the impossible. The Death Merchant carried a .380 Turkish MKE pistol in an ankle holster. In his camera bag was a 9mm Uzi semiautomatic pistol with a twenty-five-round magazine. Lana Stanley had a 9mm 92-SB Beretta in her large shoulder bag. Possession of firearms is illegal in India. Firearms "cause crime." Such repression meant that there was a brisk traffic in firearms, particularly handguns, the most prized of all being American-made weapons.

Camellion and Stanley did not have a choice. Considering recent events and the possibility that enemy agents would love to make them targets, "Professor Canover" and "wife" were not about to walk a tightrope of suicide by being unarmed anywhere in public.

It was during the middle of the afternoon that a group of tourists approached the columned veranda of the Elephanta Caves. Among them were Mr. and Mrs. Bruce Canover.

Earlier, Banupa Subramaniam, the Indian tour guide, had explained that no one knew exactly who had carved the cave temples and executed the works of art in them. A nervous little man who jumped about like a grasshopper, Subramaniam explained that shortly before the time of Elephanta's excavation, between the sixth and eighth centuries, Bombay had experienced the golden age of the late Guptas, during which time the talents of artists had free scope. Sanskrit had been finely polished, and Kalidasa and other writers—under the court's liberal patronage—had helped to bring about a revival of Hindu beliefs.

"That Siva was well loved and the many ramifications of his personality well understood is shown by the polish and refinement of the artwork in the caves," Subramaniam said.

The outside of the caves consisted of a columned veranda thirty feet wide and ten feet deep, and was approached by steps flanked by sculptured elephants, each one of natural size and carved from solid granite. At each end of the facade a pillar projected from the wall, carved in the shape of a *dwarapala,* or doorkeeper. The entire temple was 164 feet square. A series of wide stone steps led down into the earth, to the caves 176 feet below the surface.

Camellion's eyes missed nothing, even as he snapped pictures with his 35mm Nikon and its 35-200 f/3.5.4.5 zoom lens. Everything and everyone appeared normal. There were some men and women singles among the tourists, all of whom were of diverse nationalities. The Orientals were obvious. There were half a dozen Americans, and Camellion and Stanley had heard other men and women discussing the artwork in French, and in German and Spanish. Once, Camellion thought he had heard Polish, but he could not be sure.

Some of the men wore lightweight coats. Most, however, like Camellion, were in short-sleeved sport shirts and lightweight slacks. Many of the women wore shorts, and almost all of them carried parasols as protection against the unrelenting sun. Bombay is always very humid, and May is always very hot. The temperature at the moment was ninety-seven degrees Fahrenheit.

"I'll be glad when we're below in the caves," Lana said, wiping her face with a hand towel. "This heat takes all ambition from a person."

"We'll be below shortly," Camellion replied. He turned slightly, as if to adjust the strap of his Gemini camera bag on his left shoulder, and glanced at the people behind him and Lana. All was normal, or so it would seem. But East German or Soviet agents would not be wearing signs. Neither would Indian agents of DARFA.

Once the group had descended six flights of stairs and was in the caves, Banupa Subramaniam escorted them into the first temple, the Hall of Lights, 200 feet long and 80 feet wide. The artwork was incredible. The sculptures had been carved from the solid granite walls. There were giant figures of *dwarapalas,* and a manifestation of Siva combining the male and female forms. On the west wall were figures of Siva and his consort Parvati. The most outstanding sculpture of all was on the east wall. It was Mahesamurti the Great Lord, an eighteen-foot triple image, the three faces representing the Hindu trinity: Brahma the Creator on the right; Siva the Destroyer on the left; and in the center Vishnu the Preserver of life, of the universe itself.

Camellion snapped ten photographs of the Mahesamurti as grasshopper Subramaniam explained in his loud voice that the multiheaded deity was a composite of the stern, just, loving father figure—an expression of the monotheistic tendency in Hinduism.

From the Hall of Lights the group proceeded north, and then west, through a long passage, to the Temple of the Gods. Here were giant but beautiful sculptures depicting the marriage of Siva and Parvati; Ravana, the Demon King—"The Christian would call him Satan"— the heavenly abode of Siva; and the charming group of Siva and Parvati with lesser male and female divinities showering flowers on them.

The last temple was the Lingam Shrine. To reach the shrine the tourists retraced their steps from the Temple of the Gods and moved east along the wide east-west passage, then north. To have continued east would have taken the tourists to the group of caves that had only been partially touched by Indian artists and other craftsmen.

The Lingam Shrine was devoted to the sexual side of the gods. Even though the Indian people frowned on kissing and other displays of public affection, they regarded sex as normal and as natural as eating and drinking. Unlike Westerners, they did not feel guilty over sexual desire.

Highly imaginative carvings covered the wall of the Lingam Shrine, in which the *lingam* and the *yoni*, the male and the female sex organs, were prominently displayed. There was Siva with his gigantic phallus. There was Yama, the god of death; Indra, who had a thousand eyes; Ashvin, the god of the starry firmament; Varuna, who resided over the cosmos; Soma, the god of drunkenness; and a hundred other gods and goddesses, all of them with their sex organs, except the terrible Kali, who was clothed. However, she wore a girdle of dangling penises, complete with testicles.

Banupa Subramaniam explained to the group of curious and intrigued tourists—many of whom were embarrassed—that there was even a Hindu sect, the Shakta, that worshiped the male phallus.

"The Sanskrit word *shakti* means strength or power and represents the divine energy emanating from a male deity, the energy pouring from the tip of his phallus."

He then pointed to a large altar shaped like a male penis and said that Shakta priests often killed a goat on such an altar.

Many of the tourists snapped pictures, including Professor Bruce Canover. One woman, however—she looked American—muttered, "It's disgraceful. It's pure pornography!"

Camellion smiled. *Good old Edwin Meese and his "Commission on Pornography" would soon put a stop to such "filth"!*

Subramaniam then announced that the next step would be the caves. Some of the caves were connected by twisting passages; others ran into each other so that it was difficult to tell where one ended and the next one began. The floor of many of the caves dipped, to the extent that from floor to ceiling the distance was sometimes a hundred feet. There were no stalactites or stalagmites.

Scattering out, the members of the tour group moved through the short passage opening to the corridor that stretched from west to east. Every now and then the Death Merchant turned sideways as he pretended to adjust the shoulder strap of the camera bag. Halfway through the passage, he spotted the danger.

There wasn't anything unusual about a woman carrying a parasol. All the women had closed their parasols and tucked them under their arms. It was how this particular woman, coming up behind Lana Stanley, was carrying her parasol that triggered a warning in the Death Merchant. She was holding it as one would hold a sword, as though she were preparing to use the pointed tip to scratch on the stone floor.

It was the pointed tip that had started the danger signals flashing in Camellion's mind. The KGB sometimes used a special kind of umbrella to assassinate its targets (or a similar-type cane). Concealed in the tip of the center frame was a pointed needle that would pop out when one pressed a latch close to the latch that opened the umbrella.

In her middle twenties, the dark-haired woman was moving straight toward Lana Stanley and would pass her on the left. Camellion was also certain what she would do. As she passed, she would "accidentally" scratch Stanley's left leg on the outside. The needle would move easily through the thin material of Lana's powder-blue slacks.

Any number of poisons could be used on the needle, poisons that would kill within a hour or in a week. The nice part about such an assassination method was that by the time the victim felt ill and realized something was very wrong, the assassin could be a thousand miles away.

The Death Merchant was not paranoid. It was possible that the woman—no one seemed to be with her—was only an innocent tourist who just happened to be carrying her umbrella in an odd manner. Should that be the case and he grabbed the parasol, he could always give the excuse that he had stumbled and had reacted automatically, grabbing the first thing that was handy. If the woman was a wet-work agent and he did nothing, he doubted if Lana Stanley would live to see the sunset.

Mercy, mercy, Mother Percy! If Stanley has been marked for a target, so have I!

There was only one way to find out. He didn't have time to warn Stanley, or pull any weapons. He had only seconds in which to act.

As Lana and the woman behind her took another step forward, Camellion stopped and stepped wide to his left, his movement so sudden that Katerina Minsovik didn't have time to halt or raise the umbrella. The next thing she knew, Camellion had clamped his left hand around her right wrist and in a very low voice was saying in Russian, "Sorry, you pig-farmer slut. Today the KGB loses!"

At once, he saw the look of surprise on the woman's face. She had definitely understood his words. Instantly, fear and hatred bloomed in her eyes. Camellion had been right. She was a Mokryye Dela "blood wet-work" specialist.

Camellion acted immediately. As Lana Stanley—she had noticed he was not by her side—turned to see what was wrong, the Death Merchant twisted Minsovik's wrist and brought up his right fist to her chin in a short uppercut. Her head snapped back. She let out a groan and began to sag.

Stanley at once knew that something was very wrong. She reached quickly for the SB Beretta pistol in her shoulder bag. The people behind her and the Death Merchant didn't know what to think or what to do. Was it a man-and-wife quarrel? Is that why he had hit the woman? Some of the men felt that they should interfere, but, unde-cided, they hesitated. No one hesitated when they saw Stanley pull the Beretta from the shoulder bag. They darted to the walls and then began to run in the opposite direction, some of the women screaming. In front of Camellion and Stanley, Banupa Subramaniam and the rest of the tourists ran toward the caves.

Behind Camellion and Stanley, one man had not run away—a full-faced individual in sunglasses and a light tan summer suit. Not more than thirty feet behind the Death Merchant and his "wife," Nikolai Gosnihikis reached inside his coat at the same time Katerina Minsovik fell, Stanley released the safety of her Beretta, and Camellion threw himself to the stone floor, his right hand darting inside the camera bag.

Gosnihikis—Minsovik's backup—had his SIG pistol outside his coat when Lana Stanley fired, the loud crack of the Beretta sending echoes rolling and tumbling up and down the passage. The Beretta's 9mm hollow-point bullet hit the Russian between the open collar of his sport shirt, high in the chest. She pulled the trigger the second time; this time the slug slammed into the dying man's stomach. Corkscrewing around, he started to topple as the Death Merchant, the Uzi pistol in his right hand, got to his feet.

"What was she going to do?" asked Stanley in an excited voice. She glanced down in disgust at the unconscious Katerina Minsovik, then at the dead Nikolai Gosnihikis.

Camellion picked up the umbrella. "Watch the tip," he said. He gently pushed inward on the short length of metal to one side of the regular strip that opened the parasol. Instantly a half-inch needle shot outward from a tiny hole in the center and at the end of the steel tip.

"She would have 'accidentally' scratched you," Camellion explained, his lean face as hard as his voice. "Within hours—if not within minutes—you would have had an apparent heart attack. The joker behind us would have taken care of me in some way—he thought."

Stanley looked amazed. "But—how did you know? What warned you?"

"Experience. It was the way she acted, the way she was moving toward you."

"I—I don't understand how they could have m-made us so fast. It's incredible!"

Camellion jammed the tip of the umbrella on the floor, breaking off the poisoned needle. "There isn't anything incredible about it. It was only good intelligence work on the part of the KGB. All they used was deduction."

Stanley looked up and down the passage, the Beretta still in her hand. "We'll have to get out of here and fast," she said nervously.

"We can't." Camellion tossed aside the umbrella. "We don't have any transportation of our own, and I can't see us escaping in a tour bus. All we can do is tell the police that we were attacked and defended ourselves"—he gave a long sigh—"with weapons bought on the black market."

Stanley's eyes widened in dismay. "But—we'll never find Holtz. And if we admit to the police that we had guns in our possession—"

She couldn't understand why Camellion was so calm.

"The show's not over with yet," he said. "Come along, 'dear.' We'll go to the surface and wait for the police. It's all we can do."

They hurried down the passage and soon reached the east-west corridor. Turning, they started west, and at length came to the wide passage that led to the Hall of Light. No sooner had they turned the corner than they saw four men, three in suits, one in slacks and sport shirt, all four coming toward them from fifty feet to the south. Intuition told the Death Merchant who they were—KGB hit men.

The four Russians pulled up short, stared, and one of them said in Russian, "There they are. Kill them!"

"Oh, my God!" gasped Stanley, ducking behind the corner with Camellion. "What are we going to do?"

"Stay against the wall," Camellion ordered in a voice Stanley had never heard before, a strange voice, a voice without fear, a voice of cold, calculating efficiency.

The Death Merchant was aware that trained gunmen, especially KGB wet-work artists, wouldn't bunch up. They would spread out and move in with a quick zigzag. He had to slow the four gunmen, or he and Stanley would never reach the caves—and where had the four come from and how did they intend to escape?

Camellion leaned around the corner and triggered off two fast shots with the Uzi pistol, the 9mm projectiles hitting only air and the west wall. But the two rounds did cause the four enraged Russians to drop to the floor and get off rounds from a variety of weapons. Their slugs zipped into the stones at the corner and zinged off into space with loud ricochets whose screaming tailed after Camellion and Stanley, both of whom were running straight east toward the caves, their only interruption Katerina Minsovik. Regaining consciousness, she had taken Nikolai Gosnihikis's 9mm SIG autopistol, was coming out of the short passage, and was trying to aim down on Camellion when the Death Merchant fired—while he and Stanley were still on the run. His 9mm FMJ projectile popped her in the face just below the left nostril. The hunk of metal mashed its way through her upper teeth, skipped across the roof of her mouth, and bored through the back of her throat, the impact making her head snap back then jerk from side to side.

Camellion and Stanley darted through the archway into the unfinished caves only a few moments before the four Russians came around the corner and began running straight east, thinking that their two targets had darted into the short north-south passage that led to the Lingam Shrine. They realized their mistake too late. A hundred and ten feet to the east, the Death Merchant leaned out from one side of the archway and fired very quickly, having only a mini-moment in which to body-point. The Uzi roared, and Josef Bronsky, a ten-year veteran with the Soviet KGB, stopped as though he had run into an invisible steel wall. It was really the other way around. A very small 9mm "wall" had crashed into him, just below the tip of his breastbone. He gave a loud cry, dropped the Finnish 9mm Lahti pistol in his left hand, doubled over and fell.

The other three Russians were very good, very expert. Yuly Tretyakov and Victor Bugov darted to the walls. Vsevolod Prastev stopped and opened fire with a 9mm Hungarian Tokagypt v58 pistol. *Zinggggg-zinnnng!* Two slugs hit the stones only inches from Camellion's head. A third grazed the inside of his right arm. Camellion cried out in pain and jerked back, a drop of blood dropping from his arm. There were half a dozen more rapid shots and more *zinggssss* as metal flew off hard granite.

"That was close," Lana whispered, staring at the Death Merchant's arm. "They're determined to kill us. Surely they must realize that we can keep going back into the caves and that they could never get to us?"

"They're counting on us running out of ammo," Camellion said. He looked around the cavern. Work in this cave, as well as the other caves to the east, had never been completed. No one knew why. It was believed by some historians that the work had ceased because of a religious conflict between Hinduism and Buddhism. The evidence they cited was the artwork in which an attempt had been made to blend Hinduism with Buddhism.

In this cave—to the east and beyond seven slim pillars—there was a Buddha on a lotus seat supported by snake-hooded demigods. On the south side of the cave, next to the entrance that led to the cavern beyond, was a huge stone figure of Bodhisattva Padmapani, a near-Buddha and one of the forms through which Buddha passed before he reached Padmapani, or Enlightenment.

"We'll trap them in a crossfire," Camellion whispered. He stooped and pulled the MKE autopistol from its ankle holster.

"Why bother?" She looked at him in confusion. "You have plenty of ammo in the Uzi. Besides, by now someone must have called the police. The shots were heard from above."

"I don't like people shooting at me, especially damned pig farmers," Camellion replied. "Now give me your Beretta. It has a larger mag capacity than the MKE."

"I don't understand," Stanley said, more confused than ever. "You still have almost a full magazine in the Uzi. Why—"

"You're going to use the Uzi and the MKE," Camellion told her and, taking the Beretta, handed her the Turkish autoloader. He quickly explained his plan. She would get behind the Buddha and snap off four or five shots with the MKE. Then she would move to the other side of the Buddha and fire half a dozen shots with the Uzi, thereby giving the impression that there were two persons behind the granite carving.

"I'll be behind the other figure to the south and chop them down with the Beretta from there," Camellion finished, handing her the Uzi. "You get off the first shots. You don't have to hit any of them. Just fire to draw their attention."

"I hope to God you know what you're doing!" Lana said, her breath catching in her throat.

"Don't worry about it," he said with a chuckle. "Sometimes I surprise even myself."

The three Russians did not storm into the cave like a pack of gangbusters out of control. The Mokryye Dela killers used an intelligent tactic, just as Camellion knew they would. While Yuly Tretyakov and Victor Bugov fired shot after shot around the sides of the archway, Vsevolod Prastev began slithering in on his stomach, a Tokagypt in his right hand, a Lahti in his left hand.

Bugov and Tretyakov were firing in all directions but down, and Camellion and Stanley had no choice but to remain behind the statues, she in back of the Buddha, he in back of the Bodhisattva Padmapani. But came the lag time in the firing, and Lana Stanley, in spite of her deep fear, leaned around the right side of the Buddha. She didn't get a chance to fire. Prastev, spotting her, was too fast. He got off a round with his Tokagypt as she ducked back and snapped off a shot to warn Camellion. Lana then moved to the left of the enormous stone Buddha.

Regardless of his orders to the young woman, the Death Merchant always relied on his own resources. The instant lag time occurred, he stepped from behind the Bodhisattva Padmapani. He could not have picked a worse time. . . .

No amateur, Prastev had not been fooled. He had seen Stanley, and when she fired a shot upward from behind the Buddha, he had guessed that he and his two comrades had walked into what was to be a crossfire. He was swinging the Finnish Lahti pistol to his left as the Death Merchant stepped out from behind the Bodhisattva Padmapani, and Victor Bugov and Yuly Tretyakov zigzagged through the doorway. By then, Lana Stanley had reached the other side of the Buddha and was also leaning out to fire.

Spotting Camellion, Prastev didn't have time to aim. He fired blindly in the Death Merchant's direction, the 9mm bullet missing Camellion by seven inches. And any miss was as good as a mile.

During that bare shave of a second, Tretyakov, who had darted to his left, could not see Stanley, nor she—a moment later—him. However, she did have a full view of Victor Bugov, who was running to his right and who had spotted her and the Death Merchant.

The cavern exploded with gunfire. Camellion's 9mm Beretta bullet popped Prastev high in the forehead. The hollow point flattened off upon impact, bored through the Russian's skull, and buried itself in his brain only a micromoment before Victor Bugov's 9mm Para slug sped by close to Camellion's left hip and Lana Stanley's .380 MKE round punched Bugov in the stomach. A big *Ohhhh!* jumped out of his mouth. He doubled over and fell face down . . . moaning. . . .

The Death Merchant could see Yuly Tretyakov, who was too experienced to waste time by turning around and trying to snap off a shot. His sole aim was to reach the north side of the Buddha. He almost succeeded. Half of his body was to the side of the Buddha when Camellion fired, the bullet slicing into Tretyakov's right thigh and knocking his body to the floor so that he fell on his back. From Camellion's position, he could see only to the middle of the Russian's abdomen, but that was more than enough. Camellion's next bullet caught Tretyakov in the groin and whacked him with sheer shock into unconsciousness. He would be a corpse in the marketplace before he would awaken.

But Victor Bugov was still alive. Lying on his back, he was twisting back and forth and moaning. The Death Merchant—humanitarian that he was—put the Russian out of his misery. He hit him in the head with a 9mm Beretta bullet.

Silence! An eerie stillness. Camellion and Stanley crept forward, both ready for trouble of the worst kind. Could more hit agents be waiting outside? No, not likely.

Presently, Camellion and Stanley linked up and were standing together. "Five of them, six with the woman," mused the Death Merchant. "Moscow sure wanted us dead."

"I'm not looking forward to sitting in an Indian penitentiary," Lana said caustically. "I suppose you know we can't count on the Pickle Factory for help?"

Camellion shrugged. "By now, some of the people who ran back upstairs will have called the police. We might as well go to the surface and give ourselves up—and don't worry about going to a Hindu pen. We won't."

"Go up—with three guns?" Lana shook her head in disbelief.

"We'll leave them here in the caves and walk out with our hands in the air. Indian police have nervous trigger fingers. . . ."

Disguised as an elderly man with gray hair and a gray mustache, Major Boris Bukashev, who had been among the people to flee the caverns, found it difficult to believe that his crack squad had failed in their assignment. It wasn't possible. Ten minutes earlier, hearing police sirens approaching, he had turned on the tiny transmitter in his pocket and sent a signal to the helicopter hovering several hundred feet away. The pilot had revved up and flown off.

Almost numb with rage, Bukashev stood there with other tourists and watched the police, sixty feet ahead of him, put handcuffs on Bruce and Ethel Canover.

"I think it is just terrible," a woman, standing next to Bukashev, said to her husband. "They're murderers. They shot those people down in cold blood."

"Yes, that's right, dear," the husband replied.

Another man addressed his remark to Bukashev, who was watching the police shove the Canovers into separate police cars. "I think they're really communist terrorists."

Bukashev looked properly horrified. "I'll bet you're right," he said in good "American" English. "The communists are always stirring up trouble—those damned atheists. . . ."

Chapter Six

This was a first for Police Inspector Juderwal Bhilainagar, the first time he had taken Americans into custody. At first, he had not been sure of how to proceed with the questioning of Bruce and Ethel Canover, neither of whom had yet been charged with any crime. Didn't Americans have a lot of money, and didn't the American government have a lot of power? Be that as it may, it was clear that Mr. and Mrs. Canover had shot and killed six people, six Occidentals like themselves. Whether it was murder or self-defense still had to be determined.

The Indian police had taken the Canovers to police headquarters close to Town Hall in the Fort section of Bombay. For four hours, Bhilainagar had interrogated Camellion while other detectives questioned Lana Stanley. Assisting Bhilainagar in his questioning of the Death Merchant were Tanrin Kapoor and Jamil Satwaharawi, two twenty-year veterans of the Bombay Municipal Police Department.

"Let's begin again, Mr. Canover." Bhilainagar spoke with a slight British accent. "I want to know the real reason why you and your wife came to India. We know it wasn't to study Indian culture."

(You know nothing of the kind. You're only fishing, and you don't have any bait.)

"Inspector, by now you have sent men to our hotel and have seen our passports and visas. Your people have searched our rooms. You know I'm in the process of gathering material for a book on India I'm going to write. I do hope your detectives didn't frighten my son."

"They didn't," Bhilainagar said, his eyes studying Camellion.

"For a man about to be charged with six murders, you're remarkably calm, Professor Canover," said Tanrin Kapoor. A Bengali, he had skin the color of weak tea and was a Christian.

"I see no need for hysteria," said Camellion, looking straight ahead. He sat at the end of a long table. Hip-sitting in front of him, on either side of the table, were Kapoor and Satwaharawi. Behind the Death Merchant, his hands on the back of Camellion's chair, stood Bhilainagar.

"And you maintain that you and your wife didn't know the names of the people you and she shot?" said Bhilainagar.

Camellion shrugged. "How could we know their names. We had never seen them before. The woman was going to stab my wife in the back with the end of an umbrella. I prevented her from murdering my wife by taking the umbrella away from her and knocking her out."

Jamil Satwaharawi nodded. "Then you shot Maurice DePris. How long did you know him?"

"I've never heard of—what did you say his name was?"

"He was the man behind you and Mrs. Canover. He was the first man you murdered."

"Wrong! I didn't murder anyone. My wife did not murder anyone. What happened is that my wife saw him pulling a gun from underneath his coat. She shot him to save our lives. It was self-defense on her part." Camellion's voice became hard and accusatory. "Or is it against the law in India for foreign visitors to defend themselves against Indian thugs?"

"Those men and that woman weren't Indian and you know it!" Satwaharawi, who didn't like foreigners, had come right up to the edge of losing his temper. He was a Punjabi and, as a Muslim, considered Americans the epitome of materialism—brash, unprincipled hypocrites whose only god was money.

Inspector Bhilainagar warned Satwaharawi with a deep frown and a quick shake of his head. Satwaharawi became silent and quickly regained his former professional composure.

Bhilainagar intoned, "Mr. Canover, you said that your wife shot DePris with a weapon you and she bought from a taxicab driver."

"I didn't say any such thing." Camellion sounded bored and mechanical. "I did say that Mrs. Canover saved our lives with a handgun I bought from a street vendor. The vendor approached me. I don't remember the name of the street."

"It doesn't make any difference who approached whom," Bhilainagar said. "Possession of firearms is illegal in India. You and your wife committed a very serious crime when you bought three handguns, a crime that could put both of you in a penitentiary for fifteen years."

"Five years for each weapon," Tanrin Kapoor said smugly. "You did admit buying three handguns from a cabbie."

"From a street vendor."

Bhilainagar's voice was ruthless, brutal even. "I warn you, Mr. Canover. We'll see to it that you and your wife get the maximum sentence for illegal possession of firearms if you don't start telling the truth. We're getting tired of this nonsense."

Jamil Satwaharawi leaned closer to the Death Merchant, his stare two ice picks stabbing into Camellion.

"We have more than a dozen eyewitnesses who saw your wife shoot DePris, and saw you take that Uzi from your camera bag. All of them will testify against you in court."

"Fine," Camellion said pleasantly. This time he looked straight at Satwaharawi, and stared directly into his eyes. "Those same witnesses will also have to testify for us. They will have to swear that they saw —what did you say his name was?—pull a gun from underneath his coat and try to kill my wife and me. Other witnesses among the tourists will have to tell the court that they saw four other men shooting at us—and you did find weapons with this four." *(Now for the intimated threat of an international stink!)* "It's a very sad day when American tourists can't defend themselves against trash in a foreign country. It's even worse when the police of that nation blame the tourists for trying to defend themselves. The entire world should know about it!"

"I told you that—" Satwaharawi snapped his mouth shut and glared at Camellion, whose mind was racing and analyzing probabilities. If Bhilainagar and his men were only half good, they would have found part of the poisoned needle in the umbrella. Another piece of good news was that the Indian authorities couldn't prosecute without the umbrella. Nor would the authorities be able to deny that the umbrella, because of its special mechanism, was a special killing weapon.

Camellion was not concerned about Lana Stanley. He had ordered her to say nothing except *Ask my husband.*

On the wall to the left of the table was a large mirror, seven feet long and six feet high—two-way glass. Was it possible that the police suspected that he was the man who had "borrowed" the taxicab? It certainly was. Camellion assumed that Bhilainagar had already brought in the cabdriver to have a long look at him through the glass. He wasn't worried. The man would not be able to identify him; neither would Dev Nargis.

There were a lot of routes to be considered, some good, some bad. It was not likely that the Indian authorities would prosecute for murder. The Indian system of justice was based on English jurisprudence. Indian prosecutors would not be able to get a conviction. There were too many witnesses to prove that Camellion and Stanley had fired in self-defense. Furthermore, a murder trial would mean that the Indian government would have to keep dozens of foreign witnesses in Bombay for—how many months? Almost an impossibility. International law was too tangled. Another plus for Camellion and Stanley was that no native Indians had been killed.

On the dark side, Camellion could not expect any help from the United States Embassy in New Delhi. Uncle Sam was powerless when U.S. citizens committed a crime in a foreign country.

But the Indian authorities could prosecute for possession of illegal handguns. The case was open and shut.

There were other angles to be considered. Inspector Bhilainagar and his men would also wonder why two American "tourists" had been attacked by five men and one woman, all of whom carried identification from six different nations. Inspector Bhilainagar would have to realize that the "murders" smacked of something international. What would Bhilainagar do?

He'll call in the Indian Central Bureau of Identification, the Indian "FBI." The CBI will then confer with the Dijuki Aliwarikor Rijidij Fevanagari Amayratatra, the Bureau of Internal Affairs and National Security—DARFA.

The CBI and DARFA would know at once that the gun battle in the Elephanta Caves was somehow connected with international espionage. Still another reason why the Indians would not prosecute for murder—And probably not for possession of firearms: The Indian government would suspect it had been a battle between the CIA and the KGB. New Delhi would not want to be caught in the middle, between the United States and the Soviet Union. No way. The Indians, like bisexuals, liked to walk on both sides of the street.

A realist, the Death Merchant admitted to himself that the biggest hole in the dam was the cover he and Stanley were using. A prolonged trial in India would mean that the CIA would have to keep the real Canover family under wraps in the United States. For perhaps as long as a year. An impossibility. The real Canovers could not suddenly vanish. Indian newspapers would name names, and the entire cover would fall apart. Newspapers in the United States would be quick to ask what was going on. After all, how could there be two Bruce and Ethel Canovers with a son named William . . . two Canovers with the same profession, with the same address? Nonsense!

"Mr. Canover, you maintain that you are writing a book about Indian social customs," said Inspector Bhilainagar.

"No. I said I was going to write *a* book."

"Nonetheless, you are considered an authority on Indian history and social customs. Is that not so?"

"Yes."

"Tell us—what was the Gupta Empire?"

"The Gupta Empire lasted until the end of the fifth century A.D. It was the golden age of Hinduism. It was during this period that Sanskrit literature attained great heights. The name Gupta comes from Chandragupta. He was a Hindu prince from East India."

Looking defeated and disgusted, Tanrin Kapoor snapped, "Give us your definition of a Hindu."

Camellion pretended to think for a moment. "Well, gentlemen, the ancient classical definition of a Hindu is one who believes in the Vedas, and who believes in his own personal *dharma,* the thread that contributes to the larger social order."

Jamil Satwaharawi started to speak, but Camellion silenced him with "I'm not finished. The truth is that the Hindus are a people first, a religion second. I would say the Hindus are much like the Jews in today's modern world. The word *Hindu* is primarily a social term. In this respect, I feel that a Hindu is best defined by the process of elimination. A Hindu is an inhabitant of India who does not profess to belong to another religion.

"As you gentlemen know, the word *Hindu* comes from the Persian. It means 'river people.' This leads to purity. The Hindus themselves emphasize purity of birth. One cannot become a Hindu. One cannot convert to Hinduism. One is born a Hindu." Camellion smiled and gave a deep sigh. "Really, gentlemen, isn't this ridiculous? I was born in the United States, but I still can't tell you the name of George Washington's sister-in-law."

Kapoor didn't speak. Neither did Jamil Satwaharawi, who was careful not to look directly into Camellion's cold blue eyes. Once had been enough. There was something incomprehensible in those blue depths, something mysteriously alien that Satwaharawi could not define.

Inspector Bhilainagar had walked to the front of the Death Merchant and was standing to Camellion's left, his hands on his hips.

"Would you consider a polygraph test ridiculous?" he asked.

Camellion played innocent—and dumb. "Do you mean a lie detector?"

Bhilainagar smiled slyly. "Yes—and you know what a lie detector is. Will you take a polygraph test?"

"Why not. I have nothing to hide."

(And can beat any polygraph in existence.)

The Death Merchant was not at all concerned about a polygraph. The device did not "detect lies." It only recorded signs of anxiety, such as increased pulse rate, breathing rate, and perspiration. The subject might be lying, or he might be thinking of something unpleasant. Or he might be neurotic and extremely nervous.

Camellion wanted to laugh. *A lie detector works as long as the subject believes it works. A good examiner can scare the crap out of you.*

When the facts were divorced from the myths, it could be seen that the polygraph was merely a portable cousin of common medical instruments, a recorder only, a recorder of thoracic breathing, abdominal breathing, respiration, and blood pressure. Anxiety can be caused by any number of sources. Even being hooked up to a polygraph can cause anxiety because everyone feels guilty about something.

Polygraphists were the biggest liars of all. They were quick to claim that their procedure had an accuracy rate close to 95 percent. The evidence indicated otherwise and revealed that at best their results were comparable to those derived from standardized psychological exams like the Minnesota Multiphasic Personality Inventory, which claimed to be 80 percent accurate.

You might as well toss a coin!

As he was led from the interrogation room, Camellion wondered what interrogation technique the examiner would use. There was the *relevant/irrelevant (R/I) method,* which assumed that someone who was lying would have a greater physiological reaction to questions linked to a crime he had committed than to innocuous questions.

The *control question technique (CQT)* had been developed to get around some of the R/I's faults. It, too, assumed that liars would be more nervous about relevant questions. but it added to the mixture of questions that were supposed to provoke stronger responses among innocent subjects.

The third method was the *concealed information test (CIT)*. Its goal was to determine whether a subject knew something about a crime that only a guilty party could know.

The CQT method was the most common technique used in investigating crimes. The Death Merchant was more amused than worried. Stanley would also agree to take a polygraph test, and she would also know how to beat the machine. All professional CIA covert agents in the field were taught how to outwit a lie detector, taught by the very same people who taught personnel of the FBI, the Secret Service, NSA, and so on, how to *use* a polygraph and *give* polygraph tests— specialists in Building 3165 at Fort McClellan, three miles north of Anniston, Alabama, U.S.A.

Beating the polygraph involved holding one's breath during relevant questions and invoking the "pucker factor," the tightening of the anal sphincter muscle. When the anus tightened, the blood pressure would rise. Breathe right and tighten right and the machine would "prove" you were lying if you answered *Yes* to *Are you a human being?*

Chapter Seven

Bhabha Jehangir, the DARFA official, studied the polygraph charts of Bruce and Ethel Canover. Neither he nor Amtri Zumbihig, who was standing next to him, had ever seen such monumental Mount Everests of lines on a chart. The charts were filled with nothing but a constant chain of high peaks and low valleys. According to the charts the Canovers had even lied when asked such irrelevant questions as "Are you in India?" and "Are you American citizens?" More realistically, the interpretation was that the Canovers had neither lied nor told the truth.

"The Canovers used some method to trick the machine," Inspector Bhilainagar said, watching Jehangir and Zumbihig, the latter of whom was a CBI agent. "The examiner we used was trained in London by Scotland Yard and has been giving polygraph tests for nine years. He's one of the best in India."

"I don't doubt his ability," Jehangir said. "It was not his fault." Short, heavy, fat-faced, and slow-moving, Jehangir moved away from the charts on Bhilainagar's desk, a thoughtful expression on his dark face. "The Canovers have to be intelligence agents who have been trained to outwit a polygraph. They are probably CIA."

"And the six they shot?" asked Bhilainagar, not letting on that he had suspected that the entire mess had something to do with international espionage.

"I think they were Soviet KGB."

"So do I," said Amtri Zumbihig. He looked at Inspector Bhilainagar, who had poured tea and was dropping a cube of sugar into the cup. "All six were supposedly citizens of different countries—so we are supposed to believe. That's too convenient. Five men and one woman—supposedly strangers to each other—don't try to kill two Americans unless they have something in common—not only in common with each other, but also in common with the two Americans. We are definitely dealing with an intelligence matter."

After a short pause, Zumbihig asked in a curious voice, "Inspector, is your department going to recommend that the Canovers be prosecuted for murder?"

Stirring the sugar in the cup, Juderwal Bhilainagar studied Zumbihig, who, like Bhabha Jehangir, was a Hindu. Only unlike Jehangir, who was of the Vaisya or merchant caste, Zumbihig was of the Kshatriya or warrior caste. Zumbihig was different from Jehangir in another way: He was tall, quick-moving, and built like an athlete who exercised for several hours a day.

"We wouldn't be able to get a conviction for murder," Bhilainagar said in a practical voice. "There are several dozen witnesses who would swear that the Canovers only defended themselves. We're convinced that the Canovers did shoot in self-defense. Due to international law, we wouldn't be able to detain the tourists as material witnesses, but their affidavits would be sufficient. Would either of you care for tea?"

"Americans are not well liked in India," Jehangir said slowly, as if turning over each word. "A jury could convict them in spite of the affidavits. Of course, the Canovers would have one of the best American criminal lawyers, who would work with half a dozen of our own best legal minds. They would insist on at least half of the jury being Anglo-Indians." He smiled at Bhilainagar. "I don't mean to offend you, Inspector Bhilainagar."

"You haven't. I quite understand, and you're right." Bhilainagar removed his eyeglasses and squeezed the bridge of his nose between thumb and forefinger. The summer months always made his sinuses flare up. "We can easily get a conviction for illegal possession of weapons, should we charge them with that crime. They have both admitted buying the weapons and using them to kill six people."

"The Canovers haven't been charged yet?" Bhabha Jehangir glanced at Amtri Zumbihig, whose eyebrows raised slightly in surprise.

"No. I wanted to discuss the situation first with you two," Bhilainagar said mildly. "I felt there was a lot to be considered."

Because he was an Anglo-Indian—his father had been a British diplomat, his mother a Bharian—Bhilainagar always felt uncomfortable in the presence of Hindus. It was a matter of conditioning since childhood, a psychological trap from which he had never been able to free himself. At the bottom of the Indian social scale were the Untouchables. Just above them were the Anglo-Indians. . . .

Officially, the caste system had been abolished. Unofficially, it didn't make any difference. Thousands of years of customs could not be killed by a stroke of the pen. And so the Untouchables and the Anglo-Indians were in a position similar to the blacks in America—equal in theory, but unequal in practice.

Prejudice was at all levels and in all people in India. Bhilainagar found it ironic that the Indian Muslims looked down on the Hindus, even the high caste Brahmins or priests. The Muslims considered all Hindus nothing more than *babus* and *banias*—clerks and shopkeepers.

Bhabha Jehangir sounded very sly, yet very official. "Inspector, please understand that we are not trying to influence you in any way. You must do your duty as your conscience dictates. I can only tell you that you would be doing your country a disservice by recommending that the two Americans be prosecuted for any crime."

"I agree with him," Amtri Zumbihig said firmly.

"You're telling me to let them go," Bhilainagar said bluntly, enjoying putting the two Hindus in an indelicate position.

Zumbihig cleared his throat uncomfortably. Bhabha Jehangir gazed levelly at Bhilainagar.

"We are only suggesting that you release the Canovers," Jehangir said smoothly. "I've seen to it that what happened in the caves will not reach the press. There wouldn't be any problems in that direction."

"Mr. and Mrs. Canover were in possession of three handguns. They did break the law." Bhilainagar waited for a reaction, watching the two men over the rim of the cup he had raised to his lips.

Jehangir's voice lost some of its friendliness. "New Delhi would prefer that you release the Canovers on condition that they leave India immediately. With the Jains demanding autonomy, we have enough trouble here at home without becoming involved with the Americans and the Russians."

"I understand perfectly."

"I suggest you send several detectives with the Canovers to their hotel to help them pack and drive them to the airport. New Delhi would like them to leave the country as soon as possible."

"I see." Bhilainagar daubed at his lips with a handkerchief. "I would have thought that DARFA agents would wait to trail the Canovers and discover their contacts, since you feel espionage is involved."

Bhabha Jehangir shook his head. "Trailing them would be a waste of time. The Canovers realize they have blown their cover. If we permitted them to remain in the country, they would know that we were only watching and waiting. All they can do is leave the country. We'll make it easy by ordering them to leave."

Zumbihig said, "By the way, Inspector, did the cabdriver identify Bruce Canover as the man who rented his vehicle?"

"He couldn't be sure, and we couldn't locate the prostitute. It doesn't make any difference since I'll be releasing the Canovers."

Bhilainagar looked at the clock on the wall—10:36 P.M.

"Inspector, I think I'll have that tea," Bhabha Jehangir said, his former friendliness returning.

After Jehangir and Zumbihig left his office, Bhilainagar congratulated himself on being rid of the whole mess—and if they felt they had fooled him, that was fine too.

Some excuse—the central government in New Delhi not wanting to become involved with the Americans and the Russians! Since when did the Indian intelligence service ignore foreign agents operating on Indian soil?

Bhilainagar reasoned that the truth was that one or more persons had come to India and possessed information that the KGB and the CIA wanted. DARFA also wanted that information.

By sending the Canovers packing, DARFA was only eliminating a part of the opposition. . . .

Chapter Eight

There were only two police cars; yet Richard Camellion felt that he was one of the star attractions of a circus parade. He rode in the rear seat of the first vehicle. To his right was a stone-faced Tanrin Kapoor. In the front seat another *pulis vaalaa*—policeman—sat next to the driver. In the second police car was "Mrs. Ethel Canover" and three uniformed policemen.

For a time the Death Merchant had been worried. After he had taken the polygraph test, he had been locked in a basement cell. An hour later a bearded jailer had brought him a supper of *vindaloo*—meatballs in a plate of curry and rice. Hours later, three uniformed policemen had taken him back upstairs, this time to the office of Inspector Juderwal Bhilainagar, the chief of detectives.

"We are releasing you and your wife, Mr. Canover," Bhilainagar said cordially. "We have concluded that you and Mrs. Canover told the truth. After all, you and she only protected yourselves against the people trying to kill you. It was self-defense."

"And the charge of illegal firearms possession?" Camellion said, his voice and expression neutral.

"The law was broken. However, your nation and ours are allies in the struggle for world peace, and none of the people killed were citizens of India. We are going to forget the illegal firearms charge, but only on condition that you and your wife and son leave India immediately. We will take you to your hotel, then escort the three of you to Santa Cruz Airport. There will be a flight to Paris at four-thirty tomorrow morning. The three of you will be on that flight."

"Thank you, Inspector," Camellion said politely, thinking that Bhilainagar had spoken with all the sincerity of Richard Nixon getting on television and telling the American people that *I am not a crook!*

Since police headquarters was only a mile from the Shalimar Hotel on Grant Road, the drive was not lengthy. The fifty-room Shalimar was on the verge of being third-rate, but how could an underpaid professor of history afford the super deluxe hotels on Marine Drive, which curved around Back Bay?

After the two police cars had pulled up in front of the Shalimar, Detective Kapoor and a uniformed policeman escorted Camellion and Lana Stanley to an elevator, surprising a sleepy-eyed night clerk on the way.

"We certainly do appreciate the attention the police of Bombay are giving us," Camellion said with exaggerated politeness as the elevator rose. "It gives us a great feeling of comfort, doesn't it, dear?"

"Yes," Stanley said in a strained voice, feeling that Camellion was going too far.

The elevator stopped on the third floor, and the doors slid open.

Tanrin Kapoor smiled and simply motioned with his arm toward the hallway, proving he was a man who could control his emotions and not show anger. "Thank you, Mr. Canover. The police are always glad to be of help to American tourists, even those we will never see again. After you, Mr. and Mrs. Canover."

Camellion and Stanley left the elevator and, with Kapoor and the uniformed cop right behind them, started down the hall toward their suite of three rooms. Neither the Death Merchant nor Stanley had been worried about Wilbur Theimer after they had been arrested. Well trained, Weejee would have played his role well. They were positive that when the police had searched their rooms, Weejee had been the properly confused "little boy," and asking where his "Mom" and "Dad" were.

A master of deception, the Death Merchant had prepared for all eventualities even before he and his team had arrived in India. Should he and Stanley ever be arrested, she would act very concerned about her "little boy" and exhibit all the worry expected of a mother. She had done just that at police headquarters, Camellion's getting the tip-off when Inspector Bhilainagar, during the interrogation, had told him that he should not worry about ". . . your son William. A policewoman is with him at the hotel, and we have assured your wife he is all right."

Camellion thought, *It must have been more difficult for Weejee than for us.* Camellion and Stanley had been arrested at the caves at about four o'clock in the afternoon. The police would have searched the rooms by five. The policewoman would still be in the suite, which consisted of a sitting room and two bedrooms. That meant that for six and a half hours, Weejee had been forced to play the role of a twelve-year-old, a task that would not have been difficult for the twenty-nine-year-old Little Person. He was a master actor, but one single slip, verbal or otherwise, could wreck the entire performance.

Just before they reached the door of the sitting room, Kapoor said, "I'll knock, Mr. Canover. The policewoman had been instructed not to open the door, except to the police. We called ahead. She knows we are due to arrive."

Camellion stepped to one side and Kapoor gave a light rap with his knuckles. Presently a woman's voice answered in English. "Yes, identify yourself."

"This is Detective Kapoor from Central. We have the Canovers. Open the door."

The latch turned. They could hear a chain being removed. The woman opened the door and stepped to one side as Kapoor motioned for Lana Stanley to enter the suite. Once the four of them were inside the room, the middle-aged, plump policewoman closed the door.

It happened so quickly that even the Death Merchant was caught with his mental and physical defense imprisoned in limbo, so fast that he had only gotten a brief look at Weejee sitting quietly on the sofa on the north side of the room, his short legs dangling over the center cushion.

Two men—handkerchiefs over their faces forming a white triangle —reared up from behind the sofa, suppressed 9mm Hi-Power Browning autopistols in their hands. *Phyyyt!* Tanrin Kapoor cried out, jerked, and died, a bullet having torn its way through the left ventricle of his heart. *Phyyyt! Phyyyt!* The uniformed cop and the policewoman crumpled to the floor and lay still.

"The two of you raise your hands and don't move!" snapped Werner Vogel while shock and astonishment were still registered on the faces of Camellion and Stanley. Weejee sat as still as a statue, looking straight ahead.

Not having a choice, the Death Merchant and Lana Stanley, standing toward the center of the room, did as the man ordered. Camellion at once deduced what was happening and why they were facing two men, one of whom was an Indian national: He and Lana and Weejee had been tagged by either the KGB or the MfS for a black-bag job. The white man and the Indian were body snatchers. Since the KGB had made an assassination attempt in the Elephanta Caves, it was not likely that the Russians would try again so soon. Besides, the two body snatchers had killed only Kapoor and the other two Indian police. *They want us alive. They're not KGB. They're Mischa Wolf's boys.*

"We didn't expect a 'welcome home' reception," Camellion, facing Vogel and the Punjabi, said mildly in high German.

The solidly built Vogel wasn't taken back by Camellion's speaking in German. He replied in English, "We know you didn't expect us. We're even. We didn't expect the police. The point is, the three of you are going with us. Any nonsense and we'll leave the three of you dead." Vogel then said to the Indian, "Get the others from the bedrooms."

"Atcha," said Japur Mahamud. He walked around the end of the sofa to his left and moved to the door, which was also to his left in the center of the east-side wall.

Camellion saw a way out—their only chance—and he hoped Wilbur Theimer saw and took advantage of the opportunity. Weejee was sitting in the center of the sofa, and Werner Vogel, standing behind the couch, was a bit to Weejee's left. The MfS agent's right arm was extended over the top of the sofa, with the ten-inch-long silencer only eighteen inches to the left of Weejee's head.

It all depended on whether Weejee saw what Camellion saw and was willing to take the chance. He was also very fast and had the advantage of Vogel's believing he was only a child. He reached up and grabbed the rounded tube of the silencer with both hands, pulled downward, leaned more to his left and clamped his teeth on the bottom of Vogel's right hand.

Caught unexpectedly, Vogel was jerked off-balance and for the moment had to go along with Weejee's two-handed pull. He let out a cry of rage and pain and in that split second reacted automatically by trying to jerk his arm back.

The Death Merchant streaked the short distance to the sofa with such speed that he might as well have been shot from a cannon. At the same time, Lana Stanley jerked back and dropped to the side of an armchair, her hand going to the holstered pistol around the waist of the dead uniformed cop. Since 1975 the Indian police had carried 9mm Hi-Power Browning autoloaders.

Vogel was very close to freeing himself from Weejee's tenacious teeth and two-handed grip when the pistol discharged, due to the German's finger pulling against the trigger. *Phyyyt!* The slug shot downward, going in the space between the end of the center cushion and the cushion to the left.

By then, the Death Merchant had reached the sofa. His left hand shot out and his strong fingers fastened around the top and one side of the Browning. He twisted and at the same time his right arm streaked out and up and down and his hand chopped perpendicularly across Vogel's broad face. Simultaneously, Weejee released his hold and rolled off the couch, his goal the .25-caliber Seecamp II pistol he carried in an ankle holster. Still another advantage of being a "child"; no one ever bothered to search him.

The terrific sword-ridge strike succeeded, the savage blow making Vogel's hand go limp and his face explode with pain. In an instant the Death Merchant had the pistol in his left hand and was turning it toward the dazed and staggered German. *Phyyyt!* The projectile hit Vogel in the center of his chest and slammed him back against the wall before he started to slide to the floor with a stupid, surprised expression, the handkerchief over his face slowly turning red with blood bubbling out of his mouth.

Camellion swung around, tore the short distance to the bedroom door, and fired just in time as he dove to the floor. Eight feet away, Stanley made herself small by the left side of the armchair, the dead cop's Browning in her right hand. Weejee had crawled to the end of the couch by the west wall. He had pulled his little Seecamp II and was also watching the door to the bedroom.

There had been another East German agent and another Punjabi in Camellion and Stanley's bedroom. Two more Punjabi mobsters were in Weejee's bedroom. Japur Mahamud, Helmut Matthofer, and Rai Prithiraj had almost reached the sitting room. Mahamud and Matthofer, ahead of Prithiraj and about to step into the sitting room, fired off quick, frantic shots when they saw Camellion with the Browning in his hand. Mahamud's bullet tore to Camellion's right, so close to his neck that it was only a hair away from his collar. The bullet went by and thudded into the rug, only a foot from where Weejee was crouched. He couldn't fire for the moment because Camellion was in the way. Matthofer's slug cut air a foot above the Death Merchant and was wasted on the west wall. If Camellion had been standing, the metal would have hit him high in the stomach.

In contrast to Matthofer's and Mahamud's misses, the Death Merchant's first hollow point punched Mahamud in the abdomen and shoved him back against Rai Prithiraj, who was trying to get a clear view and shoot. Behind him, Babur Hudikar and Mudar Khalji had come in from Weejee's bedroom, with weapons in their hands—and wild looks on their faces.

The Death Merchant's second slug zipped upward into Helmut Matthofer's stomach. It tore all the way through the organ, hit the spine, cut the cord, and kicked him into hell with such speed that he was stone dead before he could realize he had been shot twice. The second bullet had come from Weejee, who had fired as the Death Merchant hit the floor. The .25 bullet hit Matthofer in the groin, going in so low it almost castrated him.

Jumping to his feet, the Death Merchant triggered off two more rounds, although he could only partially see the left side of the tall, bearded Rai Prithiraj, who had fired wildly a micromoment before Camellion had squeezed the trigger of his own Hi-Power Browning. Prithiraj's Browning was not equipped with a sonic suppressor, and the loud crack of the exploding cartridge echoed throughout the three rooms.

Prithiraj's hunk of hot metal passed between Camellion rib cage and the inner side of his right arm, half an inch from the bandage covering the deep graze he had received in the caves. The Death Merchant's trajectory was only a little better. His 9mm bullet tore through the door at a steep angle and grazed Prithiraj's left hip, making the man give a yell of fear and pain.

Conversely, Lana Stanley had a much better view of Prithiraj. She fired. Her hollow point hit him in the right side of the chest and smashed him to the floor.

Mudar Khalji and Babur Hudikar pulled up short. They hadn't been hired to fight a gun battle. Having nothing to gain by getting killed, they each fired several quick shots through the open door, then turned and fled into the second bedroom. They kept right on going. They opened the door of the bedroom and began racing east down the hall.

The Death Merchant raced to the doorway and looked into the bedroom. Stooping, he pulled the Browning from the hand of the dead Helmut Matthofer, all the while keeping a wary eye on the opening to Weejee's bedroom.

"Son of a bitch! This is just not our day!" cried Lana Stanley. "First the caves! Now this! If Inspector Bhilainagar ever gets his hands on us again, we'll be a thousand years old by the time we've served only a third of our sentences! How could we explain three dead Indian cops?"

"Explain—hell," Weejee squeaked. He picked up one of the Brownings and handed it to Lana. "All we can do now is run—right, 'Daddy'?"

"You'd better believe it, little man," Camellion said, disliking the way Stanley had cursed. Swearing was only the lazy person's way of expressing emotion. "To get out of this, we're going to have to be twice as good as a groom on his wedding night. The police out front heard the shots, and they'll be rushing in to investigate."

Weejee jammed the third Browning pistol in his belt. "Your boundless enthusiasm inspires me. I'll congratulate you when and if we get to the safe house."

"The one on Poon-Pon Fond Road?" asked Stanley. She hurried after the Death Merchant, who was moving into the second bedroom. "It's five miles from here."

"We're going to Green Eagle." Camellion added with fierce determination, "Don't kill any Indian police unless it's absolutely necessary to save your own lives. They're not our enemy. They're only doing their duty."

Whenever the Death Merchant was on an operation and stayed in a hotel, he always made it a rule to learn how the building was laid out. For this reason he knew the Shalimar Hotel had neither fire escapes— not that he would have used them—nor back stairs on the third floor. There was only one flight of rear stairs. They started on the second floor and led down to a short hall on the ground floor. At the south end of the hall was a door that opened to a corridor that took one toward the front of the hotel. At the north end of the hall was the door that opened to the outside rear. Why the hotel had been constructed in such a paradoxical manner was anyone's guess. After all, this was India.

Browning Hi-Power pistols in their hands—except for Weejee, who held only his Seecamp II—the Death Merchant and his crew of two ran down the hall of the third floor as fast as possible under the circumstances. With his short legs, Weejee couldn't break any records.

Surprise! They heard the sound of gunfire from the first floor as they moved down the steps to the second floor.

* * *

Unaware of the single flight of rear stairs, Mudar Khalji and Babur Hudikar had sprinted down the main stairs from the first floor and had been trapped by the four policemen who, having heard the shots from the suite of rooms, had rushed into the hotel and were in the lobby.

In the rapid exchange of slugs, Mudar Khalji was killed outright. He took three slugs in the chest. Babur Hudikar dropped to the polished hardwood floor with a bullet high in his right leg. Another 9mm projectile had broken his left arm. A third slug had stabbed him in the chest. He lay moaning and twisting in agony on the floor, calling upon Siva to save his soul.

One of the policemen was also dead. The three other uniforms raced up the steps, anxious to see what had happened to Tanrin Kapoor, the other uniform, and the policewoman. They could have taken an elevator, but they didn't want to risk walking into an ambush when the elevator doors opened.

Coming to the top of the rear steps on the second floor, the Death Merchant paused and looked down the straight flight of stairs. They appeared innocent enough. Yet he sensed there was something threatening about them.

Weejee glared up at him in dismay. "Let's not take time to admire the scenery, chum. Let's get the hell out of here."

Camellion looked up and down the hall. It was as empty as a newly robbed grave. Other people in the hotel had heard the gunfire in the apartment and in the lobby and were wisely staying in their rooms. In this case, what you couldn't see couldn't see you and couldn't harm you.

"Richard, Weejee's right," Lana said. "Now that we're this close to the outside, let's not crucify ourselves on shadows."

"And let's not jump into a trap," replied Camellion harshly. "It stands to reason that some of the fuzz out front had time to get to the back."

"We heard the shots on the first floor," said Lana. "It's clear the police came into the lobby and shot it out with the men who fled the rooms."

Weejee looked as if he were about to stamp his feet up and down on the rug. "Damn it! Those police aren't going to run around the back or the sides or anyplace else. They're going to go up to the third floor and see what happened."

"We don't know that all four went upstairs," Camellion said.

"So get to the bottom line!" growled Weejee.

"I'm going down the steps and have a look."

"Oh, Christ!" sighed Weejee in disgust.

"Christ isn't giving orders here. I am. Stay put." Camellion smiled and patted Weejee on the head. "And thank God you can be seen with me. It will improve your image."

"It will get my butt shot off—and hers too!"

The Death Merchant crept down the stairs, moving along the wall side to avoid making any of the step boards creak. Halfway down, he could see the door that opened to the outside, and by going to the other side of the steps, he could lean over, look in the opposite direction, and see the inside door that led to another corridor.

There was truth in Weejee's contention that the first concern of the four Indian cops would be Kapoor, the other uniform, and the policewoman. But attempting to predict what Indian police would do by using Western moral standards would be a mistake that could prove fatal. Even sensitive Indians considered life cheap. It was not that they were brutal and unfeeling. It was only that their moral standards and view of life and death were different from those of the West.

Confronting the Death Merchant was not a case of a woman's being able to run faster with her dress up, and a man's having to go slower with his pants down. What he and Lana and Weejee were facing was a pure gamble, a fifty-fifty balance between warm life and cold death. If only one cop was waiting in the rear—*He could snuff at least two of us the instant we opened the door!*

Because he had checked out the rear of the Shalimar, Camellion knew that there were numerous places in the alley where a policeman could hide—scores of trash cans, for instance.

The Death Merchant mentally flipped a coin, then turned and looked up the stairs and motioned for Lana and Weejee to come down. As soon as they reached him, he whispered, "We'll use the inside door, the one to the south, and leave by way of the front. And this time, try to run faster, squirt."

"Look, big man, if you don't like my speed, carry me! Or get me a pair of roller skates!"

They moved the rest of the way down the steps, crept south, and were soon at the door. Camellion slowly pulled the door open, looked out and saw a hall that stretched south for twenty feet, then turned to the west. They moved into the shorter hall, and were soon approaching the lobby.

"I'd like to know who those two white men were upstairs," whispered Lana, panting slightly. Her hair was a mess and her blue pantsuit was smudged and soaked with sweat.

"Let's go," Camellion said. "Shoot the instant you see a cop."

"But don't try to kill him," sneered Weejee. "And what makes you think keys will be in those police cars? If you ask me——"

"I'm not asking, but I'll tell you. If there aren't any keys—you can push!"

Reaching the end of the hall, they looked around. Death looked back. There was a corpse in uniform lying in the lobby. At the foot of the steps were sprawled the dead bodies of two Indians.

They glanced up the main flight of steps to the first floor, saw no one, rushed through the lobby, and soon had gone through the two doors and were on the sidewalk. Camellion knew it was not likely that the drivers of the police cars had taken the keys with them. Hearing the gunfire, the four cops would have reacted instinctively. They would have realized that something had gone wrong and would have been anxious to investigate. They wouldn't have been thinking of the possible theft of one of their vehicles. Bombay was full of thieves, but they never stole police cars.

Halfway to the two police cars, Camellion and his two companions discovered they couldn't have chosen a worse time to leave the hotel by way of the front lobby. Coming at them on Grant Road——half a block from the east——was a squad car, red lights flashing. After midnight, Bombay police never used their sirens.

No sooner had they spotted the police car than there were two loud cracks from above, and there were two loud *zinggggs* on the concrete of the sidewalk as projectiles glanced off. One bullet had hit a foot behind the Death Merchant. The second had struck between Weejee and Lana.

Earlier, while two of the cops had left the suite of three rooms to go back downstairs and call for a meat wagon, the third uniform had gone down a hall to look out a window facing Grant Road. He wanted to see if any backups were on their way. Leaning out the window, he had spotted Camellion, Stanley, and Theimer.

"Son of bitch!" snarled Stanley in an angry voice.

"Get to the first car and start her up," Camellion cut her off. "Weejee, go with her."

There were two more shots from the third floor as Lana and Weejee ran to the first patrol car facing the west. The second blue and yellow squad car was parked behind it. Both slugs hit the sidewalk to Camellion's right.

Camellion darted to the space between the back of the first police car and the front of the second vehicle, looked up at the policeman in the window on the third floor, raised his Browning, and ignored the man's next shot. The police officer was at a disadvantage because, from his position on the windowsill—actually a narrow ledge—he was looking almost straight down and could see only heads; and because he had to brace himself with one hand, he was limited in his ability to aim.

The Death Merchant was not burdened by such a limitation. He could see the man darkly silhouetted against the background of the hall light. *Phyyyt!* He fired. The 9mm bullet, going upward at an extremely steep angle, hit the policeman under the chin, the slug shattering the bone then ripping off the tip of his nose. He would have lived if he had not been leaning out of the window. The shock of the impact caused him to lose his grip and he toppled forward. Falling like a rock, he crashed to the sidewalk and lay still.

Camellion turned and, crouching by the left front of the second police car, opened fire on the approaching backup vehicle, which now was only eighty feet away, the cop next to the driver leaning out the window and about to get off a round with a Hi-Power Browning pistol.

The Death Merchant fired first. The bullet bored into the left front tire of the patrol car as the driver crouched down low, thinking that Camellion was firing at him. *Bang!* The tire blew and the vehicle swerved to the left, the driver fighting the wheel to avoid hitting several three-wheeled bicycle-type rickshaws. The cop sitting next to the driver did get off a shot, but his bullet went wild. As the patrol car turned into traffic, Camellion fired again. This time his projectile popped the right rear tire, causing the patrol car to rock back and forth.

It was Weejee who saved Camellion's life. In the rear seat of the first car, Weejee had rolled down the window on the right and was using both his hands to point his Seecamp II at the two doors of the hotel. The Death Merchant's second bullet had just exploded the second tire of the backup vehicle when the two doors of the hotel opened and the two other cops stepped out onto the sidewalk. The first thing they saw was Richard Camellion, who was turned toward the road.

Weejee aimed at the cop to his left, the first one to raise his Browning. A micromoment more and Richard Joseph Camellion would become history. Weejee squeezed the trigger; the little Seecamp II cracked.

A .25-caliber bullet does not have the stopping power of a 9mm or a .38 caliber bullet. But it can get the job done. Weejee's hundred-grain spitzer-shaped projectile hit the cop in the chest and sent him reeling back. The chunk of metal had stopped inside his right lung, and he would live. Nonetheless, the bullet had done its job; it had prevented the Bombay policeman from killing Camellion.

The second policeman, his attention diverted from Camellion by the crack of Weejee's Seecamp, swung his Browning autoloader toward the patrol car and fired twice. The first bullet tore through the right rear window, angled across the car, and left by way of the open left front window. The slug missed Weejee and Lana, both of whom were making themselves postage stamps on the seats. The cop's second bullet was low. It hit the right rear door and, after shattering the glass inside the bottom of the door, flattened itself out on part of the window-raising mechanism.

The Indian uniformed policeman who had fired at Weejee didn't have an opportunity to throw down on the Death Merchant. Warned by the shots, Camellion spun around, body-pointed, and gently squeezed the trigger of the Hi-Power Browning in his left hand. The pistol roared. The cop cried out, dropped his own autoloader, doubled over, and took a nosedive to the sidewalk. The slug had slashed into his body just above the buckle of his Sam Browne belt.

With a heart full of worry and a head full of haste, Camellion ran to the first car, jerked open the door, and got behind the wheel as Lana Stanley scooted over to the passenger side.

By now, the driver of the patrol car with the shot-out tires had managed to stop. The vehicle sat on the road across traffic, its front bumper facing the south. At the same time that the Death Merchant put the car in gear and it began to move forward, the four policemen in the backup squad car got out, guns in hand.

"Keep low," Camellion warned Lana and Weejee. "They are not friendly back there."

Stay low they did while two of the cops got off quick shots. They should have aimed at the rear tires. Instead, they aimed at the rear window. Both slugs went through the glass, leaving behind them holes from which radiated spiderwebs of cracks. One bullet cut a foot over Lana's head and buried itself in the rear of the front seat. The second projectile rocketed across the top of the seats, ripped through the short sleeve of Camellion's shirt, and streaked a burn gash on the outside of his right arm. The bullet bored through the lower part of the windshield and kept right on going.

"Man! And you said not to kill any cops unless we had to!" yelled Weejee from the rear seat. "I suppose we had to!"

"Or we could have let them shoot us!" snapped Lana, glancing at the Death Merchant, who had become strangely silent. Thinking that the whole nation of India was determined to shoot him in the right arm, he increased speed.

It was triply ironic. The Death Merchant had only one real regret in his life: that more often than not the people he worked with (and Courtland Grojean) regarded him as a master killer. It was paradoxical not only because he killed only when he had to, but because he considered all life special and precious. Even the pig-farmer trash in the Soviet Union contained a spark of the Eternal. However, there were honest Russians, many of whom were willing to fight and die for their belief in freedom.*

Lana Stanley leaned closer to him. "We can't keep this car for any length of time," she pointed out. "The police back there have already put out an alarm."

"We're going to grab another car, perhaps a taxi." Camellion made a right turn onto a small street that wasn't as brightly lighted as Grant Road, which was one of the main thoroughfares of Bombay. Anyone going home at this hour who lived in the northern part of the city would travel over Grant Road.

The Death Merchant drove two blocks south, then made a right turn onto Perchid Marg. He saw the vehicle they needed after he had driven three blocks west—a 1980 Honda Accord LX. The driver appeared to be a dark-skinned middle-aged Indian.

Weejee sniffed loudly. "What the hell are we going to do with the driver? We'd better kill him. He'll scream for the police the minute we're gone."

* See Death Merchant #67, *Escape From Gulag Taria,* also published by Dell.

Camellion finished making the U-turn. He turned on the top strobe lights of the patrol car, fed more gas to the engine, and started after the Honda, saying to Lana, "I'll pass him on your side. Flag him to the curb as we go by."

"He's going to think it strange that a white man is riding in a police car and is telling him to pull over," she said.

"Sure he will. But he'll pull to the curb. Indians respect the law."

Camellion took the vehicle past the Honda Accord LX, and Lana Stanley motioned furiously for the driver to pull over. Confused, the man proceeded to do so.

"Suppose the driver doesn't speak English?" posed Weejee.

"Any nationality understands the language of a pointed gun." Camellion pulled up in front of the Honda, stopped, pulled the two Brownings from his belt, and placed them on the seat.

"You two remain in the car until you see the driver get out," he said. "He might try to pull out if he saw pistols in your hands. Lana, bring the Brownings with you. Weejee, pass over your little peashooter."

With the .25 Seecamp II in a belt inside his shirt, Camellion got out of the patrol car, strode back to the Honda, jerked open the door, and shoved the small semiautomatic pistol in the driver's face.

"Get out of the car and get in the backseat, or I'll kill you," Camellion snarled.

The man's mouth opened like an *O.* "Y-you're not the police!" he said angrily.

"Right, old chap, but you'll still be dead if I pull the trigger. Now move!"

Ludar Kowhotibar did not argue. Glancing angrily at Camellion, he slid from the driver's position and, when Camellion opened the left rear door, got in the back. There were 150 million hungry people in India, but Kowhotibar, in a light tan suit, and even wearing a tie with a large Windsor knot, looked like an overfed merchant.

"On the floor between the seats—facedown," ordered the Death Merchant. He glanced up and down Perchid Street, which had only a small lightpost on each corner of the end of the block. Several cars were approaching in the distance, coming from the east, and Lana and Weejee were hurrying toward the Honda. Lana was carrying the three Brownings, hers and Camellion's, and she had turned off the top flashing lights of the patrol car.

"Get in back with him," Camellion said, then looked down at

Kowhotibar who, cramped between the seats, was facedown. "If he as much as moves, put a bullet in his head." He motioned to Weejee. "The same orders go for you, 'Herman.' ".

Weejee grinned and climbed into the rear seat beside Lana, who was already sitting with her feet on Kowhotibar's back. Weejee knew why Camellion had called him "Herman." The man would report to the police everything he could remember.

One of the cars from the east passed as Camellion, now behind the wheel of the Honda, turned the key in the ignition.

"Herman, take off his tie and tie his hands behind his back. Alice, after Hermie secures his hands, blindfold our guest."

"I suppose you're going straight to the warehouse?" Lana said for the benefit of Kowhotibar. She bent over and pressed the muzzle of her Browning against the back of Kowhotibar's head.

The Death Merchant's destination was Dumsat saRak in the Kamatipura district, which, like Hamburg, West Germany, was famous throughout the world for its red-light area. An estimated forty thousand girls served the vice industry of Bombay, most of them in small, filthy buildings called "cages" because the windows were small and barred. Behind those hundreds and hundreds of windows, the girls paraded for passersby, although they were not prisoners. A hundred years ago it may have been that the girls, either sold by their starving parents or kidnapped, were held against their will. Now the bars existed not because the girls wanted out but because the men wanted *in*.

In another fifteen minutes Camellion had bypassed the street of whores, had turned onto Mahalaksmi Patjha, and was driving northeast. Six blocks more and he turned left, leaving Mahalakshmi Avenue and moving onto Dumsat Road, a very long, twisting street filled with shops and produce markets. One of the more larger businesses was owned by Sri and Shrimatee Phiroze Mehta—Mr. and Mrs. Phiroze Mehta. She operated the shop for tourists. He and seven helpers tended the much larger open-air vegetable market.

To the rear, below the six rooms that Sri and Shrimatee Mehta used for living quarters, was the emergency CIA safe house—*Green Eagle.*

One question kept poking itself around in the Death Merchant's mind: What are you going to do about Edgar Bedsloe? The answer to himself was always the same: I don't know.

"What the hell are we going to do with this guy back here?" piped up Weejee. "Let's blow his head off. We can't take him with us to the warehouse!"

Chapter Nine

22.00 hours.
East Germany—the evening of the same day that the KGB and the MfS tried to kill Bruce and Ethel Canover.

Realism can always make a fool of hypothesis. In theory, while all men were considered equal in the German Democratic Republic, in practice some men and women were far more equal than others. This is why Marcus Wolf had a spacious nine-room house in the country, between East Berlin and Hohen Neuendorf.

Dressed in a blue-checked dressing gown, an angry and disgusted Wolf hurried into his study, where Heinz Hafner was waiting. Wolf was not angry at Hafner, his chief executive. The special radio report had come from India. The radio technician officer had immediately contacted Hafner. Hafner had instantly gone to MfS headquarters. He had read the report and telephoned Wolf. Even though the phone call was triple scrambled and computer coded, Hafner had said only two words: *India—failure!* Wolf had told him to come straight to his home.

The director of the MfS (and of the SSD, the Staatssicherheitsdienst, the State Security Service, the political police organ of East Germany) was angry for two reasons: because the assassination attempt against Bruce and Ethel Canover had failed, and because he hated being disturbed in his home. *Mein Gott!* It was already ten o'clock! An early riser, Wolf was always in bed by 9:30 P.M.

Without even a *Guten Abend,* Wolf, with the aid of two canes, moved laboriously to the antique table he used as a desk and sat down. He turned on the desk lamp and methodically read the report sent by

Friedrich Seckendorff. Heinz had already placed the report on the table. The more Wolf read, the angrier he became. Not only had Werner Vogel, one of the MfS's best operatives in India, failed to kill the Canovers, Bruce and Ethel Canover had turned the tables and had sent him and his Indian helpers into eternity.

Even worse, the Russians were actively interfering. In an effort to protect Franz Holtz, the KGB had attempted to use extreme measures against the two posing as Bruce and Ethel Canover. The KGB had not had any better luck than the MfS. Canover and his supposed wife had killed the entire KGB squad! Incredible!

Finished with reading the dismal report, Wolf folded the ten sheets of paper and returned them to the envelope, Heinz regarding his action as permission to speak.

"The Russians must want Holtz very badly, or the KGB would not have moved against the Canovers. As I understand the report, Seckendorff and Hossinger planned the *aussiedlung* with Vogel before they were aware of the KGB *aussiedlung* against the Canovers at the Elephanta Caves. Vogel and his gunmen must have been waiting in the Canovers' rooms when the police brought them back to their hotel."

Frowning, Wolf thought of the code word Hafner had used for assassination: *aussiedlung,* which meant "special treatment."

"Heinz, forget the *Sprachregelung.* We don't need the 'Language Rule' here," Wolf said tersely. "It's a fait accompli that Vogel failed to kill Canover and his supposed wife. No doubt what happened is that Vogel and the Indian *Schweinerei* arrived at the Shalimar Hotel during the time the Indian police were holding the Canovers in custody."

Seeing the puzzlement in Hafner's eyes, Wolf supplied the explanation: "A policewoman was killed in the Canovers' rooms at the hotel. She wouldn't have come to the Shalimar with the police who brought the Canovers home. She wouldn't have been needed. Seckendorff said in the report that he learned the Canovers had been arrested at the caves. This means that the policewoman was there before the Canovers arrived, even before Vogel and his men went to the hotel. The police sent her to the hotel to stay with the Canovers' son."

Hafner nodded slowly in understanding. "Seckendorff did say that he and Hossinger didn't learn about the KGB attempt until after Vogel and the Indians were in position in the hotel," he said thoughtfully. "By then, it was too late. At least Vogel exhibited some common sense."

Wolf's eyebrows lifted. He was fond of Heinz Hafner, who was young enough to be his son. "Common sense?" he echoed. "In what way?"

"Somehow, Vogel had to talk his way past the policewoman, or he couldn't have gotten into the apartment," Hafner said. "For all the good it did him! But how—how could two persons kill Vogel and the Indians? It's not logical! It doesn't make sense."

"Who bothers to count the letters when he's eating alphabet soup?" With his right hand, Wolf began to squeeze the joints in the fingers of his left hand. "Of importance now is the new information our station in New Delhi developed. We know that Holtz will be returning to New Delhi tomorrow. What we don't know is how he will try to make contact with the KGB in New Delhi."

For a moment Hafner surveyed his boss speculatively, then took out his pack of cigarettes. As if suddenly remembering something, he quickly returned the pack to his coat pocket.

"You may smoke, Heinz," Wolf said tolerantly. "Frau Wolf only forbids smoking in the rest of the house. But turn on the air purifier first." His eyes lifted to a small grillwork in the middle of the study's ceiling. "The switch is on the wall, the one to your left, between the two bookcases."

Hafner got up and started across the room, saying, "Sir, isn't it dangerous to put faith in the babbling of a drunken KGB officer?"

"Parveen Babbi has given us valuable information many times," Wolf said brusquely. He knew exactly what Hafner was thinking: that perhaps it was a KGB disinformation attempt to avert attention away from the true operation involving Franz Holtz, in which case Babbi would either be working with the KGB, or the KGB, aware that she was working for East German intelligence, was making clever use of her.

Having turned on the air purifier, Hafner sat back down and took a cigarette from the pack. "It's not unusual for any intelligence service to give bits and pieces of honest information to establish credibility, in preparation for a big lie that will readily be swallowed. However, I admit that Parveen Babbi has given us very valuable information in the past." He reached for his lighter.

Wolf smiled at Hafner, who was lighting his cigarette, and got to his feet. "Heinz, did I ever tell you that international espionage is similar to religion?"

Hafner's expression silently said no. With the aid of his two canes,

Wolf moved around the table and started toward a large upholstered chair.

"The key word for both is *faith*," Wolf said softly. "In this case, we have to have faith that Stefan Mikhaulsky told Babbi the truth."

Hafner didn't reply until after Wolf had seated himself comfortably in the armchair and had leaned his canes against the front of the cushion, between his legs.

Hafner said, "Apparently our people in Bombay couldn't get the information about Holtz to Hossinger and Seckendorff in time, or they would have terminated the operation against the Canovers. But, sir"—he became very intense—"why did the KGB move against the Canovers? Why bother with them if Holtz is returning to New Delhi?"

"The KGB has always been paranoid about such matters," Wolf said. "The Russians don't want to take the chance that Canover will cause trouble in New Delhi. Killing Canover—if the attempt had been successful—was a precautionary measure. Even if we had received the information about Holtz days ago, instead of this afternoon, I would not have ordered Hossinger and Seckendorff to cancel our own efforts to kill Canover and his wife."

"I've never known the CIA to use a child in any of its operations," Hafner said, a curious note in his voice. "But, sir! We are taking an enormous risk, *Herr Direktor*." When he saw Wolf's eyes narrow slightly, he added, "We're going to have to depend on Parveen Babbi to find out from Mikhaulsky how Holtz is going to meet the KGB— and when and where. If we only had more facts!"

"Yes, you are correct, Heinz," Wolf said amicably. "We do have one true reality." He gave a guttural chuckle. "We can safely say that whoever he is, the man who killed those KGB agents and Vogel is not Professor Bruce Canover. I think I know who he might be, although I don't know his name or true nationality."

Hafner closed his eyes, calculating. He had never voiced his opinion that the very concept of the plan to have Holtz steal the PAL devices from the *Amerikaner* assembly plant was foolish and nonproductive. The German Democratic Republic did not have any missiles of its own, either short-range or intercontinental. Every missile in the GDR belonged to, or else was controlled by, the Soviet Union.

Why go to the trouble to steal a Permissive Action Link device? To evaluate the device, Wolf had told his aides.

Hafner didn't believe it. He was convinced that *der Meister* had another motive. The boss was too intelligent to take giant risks unless the venture was worth it.

Hafner decided to pretend surprise over Wolf's remark.

"Who do you think the man is, sir?" he asked in just the right voice.

"There is only one person who can make the Gray Man with the black cape and the scythe work overtime," Wolf said smugly. "That person is the *Tod Kaufmann!*"

This time the expression of surprise on Hafner's face was genuine. Wolf was probably right. Only the Death Merchant had the talent for killing on a mass scale. . . . Only the Death Merchant could have fought his way out of ambushes of the type that had been set in India. . . .

Chapter Ten

As curious as a kitten investigating a dark closet, Wilbur Theimer watched Richard Camellion prepare the SS-9000 shortwave transceiver. Weejee had always had an intense interest in shortwave radio, but he had also been wise enough to know that his talents lay in other directions.

There were two other persons in the emergency safe house, which was only one long room beneath the living quarters of Phiroze and Chenna Mehta—Lana Stanley and Phiroze Mehta. Nervously puffing on a cigarette, Lana watched Mehta as he worked. Only five feet tall and as thin as a pipe stem, Phiroze Mehta had a head that looked too big for the rest of his body, and, in spite of his lack of height, legs that appeared too short.

Standing on the fourth step of the wooden folding ladder, Mehta was tying a blanket to a horizontal cross-brace stretched across the ceiling from wall to wall. The blue blanket would act as a partition between the cots of "Mr. and Mrs. Bruce Canover" and their "son William."

The Death Merchant had not explained to the Mehtas that he and Lana were only posing as man and wife. Who and what he and Stanley and Theimer were was on a need-to-know basis. However, the Mehtas had to suspect that Weejee was not a child. He may have looked like a twelve-year-old boy and have dressed like a twelve-year-old boy, but twelve-year-old boys do not smoke cigars and in manners and conversation act like adults.

Lana considered it ironic that Mr. and Mrs. Mehta thought she and Camellion were married. The CIA never laid down rules of moral conduct to its people who might be part of a husband-and-wife team, leaving it to the discretion of the operatives involved.

Lana had known there would be times when she and Camellion would have the opportunity (if not the inclination) to indulge in sexual intimacies, times when they would have to undress in front of each other and sleep in the same bed. She had expected the tall, lean Texan to make advances. After all, he was a man.

He hadn't even made a simple pass at her. Before retiring, he would sit cross-legged on the floor and do yoga breathing exercises, after which he would crawl into bed beside her, say "Good night," roll over, and instantly go to sleep.

Thinking about what had never happened, Lana ground out her cigarette and wondered if she should feel grateful or—insulted! She turned and looked at the Death Merchant ten feet away from her. He was seated at the radio table. Wearing headphones, he had just turned on the 100-watt long-range radio scrambler and the alphanumeric cipher device. Since the shortwave set was equipped with a frequency hopper and had spacing that permitted more than 7,200 VHF channels and 3,000 UHF channels, the Death Merchant could broadcast in perfect security, without Indian and Soviet listening stations being able to detect him. They would only hear short bursts of static. A teleprinter was also connected to the transceiver. It would print each word of Camellion's transmission as well as each word of his reply, for future reference on the CIA's end. Camellion had perfect and total recall, which is why he could decipher each word of the special code in his head.

Lana secretly admired Camellion. Even more secretly, she was slightly afraid of him. It wasn't that she feared for her personal safety. She was afraid of the unknown. She feared the high strangeness about him, the something that was "not quite right" about him.

She reflected that everything had gone smoothly after they reached the business establishment of Phiroze and Chenna Mehta on Dumsat Road, and Camellion had parked the Honda Accord next to the two open-bed trucks that Phiroze Mehta used to bring fruits and vegetables from the countryside. Lana and Weejee had waited in the rear of the Honda Accord with the terrified Ludar Kowhotibar.

The Death Merchant had gone to the rear of the house attached to the open fruit and vegetable market and given three rapid knocks, followed by two much longer knocks. When the door opened, the Death Merchant had found himself facing a little man with a large head, curious eyes, and a .380 Bernardelli pistol in his skeleton-like right hand.

Camellion had immediately given Phiroze Mehta the recognition signal, two lines from the tenth-century poet Nikar Sudikininap—*Jasper in the night is my love / As soft as gentle rain her kiss.*

Phiroze Mehta had sucked in his breath in surprise and given his part of the code, part of a verse from Kipling—*I am the land of their fathers / In me the virtue stays; I will bring back my children / After certain days.*

Ludar Kowhotibar had not presented much of a problem. Phiroze Mehta had awakened two of his men who slept in the fruit market. After tying Kowhotibar's arms and wrists and legs, one of them had driven the Honda Accord, the other following in Chenna Mehta's Indian-built four-door Sarvin. They would leave the Honda close to the Prince's Dock on Bombay Harbor, leaving Kowhotibar tied up in the back. Camellion had startled Phiroze Mehta by saying that he wanted to use the shortwave radio right away. Mehta did not protest. He was not being paid in rupees the equivalent of $500 American a month to argue. But Lana Stanley had been curious.

"Richard, it's almost one o'clock in the morning," she had pointed out. "Why the rush to contact the embassy station?"

"The hell with the embassy station in New Delhi," the Death Merchant had explained. "Right now it's around three o'clock in the afternoon on the East Coast of the United States. I want to contact Mr. G. at the main center."

The Death Merchant remained at the radio table for several hours. By the time he switched off the SS-9000 and the black boxes, it was 3:45 A.M. and Lana Stanley and Wilbur Theimer were dozing on cots. Phiroze Mehta had left the security house shortly after Camellion had made contact with Grojean at Langley, Virginia. He had gone back upstairs with his wife, after she had brought down a tray of lamb *biryani,* mangoes, and plain boiled rice to which had been added *dal,* a purée of boiled lentils. Also on the tray had been a pitcher of strong cinnamon tea.

Camellion awakened Lana and Weejee, then proceeded to bring them to full alert with the report that Edgar Bedsloe/Franz Holtz would be returning to New Delhi ". . . tomorrow. Well, today, now. Grojean said he was positive."

In bra and panties, her long blond hair fastened behind her head with a rubber band, Lana stared a moment at Camellion, an intenseness in her deep blue eyes.

"Did the Fox tell you how he obtained the information? Of course he didn't! We're supposed to be idiots and regard his every word as 'divine revelation'!" She reached for her cigarettes and lighter lying on the floor next to the cot on which she was sitting.

"He didn't want to reveal the source, but I told him we would not mount another 'gone with the wind' operation until we had some hard data," Camellion said, picking up another piece of lamb with his right hand. The lamb was too highly seasoned for his taste, but he was hungry. "He explained that in New Delhi there's an Indian woman named Parveen Babbi. She's a Makalshiski, the Indian version of a high-class call girl. According to the Fox, she's the mistress of a KGB officer named Stefan Mikhaulsky. He's the number two man in counterintelligence and security in one of the six lines at the KGB station at the Soviet embassy in New Delhi. Grojean—"

"What do you mean by lines?" asked Weejee.

"The Russian word for section translates into 'line,'" Camellion explained. He then told them that Stefan Mikhaulsky was not only an alcoholic but when drunk was prone to blab secrets to Parveen Babbi.

"And Babbi is working for the Company," Lana finished, an expression of disgust on her face. "How does Grojean know she's not a double agent? He probably suspects that she is. He's too cautious to put much faith in a whore."

Camellion finished chewing, then took a sip of tea. "Grojean thinks she is a double and probably has sold the same information to the East Germans. He is convinced she told the truth. Grojean swears that her information has always proved correct. The rub is that we don't know how Holtz is going to make contact with the KGB, or when. We can assume it will be as soon as possible after he arrives in New Delhi."

Weejee said, "You're going to tell us next that we won't know how and when until Parveen Babbi finds out from—what's the name of that Russian son of a bitch?"

Lana Stanley made a noise with her lips. "Even if that whore does find out where Holtz is going to link up with the KGB, how are we supposed to get the information? And we still have to get to New Delhi ourselves. So far, since we've been in Bombay all you've told us is that a plane will fly us from here to there if worse comes to worst. The way things are now, we couldn't be in a worse mess."

"I can't figure out Courtland Grojean," Weejee said. "From what

I've heard about him, he'd be cautious if the enemy were an old blind woman in a wheelchair. Yet he's taking the word of a goddamn prostitute. I suppose that's all he has."

The Death Merchant finished wiping his fingers with a handkerchief.

"When Babbi gets the information, she'll turn it over to her control at our station in New Delhi. We'll be stashed in a safe house in Old Delhi. The embassy station will radio the information to us."

Camellion opened a pocketknife, then looked over at Lana and Weejee and smiled. "It's a long shot, but look at it this way: it beats indoor body-surfing! As it is, we have to leave Bombay. By tomorrow morning, Inspector Bhilainagar will be tearing the city apart looking for us. If he finds us, he'll have to hold us, no matter what DARFA wants."

"I'll ask you again, how do we get from Bombay to New Delhi?" Lana asked, trying to sound casual and thinking that she had only six cigarettes left in her pack. "Inspector Bhilainagar will have his men trying to watch every Occidental in the city, and all airports, private and commercial, will be watched."

The Death Merchant began cutting into a mango with the blade of the pocketknife. "In reality, there is only Delhi, composed of Old Delhi and New Delhi, although for practical purposes—"

"You damn well better believe it doesn't make any difference!" Lana said angrily. "How do we get there from here? What about the plane?"

"The plane is on the plantation of a Japanese who works for the Company on-contract," Camellion told her. "It's a betel nut plantation not far from Paragadar, which is about forty kilometers northeast of Bombay."

At times the Death Merchant, always extremely sensitive to other people's body language, could detect a very subtle resistance in Lana Stanley. He felt he knew why she harbored a measure of resentment. She was a professional "employee" of the Central Intelligence Agency, a career officer. He was "on-contract" or, bluntly speaking, a mercenary, hired by the Company because of his talents for getting a job done.

"Forty kils. That's only twenty-five miles," Weejee said. "I guess— what's his name?—will have to help us get there, right? And hey! I thought the chewing of betel nuts had been outlawed because of cancer."

"Betel nuts are used in industry," Camellion replied. "His name is Anuri Takahashi."

"Richard, we'll need fresh clothes, and we'll have to be disguised," Lana said hurriedly. "And I'll need cigarettes."

"And cigars!" tacked on Weejee. "Another thing, what do we do if Holtz gets inside the Soviet embassy before that Russian agent tells the prostitute what we want to know?"

Camellion paused in eating his second mango and gave Weejee a pathetic look. "In that case, little man, we'll lose, and the Russians will have the prize. We can't win them all."

It was 4:30 P.M. of that same day that Sri and Shrimatee Phiroze Mehta and Sri and Shrimatee Bruce Canover drove north on Zhehid Ghagtisingh Road in the Sarvin, Phiroze Mehta behind the wheel, his wife next to him.

Richard Camellion and Lana Stanley sat in the rear. But in case anyone should ask, they were Sri and Shrimatee Amrat Matipura—Mr. Amrat Matipura and Mrs. Hari Matipura. Disguised as Sunni Muslims, they even looked the part, particularly Lana Stanley. She was dressed in the traditional black *chader* and resembled an animated tent when she walked. The important thing was that her face was covered by a veil, with only her eyes visible—so very necessary because of her fair skin.

The Death Merchant wore the round white *komar,* the cap preferred by male followers of Muhammad; and the *kurta,* a loose white shirt, and baggy white trousers. Extract from the alfaroose plant had been used to darken Camellion's face, hands, and arms slightly. If he had been in possession of a makeup lab, he could even have changed the structure of his face. He could even have changed the color of his blue eyes. But all the plants in India could not change the color of his eyes. His only recourse was to wear dark sunglasses.

People were always coming into or leaving Bombay on five different roads, three of which branched off to the northeast, the other two, straight north. It was impossible for the authorities to check each vehicle on these roads, or traffic would have backed up all the way to Marine Drive, facing Back Bay, within a matter of hours.

There was only a very slim possibility that the Central Motorized Police would stop the Sarvin; yet the potential was there, and that was the tiny flaw in an otherwise perfect plan. Camellion and Stanley did not carry any papers identifying them as Amrat Matipura and Hari Matipura.

Neither did Weejee—carry any ID. What to do with him had been a problem. A "child" in either the front or the rear seat would have been stretching luck way out of shape. The Sarvin did have a trunk, but it was too small. Even if it had been five times larger, the heat would have excluded Weejee from being cooped up in it. The Death Merchant had finally solved the problem, much to Weejee's displeasure.

Now Weejee was in a large trunk on *top* of the car, the trunk securely strapped to a carrier. To insure proper ventilation, holes had been drilled in the bottom of the trunk. A series of holes had also been drilled in both ends of the trunk so that the forward motion of the touring car would create a wind and force it through the holes facing the front of the vehicle.

For added protection against heat, a ten-inch square had been removed from the center of the trunk lid and had been replaced. It remained secure in the lid by means of latches underneath the lid. At any time, Weejee could remove the square should the heat become too intense.

Weejee was not happy with the arrangement. Riding upstairs in the trunk had nothing to do with his anger. Earlier in the day, when Phiroze and Chenna Mehta had gone shopping, they had bought a box of Silver Ring cigars for Weejee. Camellion had taken the cigars away from Weejee before he had climbed into the trunk.

"I'm not going to risk your puffing on one of those damned things," the Death Merchant had said, "and having someone in another car wondering why smoke is coming out of holes in the trunk!"

Lana Stanley was another unhappy member of the party. Not only did she dislike the Indian-made cigarettes the Mehtas had bought, but she was having a nicotine fit over not being able to smoke inside the car. But should someone see her—how would it look to see a Sunni Muslim female, with her veil removed, smoking a cigarette!

Phiroze and Chenna Mehta, although they had never traveled outside the Indian subcontinent, were well read and informed about the world's peoples. Both were good conversationalists.

At one point the subject drifted to mythology, with Chenna Mehta saying that Westerners, as a group, were ill-informed about the Hindu religion, most Occidentals thinking that the Hindu gods and goddesses were promiscuous.

"It's the opposite," explained Mrs. Mehta, who, several inches shorter than her husband, was a petite woman with dark, fragile features. "The gods of the Hindu pantheon are monogamous, and unlike the Greek and Roman Gods, they seldom have mistresses and concubines."

"Another false belief harbored by people of the West is that women in India are ill-treated," Phiroze Mehta said with a shrill laugh, as if enjoying an immense joke. "The truth is that respect for women is part of our culture and the philosophy of our menfolk. Do you know that a woman can travel for long distances on her own more safely in India than in many of the so-called highly civilized Western societies?"

Chenna Mehta said pleasantly, "Marital problems play only a small role in our country and divorces are extremely rare."

"I should suppose it's a difference between the psychologies of social customs," said Camellion, who wasn't really all that interested.

"It's a matter of being practical and realistic. The husband knows that it is his duty to satisfy his wife. The *Mahabharata* is quite definite that 'women enjoy sex eight times as much as men.' The wife tries to please her husband and at the same time satisfy her own needs. This is not difficult to do because frigidity is rare in India. The women of India are free from the biblical memory of Eve's apple and the Puritan nonsense that sex without conception is sinful."

Spoke up Phiroze Mehta, "To us Hindus, sex is one of the good things in life. We do not feel guilty about it. That is why we have no pornography in our nation. If the West would give up its false idea that sex is sinful and dirty, pornography would die out."

The Death Merchant asked the totally unexpected in a cheerful drawl, giving free rein to his Texas accent, "Why are the two of you working for the CIA? If you don't mind my asking!"

Even Lana Stanley, who had been silent during most of the journey, shifted position in the seat, indicating her surprise.

"For the money," Phiroze Mehta promptly answered. "That which your government is banking for us each month is a small fortune in rupees."

"My husband, you gave him only half the answer." Chenna Mehta turned in the seat and looked at the Death Merchant, her large dark eyes very serious. "He has made us sound greedy. We do enjoy the money, which shall provide for our older years. But there is another reason. The United States stands for freedom in the world. The United States is the only nation that keeps the thugs in the Soviet Union in check. If it were not for the United States, the entire world would be a slave to evil."

Camellion did not say "Gee, golly, gee!" Their replies meant little to him. He had always disliked working with and depending on traitors, with spies, who worked against their own governments for a price. He could respect intelligence officers of the Other Side; they were only doing their job for their country.

One could never fully trust traitors. Too often, they had heaven in their smiles but hell in their hearts. Too, there was always the chance that such people could be under the control of and owed their allegiance to an enemy power that might be using them to "sheep-dip," as the practice was known in the trade—placing an agent, or agents, within an organization for the purpose of establishing credentials that could be used later to penetrate or subvert other groups of like nature.

Well, now, suppose the KGB or East German Intelligence is sheep-dipping with Parveen Babbi, the Makalshiski.

Out of necessity, Camellion had to consider other possibilities. Could the Mehtas be leading them into a KGB or an MfS trap? He didn't think so. Yet it was possible, in which case, he and Lana and Weejee would have only their pistols with which to defend themselves —and a poor defense it would be. The answer would be the same if Phiroze and Chenna Mehta were working for the Indian DARFA and DARFA was after more information about the CIA network in India.

Self-contradictions, Gordian knots, and paradoxes! The entire world was one absurdity! In the United States and in Europe, overweight was a problem of millions. *Yet in the world at large, a human being dies of hunger every eight seconds!* The West was obsessed with freedom. There were constant references made to the world's most useless debating society, the United Nations—*but forty member nations in the UN do not even allow elections!*

Camellion did have some concrete facts: all it would take would be one tiny mistake—*and the three of us will become central figures in a ballet of slaughter orchestrated by the Eternal Smiler, the Cosmic Lord of Death. . . .*

Camellion mentally chuckled. He had another face. One hundred percent of all people alive breathe . . .

Chapter Eleven

11.00 hours.
Embassy of the Union of Soviet Socialist Republics.
9641 Sadar Thana Road,
New Delhi, India.

"It is Moscow's opinion that the loss of your entire special squad can only be viewed as a major catastrophe, Major Bukashev." Because Major Stefan Mikhaulsky was present in the conference room, Colonel Konstantin Shatalin spoke very formally and officially to his old friend. "General Chebrikov has requested that you send him a detailed report on the disaster at the Elephanta Caves. I order you to write the report as soon as this meeting is over. Do you understand, Major?"

"Yes, Comrade Colonel," Bukashev said listlessly. "As soon as the meeting is finished, I'll write the report, although I don't at this moment know of anything else I can add. The two posing as the Canovers were—they were too good for my people. Or maybe it was pure luck. We'll never know. Anyhow, those two killed the six members of my squad."

Stefan Mikhaulsky looked across the bubble room at Bukashev and intoned, "I wouldn't put that in the report, Boris—about the Canovers being 'too good.' Or the Center will order you home to undergo mental and emotional evaluation."

Colonel Shatalin looked sharply at Mikhaulsky, whom he had never liked. The man was too certain of himself, too priggish, too complacent. However, Shatalin always treated Mikhaulsky fairly and impersonally, not only because he never permitted his personal feel-ings to interfere with his job as *Rezident* of the embassy station at New Delhi, but also because he recognized that much of Mikhaulsky's obtuseness was part of his basic personality. It was the way he was, like the color of his hair and eyes.

Major Stefan Mikhaulsky was a first-rate officer in Section II, counterintelligence. It had been he who had thought of the plan to prove whether the man who called himself "Professor Bruce Canover" was genuine or a replacement. Mikhaulsky had suggested to Moscow that it have its agents in the United States go to the library of the Briswinn Institute of Social Studies and rent some of the tapes of Canover's lectures. Recordings could be made of the tapes and flown to Moscow Center. All that would be needed then was a recording of the voice of the "Bruce Canover" in Bombay.

This, too, had been accomplished. The voice of the Indian "Bruce Canover" had been obtained by a female agent who had struck up a conversation with Mr. and Mrs. Canover when they had visited the Krishnagiri Upavan garden near Borilivi Station in Bombay. A tape recorder in the agent's handbag had recorded every word.

The tape was flown to Moscow, where a voice-analysis comparison was made. The result of the comparison proved that the "Bruce Canover" in Bombay was not the real Professor Canover.

Colonel Shatalin cleared his throat and leaned back comfortably in the padded high-back executive swivel, his eyes swinging to Major Mikhaulsky. "Give me a report on Operation Temple."

"Comrade Colonel, as you know, Captain Zortilkov at our consulate in Bombay reported that Franz Holtz would be returning to Bombay today. Zortilkov reported that Holtz did take the chance and phone the consulate, using the name of 'Harvey Tessatall.' He had to talk in a roundabout manner because of possible taps. He did tell Zortilkov enough to prove he was Holtz. Zortilkov met with Holtz at the Jehangir Art Gallery. Holtz said—"

"Why didn't Zortilkov set a trap and grab Holtz at the museum?" interrupted Boris Bukashev half angrily. "We could have had Holtz. Of course, he didn't have the devices with him, but we could have easily made him tell where he has them hidden."

A look of annoyance flashed over Major Stefan Mikhaulsky's face. A man of medium height and weight for his thirty-nine years, he was always clean-shaven, had dark wavy hair, clear intelligent eyes, and perfect dentures, the latter an asset because he smiled a lot. He wasn't smiling now. He preferred brain power to brute power, and regarded

Boris Bukashev as a moronic thug whose only talent was killing people.

Shatalin quickly intervened, and none too gently. Damn it! Why couldn't Boris keep his mouth shut. He was an expert when it came to violence. But when it came to the surreptitiousness necessary for counterintelligence work, he was less than a rank novice.

"Major, hasn't it occurred to you that Captain Zortilkov could not take the chance of an ambush? He knew that Holtz would be on guard against a trap."

"Exactly!" Mikhaulsky said with some sharpness. "All we have to do is lose Franz Holtz once—and we'll lose him forever. He's extremely cautious and very frightened. One can't blame him, not after the way Canover almost put him to sleep."

After another warning look at Boris Bukashev, Shatalin directed his attention to Mikhaulsky, who continued as if nothing had happened.

"Holtz told Zortilkov he would return to New Delhi to make arrangements to fly to Jammu. It's a town of 135,000 people in the extreme northwest of India, close to the India–Pakistan border."

"Did Holtz mention the PAL devices?" asked Shatalin in an even voice.

"Yes, Comrade Colonel. Holtz told Zortilkov that he had the devices hidden—and I quote—'around Jammu.' He did not say *in* Jammu."

"And Zortilkov had no choice but to believe him!"

"He had to. It's possible that Holtz was telling the truth. I doubt it. Holtz said that he would meet with our people and turn the devices over to them at Fatehpur Sikri, the 'Ghost City.' Holtz also obtained a guarantee from Zortilkov that in return for the devices we would send him to Moscow and that he would be permitted to join the *Kah Gay Beh!*"

Boris Bukashev guffawed. Konstantin Shatalin smiled. Major Mikhaulsky smiled, a half-moon smile from ear to ear, showing his perfect dentures.

Highly amused, Shatalin commented, "I am constantly being amazed at the people we meet in this business. Holtz is a highly trained East German intelligence officer, reputedly one of Mischa Wolf's best—at least he was. Yet the poor fool is so unimaginative that he actually believes that he can join the *Kah Gay Beh*. We will, of course, take the festering cockroach to Moscow and protect him. *Agitatsiya* will make him look like the defecting hero he isn't."

"Our Office of Agitation and Propaganda is very good at such things," agreed Mikhaulsky matter-of-factly.

With a final laugh Shatalin pushed back the swivel chair, got to his feet, moved from behind the desk, and went over to the liquor cabinet built around a small refrigerator. He reached for a bottle of bloodred *Tcherveno*, a dry Georgian wine, then turned and glanced at Bukashev and Mikhaulsky. "Comrades, a drink?"

With a slight nod, Major Bukashev got to his feet and started across the room. He enjoyed a drink and was known to imbibe too freely a few times or so a year. However, Colonel Shatalin knew that alcohol had never been a problem with his old friend.

In contrast, some members of the Indian *Rezidentura* had remarked that Major Mikhaulsky liked far more than several drinks. Shatalin never listened to unsubstantiated rumors; he only judged the people of his network by their performance, and Mikhaulsky's work was excellent. He had never seen Mikhaulsky take more than three drinks at embassy functions.

"Thank you, Comrade Colonel," Mikhaulsky said pleasantly. "I make it a habit never to drink while on duty."

His back to Mikhaulsky, Shatalin filled a glass with the dry *Tcherveno*, interest quickening in his eye. To his left, Major Bukashev was pouring *tari*, an Indian palm wine, into a glass.

The glass in his hand, Shatalin turned to Mikhaulsky. "Major, you mentioned that you doubted if Franz Holtz told the truth during his meeting with Captain Zortilkov. Is there anything specific you think he is lying about?"

Major Mikhaulsky considered for a few moments. "Nothing that I can put my finger on," he said straightforwardly. "I believe he has the PAL devices hidden in either Jammu or the Ghost City. Holtz has to know that we wouldn't take him under our protective wing until he turned the mechanisms over to us. Unless he has no intention of going to Jammu!"

Colonel Shatalin shook his head. "That's not logical. Holtz knows we're his only hope; he has nowhere else to go."

There was a brooding look on Major Bukashev's face as he went back to his chair. "Didn't Captain Zortilkov offer to make the arrangements to fly Holtz to Jammu? If he didn't—!"

"A good question. I was about to ask the same thing," commented Shatalin, his eyes on Mikhaulsky over the rim of the glass.

"He did. Zortilkov made the offer," assented Mikhaulsky. "Holtz refused on the grounds that he preferred to use—and I quote—'my own pilot.' That's the main reason I'm suspicious of his motives. I can understand why he couldn't fly from Bombay. The Indian police are looking for him there. But why couldn't he let Zortilkov make the arrangements?"

"Holtz is up to something," Bukashev said in a harsh voice as he settled down in his chair. "He couldn't be afraid that we might kill him before he got to northern India. He has to realize we could easily kill him anytime after he turned the PALs over to us and was in our custody. He's not a fool. He knows he has to trust us. What choice does he have?"

Happy that Boris had said something intelligent in front of Major Mikhaulsky, Shatalin offered his own theory about Holtz. "We could be underestimating Holtz. He's not concerned about our killing him. He's too valuable to us as a propaganda prize—and he knows it."

Bukashev and Mikhaulsky's expressions asked Shatalin for the bottom line. He gave it to them.

"I think Holtz is coming to New Delhi for a reason not connected with us and the PAL devices. Eventually we'll know, after we have him."

Looking worried, Stefan Mikhaulsky did a lot of shifting in his chair. "But we are still going ahead with Operation Temple, and meet Holtz at Fatehpur Sikri, six days from now?"

Shatalin, who had sat down in an easy chair, cocked an eyebrow at Mikhaulsky. "We have to meet Holtz. He designated 15.00 hours, didn't he?"

"Yes, Comrade Colonel," replied Mikhaulsky. "He said three o'clock in the afternoon. We are to meet him at the Temple of the Rain."

"I presume you know where the temple is located?" Shatalin knew that after Mikhaulsky had received the report from Captain Zortilkov, he had immediately gone about gathering complete information about Fatehpur Sikri, the Ghost City.

Major Mikhaulsky smiled—more even and pearly-white dentures.

"Major Bukashev and his people and I and mine will not have any trouble finding Holtz at the Temple of the Rain. We'll use the usual 'slip-route' to get from the embassy and we'll travel in cars, disguised as tourists. Numerous tourists are always visiting Fatehpur Sikri, especially during the summer months. Jammu is a tourist city." Once more he smiled. "I don't anticipate any trouble, or—"

"We're going to have full security," Bukashev said grimly. "It's the Americans I'm worried about—and don't bring up what happened in Bombay. You weren't there, Stefan."

"I'm not going to argue with you about security, Major," Mikhaulsky said placidly. "Security is your department. Mine is counterintelligence . . . evaluating Franz Holtz after we have him. Getting him and the devices safely back to New Delhi is your problem."

Colonel Shatalin decided it was time to tell Majors Bukashev and Mikhaulsky of the travel arrangements that had been made by the Center in Moscow.

"Neither of you will be returning to New Delhi with Franz Holtz," Shatalin said casually. "The Center had made plans to fly the three of you directly to Moscow from the Jammu area."

Bukashev and Mikhaulsky stared at their chief, who said, "Here are the details. . . ."

Chapter Twelve

Water does not always pour from the sky when it rains. Sometimes it is only a slight shower or a drizzle. Similarly, luck can be slight, fairly good, or all bad. Or . . . good luck can come like a cloudburst. With the Death Merchant and his people, luck was a monsoon. The trip from Bombay to the betel nut plantation of Anuri Takahashi was made without the slightest difficulty.

There was more good fortune when Takahashi, escorting them to a guesthouse, announced that there had been a slight change in plans: The airplane would arrive six hours earlier than scheduled.

"The airplane will land shortly after dark," said Takahashi, who spoke perfect English, was almost seventy years of age, and had been a fighter pilot in the Imperial Japanese air force during World War II.

"There will be time for you to change clothes and have something to eat," Takahashi said. "That's all the time you'll have. It will take us almost forty-five minutes to reach the landing strip in the jungle." He turned to Mr. and Mrs. Mehta. "Please accept my hospitality for the night."

The time raced by. The pilot of the two-engined Robertson was a surly man in his early forties, evidently a Britisher, unless he was a genius at faking accents. His supercilious manner changed rapidly after the Death Merchant politely asked him where the aircraft would land in Delhi and what arrangements had been made for transportation from the landing site.

"I'm not a bloody information service," Alister Botts answered. "You'll see when we get there."

Botts learned instantly that his reply had not been satisfactory. The

Death Merchant slammed him up against the plane and shoved a Hi-Power Browning pistol against his throat.

"You've just become a bloody information service, friend," Camellion said quietly. "I asked a question. I expect an answer—right now."

Botts's eyes widened. He had knocked around the world quite a bit and knew Death when he was face to face with it. He drew his head back as far as he could. The Browning moved with him.

"We'll land nine kilometers southwest of Palam International Airport, in a field," Botts said nervously. "All I can tell you is that someone will meet you. That's all I know. We—we should land about ten-thirty."

Camellion lowered the pistol. "A field, you said. What about landing lights?"

"There won't be any," Botts replied. "I'll use IFR to land. Don't worry. I'm very good at night flying."

Three hours later, when Botts landed, it was like descending into a pitch-black bowl surrounded by shimmering lights. To the northeast was the glow of Palam International Airport. Much farther to the northeast and to the north was the much larger glow of Delhi, the capital of India.

One of the oldest cities in India, Delhi was the capital of an empire five hundred years old when Bombay and Madras were trading posts and Calcutta a village of mud flats. It was from Delhi that various Hindu and Moslem dynasties, and finally the Moguls, ruled India until they were conquered by the British. It was in Delhi that the British established their seat of government, from 1911 to 1947.

Delhi had been destroyed eight times by invading armies and then rebuilt. This was the original Delhi, a city that was more than two thousand years old before Columbus discovered a continent that would be misnamed "America."

Delhi became "Old Delhi" when the British built New Delhi between 1920 and 1930, the new city a combination of Oriental and European Renaissance architecture. New Delhi is still a garden city of parks, tree-shaded boulevards, and mansions swimming in a sea of lawns. The public buildings are very modern.

Alister Botts had told the truth. He was a very good pilot, bringing the six-seater down to what was almost a perfect three-point landing, and with only infrared to guide him. Next to Botts in the co's seat, the Death Merchant watched him taxi to the end of the field, turn the airplane around, and taxi fifty feet forward. Botts then cut down the two piston engines to idle.

Almost at once, Camellion—and Lana Stanley and Wilbur Theimer, in the passenger section—heard a vehicle start up to the west, the sound of the engine growing louder as the vehicle, its lights off, drew closer to the airplane.

"That's your friends," Botts said. "You and the others can get out and I'll take off."

Amused, Camellion pulled the Browning pistol and, within the soft green glow emanating from the aircraft's instrument panel, motioned with the autoloader toward the door between the cockpit and the rear of the craft.

"You're not going to fly off into the blue until I know you haven't led us into quicksand," Camellion said in a deceptively pleasant voice that was suddenly very cold. "If you have, I'll put a bullet into the back of your head. Move!"

Without a word of protest Botts moved, he and Camellion getting out of the plane first, Lana and Weejee, guns in their hands, following. All four then watched the approach of what turned out to be a 1982 British Ellington step-in delivery van with push-in double doors on the left side. The van stopped and Camellion and his "wife" and "son" saw a familiar face behind the wheel—Barry Dillman. Standing next to him was Steve Hondergriff.

On the side of the van were white letters in Hindi. Underneath the letters in Hindi were English words, also painted in white—KANGRA RASJASTHAN. PRODUCTS OF TIN. BANDA GUPTA ROAD. DELHI.

Dillman slid from the seat and stepped out of the van. "Well, are you just going to stand there and rubberneck?"

The safe house was five rooms in the rambling stone house and family factory of Kangra Rasjasthan, a Bengali who, with his wife and seventeen-year-old son, made a living manufacturing *dabbas,* the rounded tin containers used by restaurants in large cities. Every day, thousands of *dabbawallas* carried thousands of *dabbas,* each filled with a hot lunch, from restaurants to thousands of office and factory workers.

Ding Bat was not the main safe house in Delhi. The next morning, Rory Gelhart, the CIA Control in charge, told Camellion that Brass

Coin, the main safe house, was on the other side of the city. Gelhart did not say where, and Camellion knew better than to ask.

The only other permanent resident of Ding Bat was Martin Koss, a twenty-seven-year-old rookie fresh out of Langley. The cynical Gelhart, a forty-year-old, fifteen-year veteran with the Company, considered Koss a man who was too idealistic and had played too many games without his helmet.

"He was in the top ten of his class and has his precious degree in political science, but he's so damned green that he thinks the executive branch of the U.S. government some kind of saint out to 'save the world.'"

Just then, Koss, Stanley, and Theimer, the latter two dressed in Western clothes, walked up, and Koss said, "Come along and I'll show you three the outside of the station, such as it is."

Kangra Rasjasthan's house was shaped like half a swastika. There was a long perpendicular section to the north. Connected to this section was an even longer horizontal section that was laid out from east to west. At the west end of this section was the last portion of the house; it, too, was perpendicular. The five rooms of Ding Bat were in the north vertical section.

Next to Rasjasthan's house—to the east—were the rusty-red sandstone ruins of Agra Fort, which was built by the Mogul Akbar and his son Jahangir. Three city blocks square, Agra Fort was a maze of gloomy and dangerous crumbling buildings that the Indian government, because of the cost, had not seen fit to repair and turn into a tourist attraction.

Only Agra Fort's outer front wall, sixty-one feet high and thirty feet thick, was still intact. To the west, the wall moved past the end of the north section of the house, so close that the house's north wall—the perpendicular section to the north—was flush against the south side of the Fort's massive front wall. The wall then curved southeast, then south, then made a wide curve to the northeast.

"I feel like I'm in the middle of a nightmare," said Lana Stanley, staring at the enormous wall. "It's difficult to tell whether the wall is keeping us out or trying to hem us in!"

"I prefer to think that the wall is keeping us out—protecting us, really," said Martin Koss. Slim, he had thick, honey-colored hair and was deeply tanned—a puzzlement to Camellion. Blue-eyed and blond-haired people usually got only a painful sunburn and could not tan, at least not deeply.

"Those buildings inside the Fort—well, going in them would be the same as going into a tunnel in a shaft. You never know when the rock might come down. You never know, either, when one of the buildings will collapse. Every now and then we hear a rumble when something falls in the Fort."

"Let's get back inside," said Gelhart. It was more of an order than a suggestion. "We don't know who might be passing on the road."

The remainder of the day was spent with Camellion and the others, including Barry Dillman and Steve Hondergriff, discussing the problem at hand—Franz Holtz and the PALs. Earlier, Gelhart had said that the station at the embassy in New Delhi had told him to expect a very important radio communiqué.

"Or a hand-delivered microdot," Koss had said.

Gelhart, a glass of ginger ale in his hand, looked straight at the Death Merchant. "Can you tell us what is really going on, or is it NTK?"

Camellion didn't see any reason not to tell Gelhart and Koss some facts of life, as well as bring Dillman and Hondergriff up to date. In a crisp voice he explained the latest development, how he had learned that Franz Holtz was returning to New Delhi and how Parveen Babbi and Stefan Mikhaulsky were connected with the East German agent.

"Well, that's the living end!" Gelhart exclaimed in disgust. "Do you mean we're supposed to mount an operation based solely on the word of an Indian call girl? And possibly a double agent at that!"

"It's damned nonsense!" Barry Dillman snorted, his rugged face a picture of disbelief. "For all we know, the KGB might know that Babbi is working for the Company. Mikhaulsky might be lying just to lead us down a blind alley."

Koss turned and looked at Gelhart. "Why didn't the station tell us about Babbi? She operates here in Delhi."

"Because it—she—was none of our business—that's why!" replied Gelhart, almost smiling at the absurdity of Koss's question. "Wise up! We don't know a tenth of what goes on here in Delhi."

Steve Hondergriff sighed and shifted his gaze to Rory Gelhart.

"I think you have missed the most important part of what Canover said. Babbi is the only lead we have. If Mikhaulsky doesn't tell her where and when the KGB is going to meet Holtz, we'll lose him."

"That's right," Camellion admitted. "All we can do is wait and hope that Parveen Babbi obtains the information and gets it to the station in time. Even so, that doesn't mean we'll automatically be able to corner Holtz. It will depend on the situation, on the time and place and other factors."

Gelhart finished his ginger ale and placed the empty glass next to him on the floor. "Win or lose, we're skating on thin ice. I don't think it makes all that much difference in the long run. Sooner or later the Russians are going to lose control of their society. We've already lost control of ours. We're risking our lives to protect a society that is rapidly rushing toward its own destruction."

"That's a very broad generalization," said Lana Stanley, who found Gelhart's pronouncement annoying. "I think there's a lot of good in American society. You've been brainwashed by a media that focuses only on the bad." She glanced at Camellion, expecting him to reinforce her opinion. She didn't like what she got.

"Rory has a good point," he said curtly. "American society has stretched the boundaries of moral behavior so much that we're drowning in a sea of permissiveness. There is a tendency to encourage each delicate ego to become the prime center of its own universe. It's called 'personal freedom,' but it's a freedom that's totally out of control."

"He's right!" Gelhart was quick to point out. "Along with that runaway freedom is the attempt by the liberal-minority coalition to make the American people wholeheartedly accept immigration, integration, and miscegenation."

"That's a racist statement, if I ever heard one!" Stanley snapped. She also gave Camellion a dirty look.

"It's *fact,*" Gelhart insisted. "What the television specials don't tell the American people is that past immigration was almost entirely of European origin, while today it is mostly nonwhite. Today's nonwhite immigrants are coming in so fast and reproducing so rapidly that in a short time white people will become a minority in their own country."

"Nonsense!" sneered Stanley. "There have always been 'doomsday prophets,' and not one of their prophesies have ever come true. I think a lot of immigrants coming into the United States today contribute to society."

"They sure do!" laughed Gelhart. "Go to any large city and you'll see what the majority of these new immigrants contribute—crime, disease, corruption, drugs, poverty, illiteracy—the whole nine yards that's wrecking society."

The Death Merchant said mildly, "Most people don't know it, but the woman who wrote the poem that was placed on the Statue of Liberty, seventeen years after the monument's erection, was named

Emma Lazarus. She was a proletarian Marxist, and she called for Americans to accept the 'wretched refuse from your teeming shore.' It's ironic. Today we are certainly accepting that 'wretched refuse'— by the millions!"

"You had better believe it," growled Gelhart, "and if we don't stop this flood, our children will curse us in our graves!"

Weejee Theimer said in his high and now loud voice, "Getting back to Franz Holtz . . ."

The Death Merchant's good luck continued to hold. It was ten-thirty the next morning when Jamilka Bikaljoo, an Indian cabdriver who served as a liaison between the embassy station and Ding Bat, arrived with the previous day's edition of the *Delhi Times* and a coded letter. Bikaljoo, a fierce-looking Jain with a full beard, didn't know it but the coded letter was a fake; it was a security-for-cover and contained nothing of value.

After Bikaljoo left, Rory Gelhart said, "It's always the last period of the last sentence on the third page."

Ten minutes later the microdot had been removed, placed in the enlarger, and the message was on the screen. There was only a hushed silence as the Death Merchant and the others read the words from the chief of the Company's Delhi station:

> *Franz Holtz will make contact with the KGB in Fatehpur Sikri, the Ghost City. Place of meeting: Temple of the Rain. Time: 15.00 Wednesday. We are making arrangements to fly Canover and three others to Srinagar. The KGB has named their end of it Operation Temple. Additional details for departure from Delhi will follow tomorrow by courier at 10.00. Time of departure from Delhi 22.00 tomorrow.*

The long silence was finally broken by Gelhart's switching off the enlarger and then removing the microdot from the slide.

"I just saw it, but I find it difficult to believe that Parveen Babbi pulled the information from Mikhaulsky," Lana Stanley said in a small voice. "How could a trained Soviet agent be so stupid?"

"It happens," Barry Dillman said. "When sex comes in, all common sense flies out. Remember when Oleg Gordievsky defected in London? And he was the KGB chief of station! All of it over a woman. The damn fool thought the doll would follow him. When she didn't, the idiot even made a bigger fool of himself. He went back to the Soviet Union! You see, Mikhaulsky is not all that unusual."

Stanley's eyes narrowed slightly when she sensed that Richard Camellion was apparently less than enthusiastic over the information that had been on the microdot. Did he think that the information was false, or, worse, part of a clever trap set by the KGB? Knowing it would be useless to ask him, she only said, "I wonder how the station intends to get me and Weejee out of India. I don't think we'll be going to Srinagar."

Weejee bit off the end of a Silver Ring cigar. "We'll know tomorrow. I don't give a damn how we get out, just so we make it. I'm sick of this country."

His expression intense, the Death Merchant stepped closer to Rory Gelhart, who had just destroyed the microdot by dropping it into a small vat of acid.

"Rory, let's see your maps and files on India," Camellion said. "Let's see what you have on the Ghost City."

"Whatever we might have, we won't like it," replied Gelhart with his usual pessimism. He turned and walked over to a large eight-foot-wide, floor-to-ceiling bookcase against the north wall. When Gelhart had first shown Camellion, Stanley, and Theimer around the station, the Death Merchant had suspected there was something not quite right about the wooden bookcase painted green. It wasn't that it looked out of place. It looked too snug against the wall; and now, as Camellion stood only several feet from the bookcase, watching Gelhart scan the volumes, he was positive that the bookcase was a door that opened to another room, or at least another large space. He was certain because a tenth of an inch of the rear of the bookcase was inside the stone wall.

"What does the bookcase conceal?" Camellion asked Gelhart, who turned and assaulted him with a sharp look of annoyance. Curiosity bloomed in the eyes of the others in the room, except Martin Koss, who looked disappointed.

"How did you know?" Gelhart moved his tongue in his left cheek.

"I can see that a tiny portion of the back is inside the wall," Camellion said. "To me, it's a tip-off."

Gelhart turned back to the bookcase and pulled out a large book. "The bookcase opens to a long passage in the Fort's outer wall." Walking to a table with the book, Gelhart explained that the passage, four feet wide and seven feet high, was inside the massive outer wall of the Fort. The opposite end of the passage was inside Agra Fort, 580 feet to the southeast. It was Kangra Rasjasthan who had discovered the passage by finding the opening inside the Fort.

Opening the book, Gelhart said, "Since the Fort's wall is flush to the rear wall of this house, it was simple for us to knock out an opening in the wall of the house, and then make an opening in the Fort's wall. I don't think we'll ever need the escape route, but—who knows?"

"We have a van stashed in the fort, just in case," Koss said.

Gelhart, who had thumbed through the book, tapped a page and smiled at the Death Merchant with his eyes. "Here we are, Fatehpur Sikri, the Ghost City."

They quickly learned that Fatehpur Sikri was twenty-two kilometers north of the city of Jammu. In the sixteenth century, Fatehpur Sikri had exceeded London in both population and grandeur, and had been used as a capital by the great emperor Akbar. But all things end. Today, Fatehpur Sikri was deserted and left in solitude to reminisce over its past glory. Its only value was as a major tourist attraction.

There was a fold-out map of the Ghost City, and Camellion soon found what he wanted. "The Temple of the Rain is in the center of the Ghost City. I must say that location complicates the entire business."

"We'll be right smack in the middle of the KGB," Barry Dillman said peremptorily. "What are we going to do with Franz Holtz even if we get our hands on him? DARFA is looking all over India for the Canovers and their son, and if Parveen Babbi has also sold the information to the East Germans and to the Indian intelligence service . . ."

The Death Merchant nodded. "Yes, we could have more 'friends' around us in the Ghost City than flies on a fresh cow chip."

Steve Hondergriff and Lana Stanley moved closer to the table.

"How about Srinagar?" inquired Hondergriff, pronouncing the name as *Sir-nay-gar*. "The name seems familiar to me."

"It's pronounced as if it were written 'Sirrynugger,' " Camellion corrected Hondergriff. "It might be familiar because Srinagar is the summer capital of Kashmir. It's way up in northern India, in the Himalayas. Srinagar is called the 'Venice of the East,' and it does have a large airport, mainly for tourists."

"Jammu is much smaller than Srinagar," Rory Gelhart said. "Its main industry is tourism. According to this book, it does, however, have a large colony of Pahari painters."

"Well, you can count me and Weejee out of the action," Stanley announced. "DARFA will be looking for a Western couple with a little boy. I just wonder how many tourists will have a little boy with them?"

Barry Dillman directed his words at the Death Merchant. "We are going to have to have some kind of disguise. As foreigners, we'll stand out like newly splashed mud on a freshly washed car. On the other hand, there'll be tourists there from all over the world."

"The station at the embassy will provide us with passports, visas, and pocket litter," offered Martin Koss, sitting down. "I suppose they'll send everything over tomorrow morning."

The Death Merchant thought for a moment. "At this point in time it's impractical to discuss possibilities. We don't have enough data. All we can do is wait and see what the main station sends over."

His expression wintry, Barry Dillman chipped in, "I'm bothered about Holtz's returning to Delhi. You have to give that kraut credit. He may be all alone and on the run, but think about it! He did a good job of getting out of Bombay and slipping back to Delhi."

Camellion nodded. "You're really asking why Holtz returned to Delhi when he's going to meet the KGB in the Ghost City, three hundred miles northwest of Delhi. He picked the Ghost City. The KGB didn't."

Gelhart closed the reference book, his eyes flicking over the Death Merchant. "What makes you think that the KGB didn't choose the meeting spot?"

"The KGB would want speed," Camellion said. "The KGB would choose the path of least resistance. The Russians would pick Delhi. The number of options available to an organism, or to an organization, decreases in direct ratio to its increased complexity and specialization. The farther Holtz is from the KGB center in Delhi, the more complicated netting him becomes, unless the KGB intends to get him out of India by flying him out of Srinagar."

"Our own position isn't all that secure," grumped Lana Stanley.

"It's all academic," Camellion said, and stood up. "Like I said, all we can do is wait and see what the station sends over tomorrow."

Chapter Thirteen

"Tomorrow" never came for the Death Merchant and the rest of the people at Ding Bat, not in the sense that he and the others would have to wait for a courier to arrive from the U.S. Embassy center at ten o'clock in the morning. At 3:30 A.M., Rory Gelhart came into one of Ding Bat's rooms and, keeping the beam of the flashlight close to the floor, gently shook the right shoulder of the Death Merchant, who was sleeping on a folding cot.

Instantly awake, Camellion intuited that something was very wrong. Something was. Gelhart whispered that either agents of DARFA or the Indian Riot and Security police were surrounding the house.

"Four photoelectric alarms around the house began flashing lights five minutes ago," whispered Gelhart. "Damn it! Somehow we've been made. The others are already awake."

First picking up a Hi-Power Browning pistol from underneath the cot, Camellion was instantly on his feet, his eyes quickly adjusting to the near darkness. He saw Barry Dillman and Martin Koss hurry into the main room of the station, each carrying a bag of magazines and an Italian Socimi 821 submachine gun. Behind them was Steve Hondergriff, carrying several bags of magazines and three Socimi SMGs.

Bearing a striking resemblance to the Israeli Uzi, the Socimi SMG could be fired from either full auto or single shot, and operated on the primer-ignition system by means of a straight blowback principle. The magazine held thirty-two 9mm para NATO rounds.

"Here!" Hondergriff handed Camellion one of the Socimis and a dark canvas bag containing four magazines. Then he hurried off to one of the windows and took a position on one knee, to one side of the window.

"The way this house is laid out, we won't be able to hold out for any length of time," Camellion said, checking the Socimi to make sure there was a cartridge in the firing chamber. "How many rooms does Kangra Rasjasthan and his family have?"

"Four rooms in the front section of the house," replied Gelhart. He adjusted a shoulder holster in which was nestled a .357 Desert Eagle autopistol. "His little tin lunchbox factory is in three large rooms in the horizontal section. Finally, there are these five rooms of the station in the north part of the house, this large room and four smaller ones. To top it off, Rasjasthan and his family intend to make a fight of it. What a goddamn fuckin' mess!"

"Where are Stanley and the little man?" Camellion's cold expression never changed. "And how long will it take you to open that bookcase? Either we go through the passage or we're going to stay here and die."

Gelhart looked over at Martin Koss, who was down on his knees opening a wooden chest close to the bookcase against the north wall. He stepped closer to the Death Merchant, a determined set to his jaw. "Listen, we're going to do more than escape through the passage, then on to Brass Coin. We can't let the Indian police, especially DARFA, find the shortwave and the microdot equipment. We're going to blow up Ding Bat with twenty-two kilograms of Duramite."

Camellion frowned. "Duramite is fifty pounds of what?"

"It's an Indian explosive. Half is TNT; the other half is similar to RDX. It will take me and Koss about fifteen minutes to set the charges. Can you and the others hold them off for that length of time? These Indians don't have any finesse. Once they're in position, they'll storm in like wild men and hit us on all sides. But can you and the others hold them off?"

"Do we have a choice?" conceded Camellion. "Hurry it up as fast as you can. I'll get Lana and—never mind. Here they come."

Gelhart moved off to help Martin Koss prepare the Duramite, and Camellion moved over to Lana and Weejee, both of whom were armed, Stanley with a 9mm Sterling Para M7 pistol, and Theimer with a 9mm Sterling submachine gun that was only slightly shorter than he was.

"What about Rasjasthan? Is he going to make a fight of it?" Camellion glanced again at Barry Dillman, who was watching the single window to the east, and then at Hondergriff, who was on duty by a window on the west side.

"I think Rasjasthan is crazy," Lana said. "He said the police don't have any business here. He'll kill some of them and they'll kill him and his whole family. His wife and son are as nutty as he is."

"Never mind him. Hindus have a different concept of death than we do." The Death Merchant suddenly chuckled, much to the astonishment of Lana and Weejee. "But man needs the unfathomable and the infinite just as much as he does the small planet that he inhabits."

"I never should have left Ringling Brothers!" muttered Weejee fiercely. "But I did, and now I'm in India listening to a maniac spout philosophical bullshit! We're gonna get our butts shot off—you know that!"

"Little man, you and Lana take positions by the other window on the west. Don't take time to aim and hit anything. Just fire to keep them back. The bars over the windows will prevent them from getting in—at least for a while."

Lana's voice was strained and hollow. "What are you going to do, Richard?"

"I'm going to trigger off shots from the windows of the factory section," he said, and started toward the door. "The more people they think are in the house, the more time we'll gain. We only need fifteen minutes."

In the darkness, Camellion was moving through the last room of Ding Bat and was only six feet from one of the first rooms of the home-center tin factory when he heard the earsplitting chattering of either a submachine gun or an assault rifle from one of the rooms in the front of the house. Damn it! Apparently Kangra Rasjasthan had become impatient and had opened fire on the Indian police creeping toward the house. Instantly the stillness of the night was shattered by the roaring of automatic weapons from the east. More assault rifles began firing from the west and the south. Other projectiles came straight from the south, tearing into the glass of the four windows of the first factory room on the southeast, in the horizontal section of the oddly shaped house.

Tinkle, tinkle, tinkle! Instantly the windows of the room were shot out, the hail of metal tearing across the room and thudding into the opposite wall. And there were screaming ricochets as some of the 7.62mm slugs struck the flat iron bars. None of the controlled-expansion slugs came very close to Camellion, who had dropped flat the instant he had heard Rasjasthan begin firing.

The fool! The Death Merchant didn't mind Rasjasthan's decision to commit suicide with his family. A man had a right to fight and die for the things that were important to him. *But we could have gained another five minutes if that nitwit would have remained quiet.*

The long shaft of a spotlight raked across the windows, the bright beam poking into the room and probing above Camellion. Listening to Dillman and the others firing from the last room in the Ding Bat section of the house, Camellion wormed his way across the dirty floor to the window in the southeast corner. He adjusted the strap of the ammo bag, then looked out the window from the right-hand side. He didn't like what he saw.

Due south 160 feet, sitting there on Banda Gupta Road, was an Indian-built Mongoose light-armored scout car, the barrel of the 7.62mm machine gun in its turret pointed straight at the house. There were also several trucks and half a dozen cars on the road.

Catching sight of some of the Indians as they ran through the beams of spotlights attached to trucks, he saw that they wore maroon berets, dark brown smocks similar to British "Dennison" combat coats, green denim trousers, cloth puttees, and black combat boots. Each man had ammo pouches around his waist and carried a Belgian FN 7.62mm FAL assault rifle.

India's best! Paracommandos! Someone tipped off the Delhi government that the house was full of terrorists! How about that!

Camellion shoved the end of the Socimi SMG through the shattered window and very quickly triggered off six single rounds at four paras who were moving toward the northwest, apparently in an effort to get closer to the rooms of the house where Kangra Rasjasthan and his wife and son were firing British EM2 automatic rifles, their .280in SAA ball ammo wasted on trees and grass and the armored sides of the Mongoose L.A.S.C.

One of the paras let out a short, agonized scream and skidded to the dew-wet grass. The three other paracommandos only jerked and died and dropped into the Ultimate Elsewhere without a sound.

Old pro that he was at pushing aside Death, Camellion had more sense and experience than to try to fire a second volley from the same position. Smoke from the sixth shot was still curling from the muzzle of the Socimi submachine gun as Camellion jerked back, moved like chain lightning to the east wall, got down, and began crawling toward the door—and none too soon.

Major Ghazel Marchchakka, the para commander, and his officers had seen the muzzle flashes of the Socimi and, even worse, they had seen the four paras cut down by the Death Merchant's accurate firing. Now Marchchakka ordered the machine gun in the Mongoose light-armored scout car to rake the horizontal section of the house; he also ordered the gunner to toss 7.62mm projectiles at the forward vertical section harboring the three fanatical Rasjasthans.

The Indians of the 50th Parachute Brigade were very good. They knew they could only fire through the barred windows and that even light machine-gun slugs would not penetrate the thick stone walls. Accordingly, as the machine gun in the Mongoose kept up a steady firing and pinned down the Rasjasthans, other paras advanced under cover of smoke and killed the Rasjasthans by firing through the windows.

Major Marchchakka had not missed the fact that most of the enemy fire was coming from the last section of the house and directed at his men who were trying to move in from the east and the west. His plan was direct and formulated with an eye toward efficiency. Now that the front of the house had been taken, he gave orders that the men should advance room by room. To try to close in on the rear of the last section of the house under the cover of smoke would be too costly in men. Five had been killed and three wounded in killing Kangra Rasjasthan and his wife and son; and there were at least four submachine guns firing from the room in the rear section.

There were four smaller rooms in front, or to the south, of the main communications room of Ding Bat. The Death Merchant waited in the darkness in the small room to the west, the one closest to the last room of the *dabba* factory.

When the Death Merchant heard the paratroopers breaking down the front door of the Rasjasthan's home in the first perpendicular section, he rushed back to the main room of the station, which looked as if it had been hit by a tornado and in which floated a blue haze from burnt gunpowder. Hundreds of 7.62mm FAL projectiles, coming through the three windows, had ripped into the furniture. Many had struck the walls and plaster debris lay on the floor. The KG-7000 shortwave and its group of black boxes were wrecked. So was the microdot machine.

The firing from the paras had slackened, but there were still occasional bursts, the rain of slugs tearing over the prone bodies of Dillman, Hondergriff, Stanley, and Theimer.

"We're being attacked by paratroopers," Camellion said. "They've whacked out Rasjasthan and his wife and son. Either we get out of here or we'll be next."

He crawled across the room toward the bookcase that Rory Gelhart and Martin Koss had pulled open. On his way he saw that Koss was placing a block of Duramite on one side of a filing cabinet and that an electric fuse wire was trailing out behind the explosive. The wire led into the opening of the passage behind the bookcase. Something was wrong.

Camellion found Gelhart just inside the passage. With the aid of an electric lantern, Gelhart was inserting an electric blasting cap of 13.5 grains PETN into a five-pound block of Duramite.

Camellion's stare had all the force of two daggers. "I thought you were going to detonate by remote control! Don't you have D-timers with a connect to a central control?"

Gelhart pulled on the cap's bridge wire and began twisting it to the end of a fuse line. He looked up and gave Camellion a worried look.

"I've plenty of D-timers, but the battery is dead in the main control. I don't have a spare." He finished twisting the wires together, then shoved the copper cap into the putty-like material of the Duramite.

The Death Merchant had the feeling that the Cosmic Lord of Death was about to perch on his shoulder. "How long before you have everything connected?"

"Another ten minutes." Gelhart looked up again, fear in his eyes. "How close are they?"

"Practically on our doorstep," growled Camellion. "We have only one chance left and it's a slim one. Do you have a spare gun?"

Gelhart reached into his back pocket, pulled out a 9mm Detonics Super Compact autopistol and handed it to the Death Merchant. "It's fully loaded and a round is in the chamber. Just shove off the safety."

Camellion left the mouth of the passage and whispered in a loud voice to Barry Dillman and Steve Hondergriff. "You two come with me. We have to slow them down." To Weejee he said, "Watch the window to the east, little man."

No one asked him for an explanation. Not even Weejee bothered to crack one of his stale jokes. He and the others knew this was not the time or the place. It never is when one is only minutes from eternity.

Camellion and the two CIA street men raced to the first two small rooms facing the third room of the *dabba* factory. Camellion and Dillman took positions by the sides of the door to the west. Hondergriff waited by the side of the door inside the room to the east. They soon heard the paratroopers coming their way.

The paratroopers stormed forward according to the book. Two of them would dash through a door, scan the forward area, and go into a firing stance. Then two more paras would race into the room, run to the opposite wall and take positions by the next door, this a signal for the first two paras, who would rush across the room, go through the door, and begin the performance all over again.

One of the first paratroopers to rush into the last room of the *dabba* factory almost tripped over a large roll of wire on a roller frame by the side of the door. Both men jerked to a halt, went into a firing stance, looked across the area, and, in the semidarkness, saw the doors of the first two rooms of Ding Bat.

"Double team—now!" one of them called out.

At once four paratroopers, FAL assault rifles in their hands, moved into the big room and started to sprint to the two doorways, their progress slowed by various kinds of equipment in the area.

Having heard the man call out for two teams, the Death Merchant congratulated himself. He had gambled that when the first two men saw the two doors, they would call for a double team. The para had called out in Hindi, but the sound of an extra set of footsteps had told Camellion he had been right.

The four paratroopers were halfway across the room when Camellion leaned around the door frame and calmly triggered both the Detonics Super Compact autoloader and the Socimi 821 submachine gun, using the mini-SMG as a pistol and firing it on single rounds. Dillman and Hondergriff remained hidden. Camellion had ordered them not to fire until he ordered them to or until they ascertained he needed their help.

Two of the Indians were killed within several seconds by the Death Merchant's 9mm Parabellum slugs. One of them fell across a worktable and lay still. The other collapsed to the floor, his head striking the stones with a loud crack. The second pair of paratroopers cried out from pain and the shock of slugs slamming into their bodies. They were falling into unconsciousness and into the final blackness of death as the two Indians, who had first moved into the room, started to bring up their FAL assault rifles. *"Uh-ohhh!"* jumped from one man's mouth. He fell back, blood flowing from a bullet hole just above the bridge of his nose. The Death Merchant had missed the target. He had aimed at the broad part of the man's chest, but the para, starting to throw himself to the floor, had dropped a second too fast.

The other paratrooper never got to realize he was being changed into a corpse. A 9mm jacketed hollow-point poked him in the chest and punched itself through his heart. He fell with his eyes wide open and his mind closed forever.

"Cover me!" Camellion ordered Dillman. The almost empty Socimi SMG in his left hand, and the fingers of his right hand around the butt of the Detonics pistol, Camellion leaped from the doorway and started toward the end of a long worktable on the south side of the room.

Simultaneously, Barry Dillman began to sweep the sides of the doorway at the opposite end of the long room, some of his 9mm P 115-grain slugs burying themselves in the ancient wooden framework, others cutting into the sides and chopping off splinters. Dillman didn't fire more than six seconds before pulling back out of harm's way. He was convinced in his own mind that all of them—and in the large room of the station too—were as good as dead, and only going through the motions of living.

Now that the lag time was on their side, the paratroopers in the second factory room—two standing by the sides of the door and two kneeling—poked their FAL A-Rs around both sides of the door frame and began firing bursts at the doors of the first two rooms of the Ding Bat station. Because none of them suspected that one of the "terrorists" would be crazy-brave enough to charge into the room, two of the paratroopers charged in low while others took their places, and the two kneeling paras continued to toss hot 7.62 millimeter metal at Ding Bat's first two doorways.

By that time, the Death Merchant had crawled on his knees to the west end of the worktable so that he was only ten feet, at a left angle, from the door where the paratroopers, on the other side, were crouched.

Camellion hesitated out of necessity. If he miscalculated and other Indians rushed in while he was cutting down the paras across the room, he could end up being the recipient of a burst that would blast him into the next world.

He didn't have time to decide, one way or another. Because of the intense firing from the Indians, Dillman and Hondergriff were pinned down and didn't dare expose themselves. The paratroopers, feeling that they had the edge, began to pour into the room. Two Indians raced through the doorway and ducked to the left, getting down on one knee beside the other two paras. The next four came in and moved to the right; their intention was to get down by the large roll of tin and by the west end of the table.

Circumstance had decided for the Death Merchant. Almost sweating blood, Camellion reared up in a half crouch, his sudden appearance completely surprising the four Indians, three of whom were so close to the Death Merchant he could have reached out and touched them.

Therthin Rujgir, the fourth man, was on the other side of the table. He was unable to raise his FAL and fire because one of the other paratroopers was in his line of fire, between him and the Death Merchant. Rujgir did the next best thing: He dropped and started to go underneath the table at the same time that Camellion's Socimi mini-submachine gun and the Detonics pistol exploded in anger.

Two of the Indians at the end of the table died together. One of the men caught a Detonics bullet in the Adam's apple, the impact of the slug making his head jerk back and forth as though it were attached to an invisible rubber band. The second paracommando received a Socimi bullet in the chest. He made a gurgling sound. His eyes rolled back in his head and he began to sag.

Guresha Kathmerkadu, the third commando in front of the Death Merchant, was splashed with blood when the paratrooper who had been shot in the throat twisted to the right and started to sink to the stones. A thick river of red had splattered over Kathmerkadu's left shoulder, left arm, and left side, the bath of blood almost making him gag. In spite of his precarious position——he knew the white *derjunga* of a Westerner would next swing one of the weapons to him—— Kathmerkadu was unable to control his disgust at being baptized with his friend's blood. Feeling the bile building in his gut and starting to climb up in his throat, he staggered a few steps in the direction of the south wall.

During those ten seconds the Indian paracommandos lost their edge. The other four Indians across the room, to the north of Camellion, paused in their firing when they heard his SMG and pistol roar. It was the few moments' lull that gave Dillman and Hondergriff the opportunity they needed. They opened fire with their mini-sub-machine guns, pulling triggers in union with Camellion, who fired with his arms spread in a *V*. The Socimi in his left hand began spitting slugs at the doorway while the Detonics pistol in his right hand started tossing 9mm Silvertip metal across the table, at the four commandos who were now caught in a crossfire between Camellion and Dillman and Hondergriff.

One commando's head exploded in a cloud of skull bones, brain, flesh, and blood from the impact of Barry Dillman's burst of slugs. Another para started his last dive to the floor with another one of the Death Merchant's slugs lodged in his brain. Steve Hondergriff's stream of projectiles and the last of Camellion's SMH projectiles cut down the other two paracommandos across the table.

Six times the Socimi submachine gun in Camellion's hand roared, and each time an Indian, trying to come through the doorway between the two factory rooms, went down.

He had not forgotten Guresha Kathmerkadu, who had finally managed to keep from vomiting and had stepped closer and was about to level his FAL assault rifle at the one-man army confronting him.

Now, with two empty weapons in his hands, Camellion found himself in a situation that would have been impossible for the average man. But then again, the average man would not have been there. Especially dangerous since Therthin Rujgir was crawling out from underneath the worktable, on the Death Merchant's side. Seeing that Camellion would be occupied with Kathmerkadu, Rujgir made up his mind to score points with Major Marchchakka by capturing Camellion alive. A simple matter. He would slam Camellion over the head with the barrel of the FAL. The terrorist might later die from severe concussion, but if he could be made to talk first. . . .

Watching from the doorways at the other end of the room, Dillman and Hondergriff saw Rujgir coming up on Camellion from behind. However, neither could fire because Rujgir was between them and the Death Merchant. Some of the 9mm hi-vel slugs might go through the Indian antiterrorist commando and strike Camellion.

"Behind you!" yelled Gillman and Hondergriff.

Not only did Camellion hear their shouted warning, he also sensed that Therthin Rujgir was moving in behind him; yet he couldn't divert his attention from Guresha Kathmerkadu, who was only a micromoment away from pulling the trigger of his assault rifle.

Do it or die! With a speed that made lightning seem like a turtle crawl, the Death Merchant swept the barrel of Kathmerkadu's FAL to his right at almost the same instant that Kathmerkadu squeezed the trigger. The assault rifle roared and sent a stream of 7.62mm projectiles that passed a foot to the right of Camellion and several feet to the right of Rujgir, who had raised his FAL assault rifle and was in the process of bringing it down. But the barrel and the forward part of the A-R swished through empty air, missing the Death Merchant by fifteen inches. Camellion had jumped to the left.

Rujgir had time for only a flash of Camellion's pivoting on one foot and spinning around to face him. The next thing Rujgir knew, as he raised the FAL to try for a second slam, his face exploded with the worst agony he had ever known. Camellion had spun and smashed him in the face with a right-legged Savate Fouettes kick. The grand slam left Rujgir helpless. The Death Merchant's foot had broken his upper and lower jaws, knocked out his upper and lower teeth, and left him as helpless as an ice cube in a microwave oven. His face covered with blood, a pure crucifixion screaming in his brain, Rujgir found his legs buckling and his consciousness fading.

Guresha Kathmerkadu had also used up his one chance. The Death Merchant completed his spin-around so that once more he was facing Kathmerkadu, who was almost numb with fear, not understanding how any human being could move so fast. Before he could swing the barrel to the Death Merchant, Camellion had him. Camellion's left hand streaked out, grabbed the barrel, and pushed the weapon away from him. Simultaneously, his right arm moved outward, the edge of his right hand chopping down vertically, the terrific strike doing more than breaking Kathmerkadu's nose and left cheekbone. The sudden, terrific pain caused him to release his hold on the FAL assault rifle. With a savage pull the Death Merchant twisted the weapon from the dazed Indian's hands, the forward motion of the A-R forcing the trigger against Kathmerkadu's finger. The weapon roared out its last fourteen projectiles, all of them going harmlessly past the Death Merchant.

Camellion swung the assault rifle around and rammed the end of the barrel into Kathmerkadu's stomach with such force that the muzzle tip-tapped against his backbone. In shock and unable to scream, Kathmerkadu began to go down, his eyes bulging horribly.

Once more, Camellion heard mini-submachine guns roaring behind him. Another group of Indian paracommandos had shoved weapons around the edges of the doorway to the west and were about to open fire. To the music of yells and screams of pain, Camellion dropped down, picked up the Hi-Power Browning pistol that had slipped from his belt and fallen to the floor, turned, and did a fast duckwalk to the east, to the end of the table.

"Cover me," he yelled at Barry Dillman and Steve Hondergriff.

Dillman had fired the last round in his last Socimi SMG magazine, and had pulled a .44 magnum Llama Comanche-V revolver from a shoulder holster. Hondergriff, who had just shoved his last magazine into his mini SMG, opened fire, methodically sending 9mm para NATO rounds at both sides of the doorway forty feet to the west.

The Death Merchant got up from the end of the table and ran for it. He was soon standing beside Dillman and calling out to Hondergriff, "Steve, get back to the main room, and close and lock the doors in both rooms on your side." Then to Dillman, "Let's go."

Camellion closed the door and turned the latch. The Indian commandos would soon break through the door, as well as the three other doors, but it would take them time—triple time. After the slaughter in the factory room, the Indian paracommandos would use greater caution than ever.

As soon as Camellion reached the main room of Ding Bat—where shots were still coming through the windows—he began crawling straight toward the entrance of the passage in the Fort's outer wall. He was not even halfway to the northside wall when he saw Martin Koss crawling toward him on his hands and knees, stretching out a fuse wire behind him.

"I've just placed the last package," Koss breathed, his low voice skidding up and down the scale of nervousness. "All we have to do is play out this last wire through the entrance, close the bookcase and—"

Koss found that he might as well have been talking to himself. The Death Merchant had turned and was calling out in a loud whisper to Lana Stanley and Wilbur Theimer, telling them it was time to leave. Dillman and Hondergriff were already moving toward the open end of the bookcase.

Koss continued to let the spool of wire in his hands revolve, and in less than a minute he and Stanley and Theimer were moving through the opening, and Camellion and Dillman were preparing to close the bookcase by pulling on two metal handles fastened to its back side.

Koss put down the spool, picked up an all-purpose D-cell fluorescent light and turned it on. The others, except for Rory Gelhart, stood behind him.

"Pull it all the way in," Koss said to Camellion and Dillman. "When you hear several clicks, it will mean that the catches have fastened together and that the bookcase is fully closed."

"Where's Gelhart?" asked the Death Merchant as he and Dillman pulled on the handles and the bookcase began sliding toward them.

"He's gone several hundred feet inside the tunnel with the 'hellboxes,'" Koss replied. "He's already stretched out all the other lead wires. All we have to do is roll out the wire from the last package."

Click. Click. The bookcase was completely closed and the "door" to the passage in the outer wall of Agra Fort was closed. *But it won't be for long, not if we don't detonate before the Indian commandos get to the main room and find the wires leading underneath the bookcase!*

"Hold the light, please." Koss handed the all-purpose lantern to Lana Stanley and bent to pick up the spool of wire.

"Leave the wire," Camellion said sharply. "We don't have time to stretch it out. Should the commandos break through and find the explosives, they'll cut the wires." He took the light from Stanley's hand. "Follow me and move as fast as you can."

Turning, he moved into the darkness of the narrow passage, which, inside the wall itself, was four feet wide, forcing them to move in single file.

The corridor itself was remarkably cool, almost cold, and for an obvious reason. Sunlight had never penetrated into the passage; neither had heat been able to penetrate the stones, which, on each side of the passage, were thirteen feet thick; fifty-four feet thick above the ceiling of the corridor. There was not even dust underneath their feet, nor any kind of moss or lichen on the walls. There was only sound, the sound of their feet on stone, the sounds of their labored tension-breathing.

It seemed like an hour, but it took only four minutes to reach Rory Gelhart, who, by the light of an electric lantern, was waiting with four hellboxes (or four DuPont pocket-type ten-cap blasting machines) and the ends of nine double wires.

"Where's the tenth fuse?" Gelhart wanted to know when he saw that Koss was empty-handed.

The Death Merchant told him. "We didn't have time to play out the last wire. We have to detonate. The Indians should be coming through the four small rooms right now." He got down on one knee. "I'll help you."

With the others watching, Camellion and Gelhart began twisting the double wires around the stems protruding from the tops of the hellboxes, which were actually modified generators. In less time than it takes to boil a three minute egg, Camellion and Gelhart had twisted the wires around the stems and had tightened the round brass nuts over the wires. There were three sets of wires fastened to each hellbox.

Holding one of the blasting machines, Camellion said, "Go ahead, Rory. You first. Do it."

"First, I'll seal the entrance in the house and in the wall." Gelhart gave a quick twist of the handle of the hellbox in his hands.

BLAAAMMMMMM - BLAAAMMMMMM - BLAAAMMM- MMM! The first three packages of explosives—fifteen pounds of Duramite—exploded with a terrific blast that not only brought down the stones in the north wall of the last room of the house and on the south side of the Fort's outer wall, but also killed six Indians by concussion and flying debris. Five more were wounded. Three would later die before sunset. Amid smoke so thick it appeared to be a solid gray wall, the rest of the commandos, coughing and half choking from dust and smoke, staggered back toward the smaller rooms.

Inside the passage in the wall, the Death Merchant and his group heard only a kind of deep, rolling thunder, the thick stones blocking out most of the sound. The stones of the wall, on either side of the corridor, didn't even shake.

The Death Merchant twisted the Bakelite handle of his hellbox.

BLammmmm - BLAAMMMMMM - BLLAAMMMMMMM. Again there was that low sound of muted tumbling thunder, but only inside the narrow corridor. Outside, the sound of the exploding fifteen-pounds of Duramite was earsplitting. Major Ghazel March-chakka and his officers and men saw three bright red flashes followed by a cloud of smoke and dust. When the cloud cleared, they saw that most of the walls of the last room of the house were gone, blown away by the blast. A moment later there was another explosion, another intense flash that seemed to be composed of three parts, and another instant birth of a dust-and-smoke cloud that seemed to threaten the pale light of the half-moon.

This time after the cloud cleared (and by then Gelhart had tossed down the third hellbox), there was no sign of the walls or the furnishings. Even part of the floor had vanished, the stones turned to jagged shrapnel.

"Colonel Marchchakka, they blew themselves up," said Captain Shunta Bliskalmar in awe, staring in disbelief at the destruction. "The first explosion killed them. The other two had to be timed."

The grim-faced Marchchakka did not reply.

The corridor inside the fort's wall was 580 feet long. The Death Merchant and his group covered the remaining 380 feet in ten minutes and approached the entrance inside the Fort with caution. Although they had blown up the entrance in the north wall of the house and in the south side of the Fort's wall, each one knew that a great deal of danger was still present. The entrance inside the Fort, to the southeast, was inside a building. Suppose rubble was blocking the entrance? ("Well, it wasn't blocked a few weeks ago," Martin Koss had said.) Or suppose the Indian commander of the paratroopers had stationed even two or three of his men inside the Fort?

Rubble did not block the entrance. The Death Merchant and Barry Dillman easily pushed open the two-ton perfectly hinged stone covering the entrance, and looked out into the darkness.

"Turn out the lanterns," Camellion said, "and no smoking. I especially mean you, Weejee, and those stinking cigars of yours. Weeds burning in Texas have a better odor."

"It's not my fault they're a cheap Indian brand," retorted Theimer.

"I don't care if they're pre-Castro Havanas that cost fifty bucks a box—no smoking. The glow of a cigarette—particularly of a cigar—can be seen for half a mile. Positively no flashlights. There's enough moonlight to see by."

Weapons drawn, they moved across the dusty floor and, soon reaching the outside, saw that they were surrounded by structures of massive stone, buildings that had high, dark, and sculptured walls with high windows and imposing doorways—all of it imprisoned in vines, some as thick as a man's arm.

The architecture appeared to be a cross between the Dravidian Madurai and the North Indian Khajuraho and was truly colossal, ponderous with the fronts and corners of buildings decorated with stone-carved animals, dwarfs, goblins, devils, and snake gods. There were also frequent niches of huge dimensions, all of them empty. Once they had contained statues of saints, but these had been removed and carted off to other tourist sites.

Rory Gelhart and Martin Koss led the way through streets that had been deserted for hundreds of years, streets in which vegetation had pushed its way through hairline cracks in the stones. In some places, even trees had grown and developed.

"God, I'd hate to be buried in a place like this," whispered Lana Stanley, looking around her at the massive buildings.

The Death Merchant gave a strange little chuckle. "But think of the nice flowers you would help make."

Lana was curious. "What do you mean?"

"Flowers that grow on graves are always the prettiest. From sweet graves grow sweet flowers. In fact, we're passing through a boneyard right now."

Lana acted as if she had been stuck in the butt with a needle.

"A graveyard! You mean these round stone mounds?"

"Yes. They're called *stupas*. The dead ducks were buried sitting up."

It was then that they noticed a slight red glow flickering over the *stupas* and the buildings ahead and on each side. A look behind them revealed a brighter glow three thousand feet to the southwest. The explosions had started a fire and the rubble and the rest of the house were burning.

"The fire will keep the commandos busy," said Steve Hondergriff. "Rory, do you know the way to the main safe house from here?"

"I know the way." A professional, Gelhart continued to be cautious. "You'll know when we get there. The van is ahead, a hundred feet, by the side of that domed building. We have it covered with branches."

As soon as they reached the van, the Death Merchant saw that instead of the ancient British Ellington, the van was a modern Indian-manufactured Gurjan that looked almost new. There wasn't any lettering on the side.

"I have a question," Weejee said as they started to remove the dead branches from the sides and top of the vehicle. "How did DARFA learn about Ding Bat?"

Chapter Fourteen

If a foot in the door is worth two on the deck, the Death Merchant and the people gambling on life with him were safe—for the moment, even if they were under the very noses of DARFA, the Indian intelligence service.

Brass Coin, the main CIA safe house, was in the colonial home of Malcombe Pratt Walsingham, a spry and dapper seventy-nine-year-old Englishman who had once been an official in the Central British Office of Administration in Delhi. After the Indian people obtained their independence in August 1947, Walsingham remained in India and went into business as an exporter of Indian art and sculpture.

Called MP by his friends, Walsingham was a "fixture" in Delhi. Few people knew it, but he was also a direct descendant of Sir Francis Walsingham, who, as Queen Elizabeth's joint secretary of state—four hundred years earlier—had honeycombed Europe with his agents and whose first triumph had been to obtain minute details of the impending attack by the Spanish Armada.

MP's place of business was in his home on Karak Singh Avenue, only four blocks from the majestic Raj Path, the broadest thoroughfare in Delhi. It was on Raj Path that the buildings of the Indian government were located—the Secretariat Buildings, the "Oriental Whitehall" in red and gray sandstone; India's Parliament House, and the two Houses of Parliament: Lok Sabha, the House of the People, and the Rajya Sabha, the Council of States. The main office of DARFA was in the Internal Administration Building, exactly six blocks from MP's house.

For eleven years MP had been on-contract to the CIA, his motivation two-pronged: He knew that the United States stood for freedom and was the hope of the world. His second reason was money. His Walsingham, Limited export business did not do all that well.

Going over the situation in his mind as he and the others listened to Walford Cledde explain the schedule, the Death Merchant had to admit that Brass Coin was well organized. In the attic that had been turned into one large room and one small room, the safe house looked like an ordinary apartment, except that the walls slanted upward, due to the gabled roof. There wasn't, however, anything that might reveal and/or make one suspect that the apartment was a vital part of any foreign intelligence organization.

A third "room" was hidden behind a forty-foot-long false wall on the north side of the room. There was a five-foot-seven-inch space between the roof and the plasterboard wall that matched the peach walls on the other three sides of the room.

Inside the space were the communications components—an RX-327 FM, VHF transceiver with all the necessary "black boxes"—there were two CVB-6000 rolling code scramblers tied in with a Suracom-7 decoder; a twenty-four-hour tape recorder, and a special IATA "condenser" that could "squirt" messages into the airwaves. A two-minute coded message would come out in four seconds of static.

"Mr. Canover, do you have anything to add?" Walford Cledde turned and looked at Camellion through his horn-rimmed glasses. A lilt came into his voice. "After all, this is your operation. You are the lead agent."

Camellion didn't have to think it over. "The station at the embassy has made all the arrangements. We'll be in Srinagar before sunrise tomorrow. From there we fly to Jammu. I couldn't change anything if I wanted to. The day after tomorrow we have to be at the Temple of the Rain to intercept Franz Holtz."

"A ridiculous operation!" was Barry Dillman's enigmatic response. "He might be disguised as anybody."

"We have his photograph, front and profile," Camellion said. "Admittedly, still photographs aren't much to go on. He might have changed his hair style or grown a mustache and a beard. But I'll know him."

"Then you agree with the flight arrangements?" asked Cledde. Tall, in his middle fifties, he would have been distinguished-looking if it had not been for his teeth. They were not only too large, they protruded, giving him the appearance of a man who could eat fresh corn on the cob through a picket fence.

Cledde's real name was Raymond Charles Collins and he was the CIA professional who operated Brass Coin, and who for eleven years had posed as an Englishman from London. He had to have a legitimate reason for living in Malcombe Pratt Walsingham's house; and so he was Walsingham's assistant, and at times did help Walsingham in his exporting business.

"I didn't say I agreed," Camellion answered understandingly. "I said there wasn't anything I could do about it. On the surface, I would say that we will be losing valuable time by first flying to Srinagar just because Stanley and Theimer are scheduled to leave from there and fly to Pakistan. I don't know what is going on behind the scenes—it must be a matter of security—but I think it would save time if the plane first let us off at Jammu, then proceeded with Lana and Weejee to Srinagar. But that's how our luck has to run."

The Death Merchant hoped that their fortune in the immediate future would also be a big smile. There had not been any difficulty in their escaping from the Agra Fort area and in Rory Gelhart's driving the Gurjan van to Brass Coin—Malcombe Walsingham's home in the "new city" of Delhi. While Camellion and the others had remained down in the seats, Gelhart—Lana Stanley sitting next to him—had driven the vehicle into the garage attached to the tiny warehouse to the rear of Walsingham's home.

An hour later, Camellion had used the shortwave to report the destruction to the U.S. Embassy company station. He had also used a Code Red priority to ask if the station had any information on how DARFA had discovered Ding Bat.

Answer: negative. The only possibility was that one of the Indian couriers, either Jamilka Bikaljoo or Baso Churimbup, had sold out for money. Reason: unknown. But neither Indian suspected the existence of Brass Coin, which had only a staff of one—Walford Cledde—and did not use any native Indian couriers. DARFA could not know about the CIA safe house only six blocks from its headquarters.

Camellion had then demanded to know the details of the operation to close in on Franz Joseph Holtz. The embassy station had then informed Camellion that he and the others would leave Delhi at 23.00 hours the next day (actually the same day, since he had not made radio contact until two o'clock in the morning of the day after he and the others had escaped from the Agra Fort area). His party would also include Rory Gelhart and Martin Koss, both of whom were without a "home," now that Ding Bat no longer existed.

The aircraft would fly straight to Srinagar and land on a secret airfield. Everyone but Lana Stanley and Wilbur Theimer would deplane. The same plane would then fly Lana and Weejee to Pakistan. The destination was on a need-to-know basis. Another aircraft would be waiting on the same airfield. It would fly the Death Merchant and the other four men to an area ten klicks south of Jammu. Waiting at the drop down point would be an Indian-American on contract to the CIA. He would have further instructions.

At the time of the transmission, Camellion had known better than to ask why preparations were being put together like a complicated jigsaw puzzle of only one color. He knew why: It was a matter of security.

He tapped out on the high-speed code key:

We don't dare go to the target area dressed as Occidentals. We will go to Fatehpur Sikri, the Ghost City, as Indians. We will need the appropriate clothes and a complete portable makeup and cosmetic laboratory. Can you supply?

Affirmative on the kit and clothes. Give us the exact sizes of each individual, and do you have any preference as to Indian types you will use in your disguises. The clothes must fit the type used by each individual.

Affirmative. I'll call back in ten minutes. Out. Brass Coin-1.

Camellion had then obtained everyone's size in clothes—inseam, waist, chest ("bust" in Lana's case), sleeve length, hat size, shoe size. The whole nine yards.

Again he had established radio contact with the embassy station. He gave them the clothing sizes for three Sikhs, a Punjabi, and a Bengali—*I repeat: do not forget the four beards.*

Next he had tapped out:

. – – ./ . – – .. . – . – . / – . . . . – . – . / . – – . . – . – . . – – – –. . . .

Reply: *We are aware that you will need weapons. We will send handguns when we send the clothes and the makeup laboratory. Do you have questions?*

Affirmative. Once we have Holtz, if we get him, how do we get him out of India. Or should we use executive measures? This will not be possible if he does not have the PALs with him. Advise.

Use your own judgment regarding the target. You and the others will be lifted out of India by helicopter and flown to Pakistan. Full instructions for the lift-out operations will be given when you reach Jammu. Code name of contact at Jammu: DOG STAR. *Yours:* JUNKYARD DOG. *Any more questions? Do you have any requests?*

Affirmative: Send a box of cigars that have not been manufactured in India. If you cannot supply, send the best Indian-manufactured cigars. Can you supply the former.

Affirmative—out.

The clothes and the weapons (and a box of King Edward cigars) had arrived at 11:45 P.M., the delivery effected by a pickup truck's pulling up to the delivery entrance and the driver's using a hand truck to wheel in four wooden boxes marked HANDLE WITH CARE. VERY FRAGILE. OBJECTS OF ART. The driver was an Indian, a full-blooded northern Goan!

When the Death Merchant saw the boxes, he realized that the CIA station in Delhi was very efficient. Supposedly shipped from Calcutta, each wooden box had the proper shipping label. How the CIA had managed to smuggle the boxes into the shipping company depot was anyone's guess. The Death Merchant and the rest of them knew that the embassy station had to have very good contacts in the trucking company, although there was a flaw. Whoever the official (or officials) of the trucking company might be, he (or they) now knew that Walsingham, Limited was up to something illegal.

The most worried person of all was Malcombe Pratt Walsingham. He didn't mind the CIA's using his house as a message and radio center; and should an individual stop by to be secure for a week or so, that all bloody well all right too. But *seven* fugitives in Cledde's apartment was another matter.

The *Delhi Times* was full of the news about the "terrorists" blowing themselves up in the house on Banda Gupta Road. Fine. There would not have to be a trial. But the loss of twenty-six paratroopers was a tragedy. Another sixteen had been wounded, ten severely. Some members of the Lok Sabha were demanding a government investigation. Didn't the paracommandos, trained in counterterrorist techniques, know how to fight?

* * *

Martin Koss looked at his watch, then turned his head toward Walford Cledde. "We have to be at the field by eleven tonight. What kind of transportation will we have?"

"We'll use the same van you arrived in," said Cledde. "It's 'clean,' and the authorities won't even notice us. You're not in a police state, and there are almost five million people in Delhi."

"How do you find a particular drop in the ocean when it looks like the rest of the water," mused Camellion, a thoughtful look on his lean, tanned face. "The real problem could be the area where the plane lands. I didn't think much of the area southwest of Palam Airport. It was too open, too convenient for an ambush."

"Sorry, but you'll leave from the same area," responded Cledde, looking insulted and as if he were about to take another bite through the picket fence. "There's always a risk. That section is deserted and is never patrolled by the regular police. The Indians are a superstitious lot. They're convinced that deserted areas are inhabited by evil spirits that are very malevolent at night."

Barry Dillman contemplated the smoke from his drifting cigarette. "One has to be rather simple to believe in demons and devils and other things that go bump in the night."

"Amen to that!" chuckled Hondergriff. "All any religion wants is mind-control over sheep afraid to die. I never could understand it."

The Death Merchant smiled softly. "People believe because they've been brainwashed. But they seldom know any real truth about their own religion. For example, Steve said 'amen' a while ago. The word *amen* means 'hidden one' or the 'secret one.' It came down to us from the ancient Egyptian Brotherhood of Amen. In the Egyptian *Book of the Dead* one may read a prayer that begins, 'Amen, Amen, which art in heaven . . .' Does it sound familiar?"

" 'The meek shall inherit the earth' is more crap," growled Hondergriff. "All the 'meek' ever inherited was misery."

The Death Merchant sighed. "You're a little wrong there, old buddy." Camellion then pointed out that it was a matter of language use, that two thousand years ago the word *meek* was a word used to describe a chariot horse so well disciplined that with the lightest touch of the rein on the right side of its neck, the horse would instantly respond and turn to the right. At that time the word meant 'well disciplined.'

"So when Christ said, 'Blessed are the meek,' he was really saying,

'Blessed are the well disciplined.' Only it takes far more than discipline to inherit the earth, to inherit the future."

"Uh-huh, such as what?" popped up Lana Stanley, wondering what Camellion's reply might be. "It's certainly not brute force. And it's not intelligence! The world's in a mess now because of the idiots who can't keep their impractical theories in books where they belong."

"I'll tell you some day," Camellion said. "Right now, let's get to work and change your faces. . . ."

Chapter Fifteen

23.34 hours. The two-engine prop-driven Beech C99 left the long, grassy area, climbed sharply into the dark sky, and headed south, Alister Botts at the controls. He had informed the Death Merchant, whom he had not recognized until Camellion had spoken, that he would fly straight south for sixty miles—"to avoid the traffic from Palam"—then turn west for thirty miles. "I'll then make a straight flight to Srinagar, 324 miles from Delhi." The flight would last three hours.

Within the darkness of the aircraft there was little conversation, each person with his and her own thoughts. Lana Stanley and Wilbur Theimer were elated in the knowledge that soon they would be on their way home, if all went as planned. It was that *if*— the biggest word in the English language—that troubled them.

Dillman and Hondergriff, Koss and Gelhart, wondered what awaited them in Jammu and in Fatehpur Sikri, the Ghost City. There were so many factors to be considered. If they cornered Franz Holtz, would they be able to keep him? Would they even be able to *find* him? No doubt about it, KGB agents—the best available in India—would be present. And in everyone's mind was the nagging fear that Parveen Babbi had sold the same information about the linkup to the East German MfS and to DARFA. If she had, then everyone on the plane, except the pilot and Stanley and Theimer, was flying straight into hell!

Having put his seat back and half dozing, the Death Merchant— not too concerned because he knew that death is the price the human race must pay for purpose and progress—was proud of the job of disguise he had done on himself and the four men who would accompany him.

The CIA station at the embassy in Delhi had made a mistake. The station had sent only three beards. This meant that only two men could be disguised as aggressive Sikhs and one man as a Bengali. Sikhs never shave and often wear their full beards in a little net. The Bengalese also wore beards.

The lack of one beard did not pose that much of a problem. The Death Merchant, who had intended to disguise himself as a Sikh, had become a Brahmin, the highest of the Hindu priests. His well-muscled body was clad in light blue tight pants and a thigh-length loose-fitting blue coat. On his head was a *juho,* a round cotton cap. On his forehead was the mark of Vishnu, the Preserver, rising from the bridge of his nose like two thin white horns.

Dillman and Hondergriff were Sikhs, complete with red and green frock coats, tight trousers to match, and white and yellow turbans. The Bengali was poor Martin Ross, who had worried how he would shave with a full beard firmly fastened to his face. Camellion's reply had not filled him with joy—"By the time you have to shave, the beard will come off. Or you'll be dead and it won't make any difference." Ross was dressed in a *dhoti,* a long, all-purpose white garment, over which was a short coat. Underneath the *dhoti,* he wore pants.

Rory Gelhart was decked out as a Punjabi, clad in a *kurta,* a loose white shirt, and baggy off-white trousers.

The Death Merchant and the four other men did not look like Occidentals. Camellion had expertly used emulsion to darken their faces, necks, hands, and wrists. With solvents and plastic putty, with eyeliners, fatty foundation, and other materials, he had changed the shape of their faces. Transparent lenses had changed the color of their eyes. The disguises were perfect.

Unless they were stopped for some reason by the police and asked to identify themselves! There had not been time for the station to forge the proper identification papers.

Unless they had to speak Hindi. Not one of them knew more than a dozen words.

They were armed. With the clothes and the makeup kit had come the brand new 9-millimeter Ruger autoloader, a dozen of the pistols and five magazines for each weapon. They carried the pistols in the green and white Air India shoulder bags the station had sent.

Listening to the drone of the engines, the Death Merchant thought of Martin Koss. The poor guy had a lot to learn. He believed he was fighting for "freedom," for "democracy," and for that nebulous entity called the "American people." If Koss lived long enough, he would come to realize that, for comparatively little pay, he was risking his neck for self-serving hypocrites who worshiped money and power, for a system too eager to protect and too reluctant to punish, too "equality" happy to be realistic, yet too selfish to really care. A tinsel town of materialistic morons who thought more of half-illiterate sports figures than they did of scientists—*That's what that fool Koss is fighting for!*

An hour and a half later as Alister Botts brought the plane down for a landing, the Death Merchant was more convinced than ever that the human species was a sorry lot. They had turned their little speck of a planet into a charnel house, steaming and reeking with human gore . . . half of it in the name of politics, the other half in the name of religion.

As soon as Botts had landed the plane and had taxied around for another takeoff, keeping the engines idling, there was a signal three hundred feet to the left. A flashlight with a red lens flashed on and off three times in rapid succession. Botts replied with a similar red lens signal.

Brief were the good-byes to Lana Stanley and Wilbur Theimer, both of whom remained in the aircraft. The Death Merchant was the last to leave the aircraft, his Air India bag over his shoulder.

"Good-bye, little man," he said warmly to Weejee, who was puffing away happily on a cigar. "For a runt you're a big man." To Lana, he said in a softer tone, "Keep your nose clean and your mind dirty. It's the only way to live."

Lana smiled up at him in the semidarkness. "You never did tell me who will inherit the future."

"There isn't any future. There is only the constant now. All of us inherit the 'future,' moment by moment. I'll see you, kid."

Camellion turned and headed for the portside door, Lana calling after him, "Good luck, Richard."

As soon as the Death Merchant and his force of four had moved back from the Beech C99, Alister Botts took off, and by the time Camellion and his group were approaching the contact from the next plane, a Cessna 421 whose sleek outline they could see in the distance, Botts had pulled by on the control column and the craft was lifting off the ground. In only seconds it was gone, lost in the darkness, the sound of its engines fading.

When Camellion and his small group reached Kenny "Cowboy" Acadimmy, the pilot of the Cessna 421 Golden Eagle, found himself facing a Brahmin with a 9mm Ruger in his right hand, the muzzle of the pistol pointed at his stomach.

"No need for iron; I'm on your side," Acadimmy said lazily. As square as a fireplug, he had several days of light brown beard and wore a zip-up polyester windbreaker jacket and a plantation hat with the brim upturned on each side.

The Death Merchant and his four men were grateful for their coats. The temperature was sixty-two degrees, and the stiff breeze was almost cold. They had left the oppressive heat of summer behind them, far to the south, and were now at a 3,500-foot elevation in the foothills of the mighty Himalayas, in west Kashmir, a state in extreme north India. To the east was Red China. Due north was the Soviet Union. West was northern Pakistan. One hundred and eighteen miles to the south was Jammu.

And Fatehpur Sikri, the Ghost City—and, maybe, Franz Holtz.

"What are your instructions?" Camellion demanded of Acadimmy, who did a double take when he heard the four words, clothed in a Texas drawl, come from the mouth of the man he had thought was a Hindu priest.

"My orders are to fly you guys to a field fifteen miles south of Jammu," the pilot said quickly. "All I can tell you is that you'll be met on the ground with grand transportation. You guys ready? I don't wanna hang around here."

"Lead the way," Camellion said, and shoved the Ruger autoloader into his tight waistband.

Because the two propellers of the GTSIO-520-N piston engines could pull the Golden Eagle through the black sky at 297 knots at 23,000 feet, the flight lasted less than an hour and a half. Ten minutes after Acadimmy checked his chart, he was bringing the craft in for a landing.

Again there was an exchange of signals with flashlights. In only minutes, Camellion and his men had left the plane and were walking over rocky ground toward two men who were approaching them. Behind them, Acadimmy was taking off and going back to wherever it was he came from.

In the air was the sweet smell of jackfruit trees and the faint odor of mustard. In the distance, in front of them, Camellion and his men could see the outlines of a minibus. Far to the north was the glow that indicated the city of Jammu.

One of the men was of medium height, fleshly, white, and elderly, although in the darkness it was difficult to ascertain his age. He wore a utility cap, khaki pants and shirt, and a suede jacket. The other man, much younger, was an Indian in gray pants, a steel-gray corduroy jacket, and a corduroy hat.

The first to reach the Death Merchant and his men, the Indian said matter-of-factly, as if giving a greeting—"Dog Star."

"Junkyard Dog," Camellion replied, surprised at the accent in the Indian's voice. It sounded like East Coast U.S.A.

"Let's get to the bus," the Indian said with authority. "I'll explain everything after we're under way."

On the way to the Volkswagen minibus the Indian introduced himself as Hatama Vivekananda and said that the other man was Ernst Wilhelm Ebreichsdorf.

"I own this land we're on," Ebreichsdorf said with a thick German accent. "I raise mustard and sheep and goats. You will stay at my farm. You will be safe there until you have to go to the Ghost City tomorrow afternoon."

Trying to make conversation, Martin Koss commented, "I guess the wool from your sheep go into making the famous cashmere wool the world has heard so much about?"

"The wool of cashmere comes from the underside of Kashmir's goats," Ernst Ebreichsdorf said tonelessly, then opened the door of the minibus on the driver's side.

Getting in the Volkswagen, Rory Gelhart gave Camellion a long, knowing look, as much as to say, Where in hell did this kraut come from? Grojean didn't say anything about him! Neither did the embassy station.

Hatama Vivekananda laid out the plan as Ebreichsdorf drove the minibus to his farmhouse several kilometers away. There were additional weapons at the farmhouse, he said, new type 9mm Spectre submachine guns and plenty of ammunition.

"The Spectres are only fourteen inches long, but they won't fit in those Air India bags you're carrying," Vivekananda said. "It's not a problem. There's time to supply larger shoulder bags. Now about the helicopter. It—"

"Wait!" Camellion spoke the word not as a request but as an order that carried the implication of "And you had better do it! I don't like operating in the dark, and that's not meant as a pun. I want to know how you became involved in this operation."

"We weren't told about Herr Ebreichsdorf, either," Gelhart said easily, but emphasizing *Herr*. Watching Ebreichsdorf in the rearview mirror, he noticed how the German's eyes went up.

If Vivekananda was angry at Camellion's and Gelhart's words, he didn't show it. "What's to tell?" He shrugged and finished lighting a Winston cigarette. "I spent fourteen years in the United States and became a naturalized citizen in 1982. I'm in contact with the same organization you and these other gentlemen are working for. Beyond that, what's the difference? Are we asking you for your life's history?"

"They are afraid you might be an agent of DARFA," Ebreichsdorf said with a guttural and malicious chuckle, "and that I might be working with the East German MfS because I'm German."

"The thought had occurred to us," Steve Hondergriff said dryly.

The Death Merchant saw a deep bitterness flash over Hatama Vivekananda's dark-skinned face. There was the same virulence in Vivekananda's voice as he turned and looked directly at the Death Merchant.

"It was because of DARFA that my father was hanged for treason and why my mother, my brothers, and I left India. My father was innocent. No man ever loved India more than he did. Helping the CIA is my way of paying back a debt I owe to DARFA."

"What's your story, Herr Ebreichsdorf?" asked Camellion.

"It's none of your business," the German replied arrogantly. "That I am helping is enough. There is my house up ahead."

The Death Merchant and his men received the shock of their stay in India after they were in Ebreichsdorf's large Indian-style wooden house and he had ushered them into the large central sitting room, which was a combination of East and West in the furnishings.

"I'll be damned!" muttered Barry Dillman. He put his hands on his hips and stared. On the south wall seven- by five-foot bloodred Nazi flag, the standard party banner, the jet-black swastika in a circle of white. Next to the party flag was an *SS Leibstandarte Adolf Hitler* battle flag, the white SS runes against a background of black. In the upper left-hand corner of the dead-black banner was a small, grinning white skull. Below the skull was a white *l*. To top it off, and to prove where Ebreichsdorf's sympathy lay, there was a large bust of Adolf Hitler on a side table.

Camellion and his men now understood. Ernst Wilhelm Ebreichsdorf was a Nazi, and probably on a war criminals' list. The CIA often made use of such men, protecting them for its own purposes. So did the KGB.

Seeing their astonishment, Ebreichsdorf drew himself up to his full height and said proudly, "I was a *Standartenführer*—your rank of colonel—in the Reichssicherheitshauptamt, or RSHA, the head Department for the Security of the Reich."

Now in the light, Camellion and his men could see that the German was in his seventies and almost bald. What little hair he did have was a dirty white; yet he appeared to be in excellent health.

"I don't have any housemen," Ebreichsdorf said. "I'll prepare tea and a meal for us."

After Ebreichsdorf left the room, Rory Gelhart said, "We sure meet the creeps in this business. But who cares, if he can help us get the job done."

They settled comfortably on cushions and Hatama Vivekananda, who couldn't have been more than forty, spread out a large map of northern India, and explained that a helicopter would fly the party from the Ghost City to Sialkot, which was right across the border in northeastern Pakistan. Vivekananda added enthusiastically, "We already have chosen a landing site. It's only a few hundred feet north of the Temple of the Rain."

Gelhart let out a string of obscenity. "This is crazy!"

The Death Merchant knew it was not "crazy." The Central Intelligence Agency did not plan haphazardly—ever. He suspected that the lift-out plan sounded ridiculous only because of how Vivekananda was presenting it, sort of backassward.

Moving his finger an inch along the map, Camellion said patiently, "From Sialkot in Pakistan to the Ghost City, the distance is sixty-two miles. I would presume that the pilot and copilot have a crystal ball and will know exactly, right to the minute, when to lift off from Sialkot and fly across the border and pick us up?"

Gelhart glared at Vivekananda, "We're going to turn out to be nickels and dimes in a dollar world! Do you realize how long it takes even a fast eggbeater to fly sixty-two miles?"

"That's the beauty of it." Vivekananda gave a broad smile. "The helicopter will only have to fly twenty-four miles to the Ghost City. You see, the chopper is here at the farm. It flew across the Pak border last night. From here to Jammu is ten miles. Fatehpur Sokri is fourteen miles north of Jammu. That's a total of twenty-four miles. A helicopter can fly that short distance in less than ten minutes. All we have to do is call the crew on a long-range walkie-talkie."

"It could work," Gelhart said reflectively, studying the map. "From the Ghost City to the Indian-Pak border the distance is roughly thirty miles. We could be across the border and in Pakistan before anyone realized what was going on—if we're lucky and grab Holtz without getting killed!"

"What do you mean by 'we?'" Camellion asked, feeling a slight twinge of apprehension.

"I'm going to the Temple of the Rain and fly out of India with you," Vivekananda said soberly. "My job here is finished, or will be when you men pull out."

Steve Hondergriff posed a rhetorical question. "I wonder what the Company is giving Pakistan for their letting Big Uncle fly out of their country?"

"Who cares," Barry Dillman said irritably. "I want to see that chopper. It had better not be some beat-up old bird off the junk pile!"

After seven hours of sleep, they did see the helicopter, at 13.15 hours in the afternoon. The "beat-up old bird" was a very modern Westland Commando-2 that had landed in a clearing in a wooded area. The three-man crew and four of Standartenführer Ebreichsdorf's trusted workers had promptly erected a wooden "shed" around the warbird, covering the ceiling with tough netting that supported light branches.

Camellion had to admit the big bird was in order. Not only was it painted brown, like other Westlands in the Indian air force, but it also had the white, blue, and orange Indian markings. There was armament—an electric 16-Y "Ubba" chain gun and a brace of 50-caliber heavy machine guns mounted in the starboard opening.

Captain Chuck Benson, the pilot, Pete Trapp, the copilot, and Bernie Hunter, the radio/gunner and nav. man, were young, tough-looking, and had about them an air of swift efficiency. Benson, a two hundred pounder, couldn't have been more than thirty; the other two were in their middle or late twenties. From their military-type haircuts and demeanor, the Death Merchant sized them up as members of some U.S. Special Forces outfit.

"Figure three minutes to rev up and lift off," Benson said. "Once in the air we can travel twenty-two klicks in eight minutes. Then figure another three to four minutes for the sit-down. That's fifteen minutes from the time we get your Come-and-get-us call. How does that grab you by the balls, Canover?"

"What kind of communications equipment will we have?" Camellion asked. "There's a lot of stone in the Ghost City, and even with the best of W-Ts, you can figure on a one to two percent drift. We need hand-held radios."

"Yeah, you're right," Benson agreed. "It's hand-held jobs you'll have—two Racal-Tacticoms. I mean, you and your people will have two and we'll have two, just in case one might break down. An R-T hand-held job at only thirty klicks will work beautifully. You'll come in and vice versa as clear as rainwater."

The Death Merchant caught Koss's and Dillman's eyes. He could almost feel what they were thinking: that none of it meant a damn thing until it was tested. There were the X factors to be considered: the linkup between the KGB and Holtz in the Temple of the Rain could be a smoke screen. Holtz might already be on his way to the Soviet Union with the precious PALs.

"Canover, what time will we leave the farm tomorrow?" Rory Gelhart lit a cigarette. "My opinion is that Holtz and the KGB will be there on the dot, promptly at three o'clock in the afternoon."

Martin Koss said quickly, "We should get there an hour early." He added excitedly, as the thought was born in his head, "Or why not leave tonight and go to the Ghost City? We could hide out all day tomorrow and wait for Holtz."

Hatama Vivekananda was quick to say no. "It would be entirely too dangerous. Besides, Muslim guards patrol all of Fatehpur Sikri, day and night."

No one bothered to ask why the guards were Muslim, but the Death Merchant knew why. The Vale of Kashmir, eighty-five miles long and twenty-five miles broad, was, with its mountain glaciers, caverns, dazzling waterfalls, and streams and lakes, dominated by the Muslims, with a few Hindus living alongside them.

After India, the Vale of Kashmir is coolness and color. There are yellow mustard fields, snow-capped mountains and a milky blue sky filled with racing clouds. Kashmiri men are wrapped in brown blankets against the morning mist, and barefooted shepherd boys, with caps and covered ears, huddle on steep, rocky slopes. In the villages, dusty in the sunlight, the disorderly bazaars are filled with crowds and the air has the clinging smells of charcoal and tobacco, cooking oil, and ancient dirt. Grass grows on the mud-packed roofs of cottages, and buses rattle past, or halt and are quickly surrounded by small boys begging coins.

"We'll leave the farm so that we arrive at the temple at three in the afternoon," the Death Merchant said. He swung his eyes to Hatama Vivekananda. "Or do visitors to the Ghost City have to stay with the official tour? If they do, we have a problem."

"Buses take tourists to Fatehpur Sikri, but once the tourists are there, they are free to wander around—still around reason for the Muslim guards: to make sure everyone is out by nightfall."

"Let's get back to the house and do some fine-planning," suggested the Death Merchant. Without waiting for an answer, he turned and started walking toward the two Land-Rovers.

Chapter Sixteen

Welcome to the human zoo! The Death Merchant walked alone on crowded Burm Tezpur Gol, the main road of Jammu, toward the area where tourists would board the bright orange buses that would take them to the mysterious Fatehpur Sikri, the "Ghost City." He had to remain by himself. Brahmins associate only with other Brahmins. In the Ghost City it wouldn't matter. Out of necessity, everyone had to mingle. Even members of different castes would speak to each other.

Twenty feet in front of Camellion were Martin Koss, the "Bengali," and Hatama Vivekananda, who was a genuine Bengali and who knew the way to the bus assembly area.

Ernst Wilhelm Ebreichsdorf and one of his trusted Indians had driven the Death Merchant and the five other men to the outskirts of Jammu in one of the Land-Rovers and in the Volkswagen minibus. The group had then split up. Dillman and Hondergriff, the two "Sikhs," had remained together. They were only a short distance behind Rory Gelhart, the "Punjabi," who, also alone, could not associate with Brahmins, Sikhs, and Bengalis. Gelhart was ten feet or so behind Camellion.

I used to be disgusted with the world; now I'm only amused. The Death Merchant often wished that some of the liberal unrealists in the United States could see the reality of the rest of the world. *They would know that there can never be total equality. Each group has its own talents and intelligence level. What makes a people great is not "theory," but what they have accomplished. The world belongs not to "people" but to those who have made civilization.*

No one paid the slightest attention to the Death Merchant and his men, for Jammu was always crowded, not only with Indians of the various tribes, but also with Europeans, Arabs, Orientals, and people from other areas of the blood-drenched planet called Earth; and always there was that juxtaposition of wealth and degredation.

Long stretches of the street were littered with the prostrate bodies of beggars and cripples, and always there were the hawkers selling everything from cheap fountain pens and garish pictures of the Indian gods and film stars to airmail editions of foreign newspapers. There were the sellers of *pani puri:* small, hollow ovals of light pastry, fried and pierced, then filled with a thin, spicy sauce of which the main ingredient was tamarind water.

Now and then a boy, young in years but ancient in the ways of staying alive, would dart out to a male tourist, tug at his sleeve, and whisper. The offer was always the same: for a few rupees the tourist could have his sister, who was always *jikok,* a virgin. . . .

Camellion went past coffeeshops and flower sellers (and twice strode by sex rejuvenation clinics). There were stalls filled with melons, tomatoes, cucumbers and other vegetables. In the markets were the smells of wool and new clothes hanging from shop fronts, these odors mingling with a thousand other scents, the stink of openly dumped refuse, the perfume of flowers and joss sticks. And every single bit of it overlaid with that overwhelming sense of chaos that the Indians called "life." To the Death Merchant, the average Indian was living by inches and dying by yards.

As people of various races and nationalities brushed by the Death Merchant, he could only speculate who might be DARFA, or KGB, or MfS. Parveen Babbi had sold the information about Holtz to the CIA. Fine, but only if she had not sold the same information to Mischa Wolf's East German intelligence apparatus. And DARFA? *She could not have tipped off DARFA without exposing herself as a traitor, unless she's a member of Indian Intelligence and DARFA wants to trap not only us but the East Germans and the Russians as well! Is it possible that DARFA knows about the PALs and is after them? Did Goldilocks go innocently into the house of the Bears? Or was the little broad only a clever second-story man?*

Twenty-one minutes later, the Death Merchant and two of his men were on one of the buses in front of the tour depot. The three other men were on another bus. It was a chilling thought, but for all the Death Merchant and his men knew, Franz Holtz and KGB agents were on the same buses. There were numerous Occidentals and almost everyone carried a shoulder bag—some large, some small—and like Camellion and his men held the bags in their laps.

In the shoulder bags of the Death Merchant and his men were 9mm Ruger autopistols and Spectre submachine guns, along with three magazines for each compact SMG, which could claim to be the flattest automatic weapon in the world, since it was only 35mm thick. Each magazine held thirty 9x19mm rounds. The Spectre had a back grip and a foregrip; yet the weapon was so light it could be fired with one hand, like a pistol.

The Death Merchant's shoulder bag—and Rory Gelhart's—were fuller than the bags of the four other men. Camellion and Gelhart each carried a Racal-Tacticom hand-held radio. The Racal-Tacticom had an FM mode with simplex three, narrow-band frequency, and six preset channels. Frequency coverage was 40-55MHz.

On the way to Fatehpur Sikri, the fabled Ghost City, one could see poplars and willows and now and then a grove of casuarina trees. Far back from the twisting road were tiny villages with their sagging, wood-frame houses. The buses passed fields that were also backed by the misty, snow-painted Himalayas far in the distance.

Halfway to the Ghost City the engines of the five buses began to labor, for the gravel road led upward. Fatehpur Sikri lay on a rocky ridge that was four miles long and two miles wide, the total elevation almost 2,300 feet higher than Jammu.

Finally the ancient city loomed ahead, first as a hazy semblance, but very gradually as separate structures, with individual features distinct to the naked eye. The Ghost City would have shimmered in the sun if there had been a sun. Overhead there was only a sky of lead, a flat ceiling of dark gray sealing out the deep blue. There were no dry and wet seasons in Kashmir, no monsoon to flood the streets and streams and lakes. Because of the constant updrafts and downdrafts generated by the Himalayas, rain could come very fast in summer. Clouds would gather and the sky would open and release pure liquid crystal in a downpour, or else send down only an opaline drizzle.

One after the other, the buses pulled through the Buland Darwaza, the Gate of Victory, and stopped. The Death Merchant looked at his wristwatch—2:21 P.M. Right on schedule. After all, they couldn't "race" straight to the Temple of the Rain. Camellion and his people would have to move leisurely.

Once the tourists were out of the five buses, the drivers announced through bullhorns, in English, that those who might want to wander about on their own would have to be back at the buses no later than five o'clock.

Placing the strap of his bag over his right shoulder, with the bag itself resting snugly against his left hip, Camellion walked slowly, to give Dillman and Hondergriff and the other three time to catch up with him. His direction was northeast, toward the center of the city.

From inside his long blue coat, Camellion pulled a tourist map of Fatehpur Sikri. At the same time, he was amused at seeing vendors selling their wares just inside the giant Gate of Victory. Unlike Americans and Europeans, Indians attached a particular importance to food and for good reason: the threat of famine was always present.

These vendors had glass-topped boxes on wheels and were selling sweetmeats—wheel-shaped *jalebis* of fried chick-pea flour batter dripping with sugar syrup, tiny *laddoos* made of the same two ingredients but covered also in melon seeds, and pieces of peanut brittle called *chikkis*.

Travel to exotic, distant lands, meet exciting and unusual people—then kill the bastards! The Death Merchant sighed, stopped, opened the diagram and looked at it. There was the entire city in neat blue and red squares and pink lines. The explanations in black, both in Hindi and in English. The Jamil Masjid Mosque caught Camellion's eye. Designed to hold ten thousand worshipers, it contained the tomb of Shaikh Salim Chisti under an elaborate canopy inlaid with mother-of-pearl.

The other public building of the Ghost City was to the west, not far from the main gate. This was the Diwan-i-Am, the Hall of Public Audience. Almost four hundred feet long, it consisted of cloisters surrounding a courtyard that contained the Hall of Judgment. There, the mighty Akbar had sat on his throne flanked by marble screens and handed down his decisions as the head honcho of his adoring subjects. In a lighter vein, he had played chess with slave girls as living pieces on the pachisi courtyard behind the Diwan-i-Am.

According to the diagram, a feminine touch could be found in Jodh Bai's palace, built for Akbar's Hindu wife. Muslim and Hindu architecture met here once more. The main room of the palace was the Cave of the Winds. The wording on the diagram said it "may have been a cool vantage point to enable ladies of the court to see without being seen."

By then, Hatama Vivekananda and Martin Koss—they had been ahead of Camellion and had turned around—had reached the Death

Merchant and were standing only five feet away, looking at their own maps. Dillman and Hondergriff had also caught up with Camellion, and coming in behind them was Rory Gelhart.

The whole 9 yards (and 2.6 inches) was one gamble, one big risk, as if a blind man with hammers in his hands were feeling his way along in a glass factory. All around Camellion and his people were men and women of every race and creed, many with maps of the city, most with cameras. Old and young, tall and short, fat and thin— people who believed in every god possible! However, none of them seemed to notice the small group of men gathered around the tall Brahmin. Nor did the Muslim guards who, in their baggy white trousers, were posted by the entrances of the ancient buildings.

Hatama Vivekananda said in a low voice, directing his words at the Death Merchant, "The Temple of the Rain is roughly 457 meters to the northeast. That's 1,500 feet. I suggest we start 'sightseeing' in that direction."

Martin Koss said innocently, "If we have the time, I'd like to see Birbal's palace. It was named after Akbar's minister. Then there's the house of Akbar's first wife. The information on the map said that she was a Turk who—"

"God damn it, Martin! How in hell did you ever manage to get into the Company?" snapped Gelhart savagely. "Know what you're doing. Think about it! We're not here to enjoy ourselves; we have an important job to do."

Even slow-thinking people are capable now and then of cutting down a critic with razor-sharp rhetoric, if only by accident.

"I know one thing," Koss said with an unfamiliar pinched expression. "I know that people who think they know it all are particularly annoying to those of us who do!"

No one saw Gelhart redden. The Death Merchant and Vivekananda were concerned with the diagram of Fatehpur Sikri. Dillman and Hondergriff, only pretending to study the maps in their hands, were watching the people around them.

The Death Merchant consulted his wristwatch—two thirty-four.

"We'll go first to the Hall of Public Audience, then on to the House of the Astrologers, which is next to the Temple of the Rain," he said. "Once we're inside the Hall of Public Audience, we'll be able to take out our Rugers. Be careful how you do it. Don't become overanxious."

He looked up at the sky. People who spend a lot of time out of doors develop special senses, the way a farmer can glance at the sun and tell the time. Camellion could "feel" rain. The sky was lead, and the breeze had quickened, bringing with it a strong odor of *jalebis* from the food sellers by the gate.

Spread out five feet from each other, but not in any particular order, the group walked slowly toward the Hall of Public Audience and was soon inside the building with several hundred other tourists, many of whom were Europeans; at least they were Occidental. KGB or MfS? For that matter, could some of these tourists be CIA? There wasn't any way of knowing.

The interior of the stone and marble hall was none too impressive. The main hall itself was divided by galleries. In the center of the Hall was the Hawwi Jubque, a strange stone column. There were elaborate designs on the column, which blossomed upward and out into a flat-topped flower. At the very top, on the giant stone flower, was nothing less than Akbar's throne, used when he had received nobles and ambassadors. Four stone bridges connected the top of the pillar to the surrounding galleries.

Not too many of the tourists seemed interested in visiting the galleries. However, the Death Merchant and his group couldn't wait to get to one of the promenades. It was on the first one to the south that they transferred the 9mm Rugers from their shoulder bags to the inside breast pockets of their coats.

All the while, the Death Merchant and his men had watched the tourists, looking for Franz Joseph Holtz, the East German intelligence agent who, in the United States, had posed as "Edgar Bedsloe." Before they had left Ernst Ebreichsdorf's farm, each man had studied four photographs, two full view front and profile. One set was of how Holtz had looked in the United States. The other set, how Holtz would look with a beard and a mustache and dark glasses. Holtz would have to have a large shoulder bag with him for the PALs. But not necessarily. The PALs could be stashed in Jammu—or—? Another unknown with which the Death Merchant and his men had to contend.

It was a long shot, the possibility that Camellion and his five men would spot Franz Holtz before the MfS agent could meet the Soviet KGB. *But only if he uses the same technique as us and stalls around so that he can be at the temple at exactly three o'clock.*

They headed toward the Hall of the Astrologers, free-flowing adrenaline quickening their steps. Unless the meet was a KGB smoke screen, Franz Holtz and the PALs had to be close by, less than 350 feet away.

The Death Merchant and his men had already evolved a plan, if it could be called a plan. They would have to play it the way the cards fell. Number one: Go after any bags that Holtz or the Russians might be carrying, but only after getting in as close as possible. Holtz was number two on the agenda. It would be nice to take him back to the United States, but not vital that he be made a prisoner. However, if no shoulder bags or suitcases were in evidence, then Holtz would become number one. They would have to take him alive to learn where he had hidden the PALs.

The Death Merchant had given one final order: *The KGB will try to stop us. Kill 'em!*

Time: two forty-nine—when Camellion and his people entered the Hall of the Astrologers, which was a long, low building where, hundreds of years earlier, two-dozen astrologers had decided the course of action Akbar would take against his enemies. The dabblers in starry superstition had even given him advice on what color robes he should wear during the day.

Camellion said casually to Rory Gelhart walking next to him, "We'll cross the astrology building and go straight to the Temple of the Rain. The map shows a side entrance on the west side. Pass the word along. By the time we get there, it will be three on the dot."

Camellion and his men moved easily through the tourists. They walked across a hundred-foot open area, and entered the Temple of the Rain through its first entrance on the west side. It was a large building and reminded Camellion of a Greek or Roman temple that was enclosed. In the center was a hundred-foot-long, sixty-foot wide pool. Above, in the flat ceiling, was an open space of similar dimensions. On all four sides, thirty feet from the wall, were huge, square stone columns whose four sides were decorated with carvings.

Again Camellion and his crew found tourists wandering idly in the building. But there were not too many. Those who were present didn't seem interested. Who wants to waste time staring at a large pool of rainwater and fifty-two stone columns?

"If Holtz is here, he's invisible." Barry Dillman leaned toward Camellion and looked at his watch. It was two minutes after three.

"I think we've been suckered," said Barry Dillman, his jaw drooping slightly. He slid his hand inside his coat, pulled the Ruger pistol from the pocket, and shoved it into the left side of his waistband.

The Death Merchant looked slowly all around the interior of the building. Sixty feet to the east, walking along the west side of the pool toward the main entrance in the south end of the temple, was a group of seven men. Four of the men were decked out in Indian dress, the other three in Western clothes. With them, in the center of the group, was a woman dressed in a beautiful red and green sari, her long black hair hanging down her back. Two of the men—one in Indian dress—were to the rear of the woman and the man with her; he was also in Indian clothing. Three of the men—two in the clothes of Punjabis and one in a pinstripe summer suit—were in front of the man and the woman, their heels clicking on the stones of the floor. The sixth man was in the center front of the first three.

All seven men carried European-type shoulder bags. One man—in the group of three in front of the man walking with the woman—was also carrying a gray attaché case.

The Death Merchant and Rory Gelhart said at the same time, "That had to be the Russians and Holtz!" Only Gelhart added, "But who's the woman? She's certain got a pattable arse on her!"

Koss sounded worried and intense. "How can we be sure? We haven't seen their faces. To be safe, maybe we should—"

"Rules are made by safe men in safe offices, tucked far away in the U.S. in safe buildings," Camellion said roughly, his keen eyes following after the seven men and one woman.

"Damn it, let's do something fast!" Hondergriff said urgently. "They're moving away from us, and we don't want them to get outside the temple."

"Steve, you come with me," Camellion said decisively, a cold determination in his low voice. "We still have time to come in on them from the front. Rory, you and the rest of the men close in on them from the rear. Don't make any moves until I do, and don't get too close, or you'll tip your hand."

Gelhart had his doubts. "Look, you and Hondergriff don't have time to get to the front, not unless you go outside and run. You can't do that!"

"No? Watch us!" Camellion sounded happy. "Let's go, Steve."

Camellion and Hondergriff almost sprinted for the west side entrance, and once they were outside, they did run south, oblivious to the startled stares of tourists, their shoulder bags punching against their left sides. They pulled up short just before they came to the southwest corner, then calmly walked around the corner and moved east toward the wide entrance of the temple. Two Muslim guards were stationed on each side of the sixty-foot-high entrance. They were, however, civilian employees of the Indian Tourist Office and did not carry guns.

"You go down one side to the left. I'll take the right," Camellion said to Hondergriff. "I'll slam the man with the attaché case. The case must contain the PALs."

"Slam him?" The CIA street man was horrified. "Why not shoot the KGB shithead and get it over with?"

"I don't want any gunplay, not if we can help it," Camellion replied. "There are six of us and seven of them. If we can't chop them down with simple hand-power, we should go back to the States and pump gas!"

Hondergriff sighed. "Jesus! All this trouble—and at today's interest rates. . . ."

They walked past one of the guards, turned into the entrance, and, with ten other tourists, moved into the temple, Camellion moving to the right, Hondergriff to the left. Inside the temple there were tourists walking up and down the length of the building, to the north and to the south. The Death Merchant reasoned that the Soviet agents wouldn't notice him and Hondergriff because they were keeping pace with the tourists moving north. To the KGB agents, Camellion and Hondergriff would be just another Brahmin and another Sikh.

Second by second, Camellion and Hondergriff drew closer to the group of Soviet agents, and to the man and the woman in the center. Very soon Camellion and Hondergriff could see that the man in the center, dressed in the loose white shirt, baggy pants, and short coat of a Punjabi, was Franz Holtz. He was bearded, without a mustache, and was wearing sunglasses. However, he had dyed his hair—grown much longer since he had fled from the United States—black.

The woman with him was Indian. Young, her skin the color of custard, she was slim and possessed of that mysterious beauty some Indian women have. Her expression was tight and fearful, as if she was expecting a bomb to go off; and somehow she seemed familiar to the Death Merchant. Yet he was certain that he had never seen her before.

Rory Gelhart and the other three men, seeing Camellion and Hondergriff, quickened their pace, so that when the Death Merchant and Hondergriff were only ten feet in front of the Soviet agents,

Gelhart, Koss, Dillman, and Vivekananda were only a very short distance behind the last two Russians.

Major Boris Bukashev was not a man to confuse destiny with bad management. He had planned the meet with Franz Holtz in detail. The arrangement had been that Bukashev would stand by the southeast corner of the pool in the Temple of the Rain. Holtz would recognize him as the KGB contact by his Indian dress—light gray trousers, an *achkan,* a high-collared tunic, and a bright red *nritrya,* or "rye-try-a" as Caucasians called the round and peaked but brimless hat. A blue vinyl shoulder bag would complete the identification.

It had also been agreed that Holtz, who would also be dressed as an Indian, would approach Bukashev no later than ten minutes after three. The contact had not worked out that way. Instead of Holtz, it had been Suri'an Nushinobey, Holtz's girl friend, who had approached the KGB assassination expert. Five minutes later, after Bukashev had assured the young Hindu woman that it was he who was supposed to meet Holtz, the East German agent had appeared, and Bukashev had signaled to his men scattered around the interior of the temple, including two "backdrop" agents who had been far to the northeast corner and who had been trailing at a distance.

It was Semen Ageev and Mikhail Tavigun, following seventy feet behind, who first suspected that something was wrong, when they saw Gelhart, Dillman, Koss, and Vivekananda moving in rapidly behind Major Bukashev and his group. Undecided what to do, the two agents hesitated, thinking of Bukashev's orders: Do not draw attention of any kind to yourselves—and they were too far away to shout a warning—and no weapons unless absolutely necessary.

Then it was too late. Gelhart and the three other men were almost on top of the six Soviet agents, and Camellion and Hondergriff, to the south, were so close to Major Bukashev and Lieutenant Vasily Tikhon —the latter the "point" man with the Russians—that they could have leaned out and kissed the two KGB agents.

The Death Merchant and Steve Hondergriff had other surprises in mind. Hondergriff, when he was acting as though he would walk past Tikhon, moved suddenly in front of the surprised Russian and aimed a short snap-kick at the Russian's groin. He missed, the sole of his foot only grazing the front of the Russian's pants and the front of the lower part of his coat. A man who was extremely fast, Tikhon had stepped back. Now, snarling bitter curses, Tikhon and Zhores Unshlikht—Unshlikht was one of the first three Russians and was dressed as an Indian—moved toward Hondergriff, who was wishing he was somewhere else.

Simultaneously, Richard Camellion used a left knee-lift and a right-handed *Seiken* forefist to whack out Boris Bukashev. The flaw was that, while the Death Merchant was extremely fast, the not too heavily built Bukashev was a lot faster and tougher than he looked, plus the fact that Camellion had misjudged the knee-lift a fraction of an inch. However, Camellion's right *Seiken* blow connected solidly with the lower part of the Soviet agent's forehead and staggered him, forcing from him a cry of rage and pain. Very rapidly but very cautiously the Death Merchant moved in on the Russian expert.

"Donnerwetter!" snarled Franz Holtz, his tone one of anger and fear. Reaching for a SIG-Sauer DA pistol concealed underneath his shirt, he spun around and saw a cold-eyed Sikh coming in fast. *Mein Gott!* They were surrounded. A Punjabi had almost reached Alexander Kogan, and a Bengali and another Indian were closing in on Branko Medvedev, one of the two KGB men who had been to the rear.

In desperation, terror in her eyes, Suri'an Nushinobey unzipped her shoulder bag and reached for a .25 ACP Fraser semiautomatic pistol.

Yulin Dekanozov, between Unshlikht and Bukashev, reached for the silenced Makarov underneath the coat of his pinstripe suit.

The Death Merchant didn't walk into Major Bukashev's trap. Bukashev, realizing instantly that he and his men had walked into a trap, was too much of a street fighter to think he could defend himself and still hold on to the attaché case with his right hand. He let the handle of the case slip from his hand, feigned a left inside roundhouse kick and a right edge-of-the-hand strike to the left side of the Death Merchant's neck. At the same time, he tried a left hand two-finger spear strike straight for Camellion's throat. The Death Merchant didn't fall into the cleverly executed trap. He blocked the roundhouse kick with a right-legged *chado* sweep and easily brushed aside Bukashev's knife-hand strike by bringing up his left arm, his forearm slamming against the inside of the Russian's right wrist and throwing the arm outward. The two-finger spear strike was not a problem either. Camellion stepped to his left and the Russian's hand went harmlessly by the right side of his neck.

Bukashev did not have time to reorganize a new attack. The Death Merchant was far too fast, and Major Bukashev had left himself wide open. Camellion used a double-strike. He raised his right arm, and brought the edge of his hand down against the left side of Bukashev's neck in a *Shuto* sword-ridge slam. Simultaneously, he used his left hand in a *Yubi Basami* knuckle-fingertip strike.

Major Boris Bukashev might as well have been hit by a fifty-ton tank. Camellion's right-handed strike crashed into the Russian agent's sternocleidomastoid muscle and shook his jugular vein and carotid artery to the extent that, for a second, blood was cut off from the brain.

It was the knuckle-fingertip "claw" that switched off Bukashev's life. Camellion's thumb and first two fingers crushed the thyroid cartilage. Faster than one could say "Praise be to Lenin," there was hemorrhage, and as blood burst from veins the soft tissues in Bukashev's throat began to swell, cutting off all air. Bukashev's eyes began to expand out of his head as loud gasping and choking sounds poured from his mouth. The hinges in his knees began to fold and he began to sink to the floor. He'd be stone dead within twenty seconds.

Alexander Kogan was having his problems, and Franz Holtz and Suri'an Nushinobey were having theirs. A big man, Kogan had not counted on the speed with which Rory Celhart would employ a right-legged inside roundhouse kick, any more than Holtz and his Hindu girl friend had anticipated Dillman's cyclone-quick attack.

Almost 90 percent of Rory Gelhart's weight was behind the roundhouse slam, his foot almost burying itself in Kogan's lower stomach and upper abdomen. Blue-hot agony shot all the way to Kogan's face and down to his testicles and through each leg. His bladder and part of his lower intestine were mashed. The femoral arteries were as flat as paper, and the spinal nerves were sending giant impulses of shock waves to the brain. Unable to withstand such an assault of pure pain, the brain exploded psychically. A corpse, Alexander Kogan fell backward.

Only a few feet from Holtz and the woman, Dillman became angry when he saw the MfS agent swing around and start to pull a pistol from underneath his shirt—the damned kraut! He became even more enraged as he noticed that Nushinobey had unzipped her shoulder bag and was reaching inside for a weapon—the damned Hindu slut!

"We don't need you, bitch!" spat out Dillman. At the same time as he reached out with his left hand toward Holtz, he slammed his right fist straight into Nushinobey's face, feeling her lip, upper teeth, and nose give under his closed hand. With a gagged scream, she staggered back, blood pouring from her nose and mouth—straight into the path of the dead Kogan. She and the dead man went down together, the corpse smashing her to the stones of the floor.

If Dillman had been one or two seconds slower, Franz Holtz would have succeeded in putting two FMJ .380 slugs into his chest. As it turned out, Dillman grabbed the East German's right wrist and pushed the arm and the weapon to one side just as Holtz's finger contracted against the trigger. The SIG-Sauer autopistol cracked, the bullet hitting the floor between the legs of Branko Medvedev, who had both his big hands around Hatama Vivekananda's throat and was choking the Indian-American to death.

Holtz did his best to jerk his arm away and at the same time let Dillman have an uppercut to the chin. Dillman ducked the fist and slammed his own right fist into the East German's solar plexus, thinking that it was a shame that he couldn't kill the son of a bitch on the spot with a couple of *Nukite* spear stabs to the sensitive region. But Canover wanted the kraut kittylitter alive.

The powerful slam took all the strength and the fight out of Holtz, who could only gasp in agony and start to sink from his knees. Dillman pulled the .380 autoloader from Holtz's limp fingers and looked around, first to the north.

Several minutes earlier, as soon as the fight had started, tourists had begun moving away. The sharp crack of Franz Holtz's .380 SIG-Sauer increased the speed of the exodus, so that by now most of the Temple of the Rain was deserted. Dillman also saw two other things during that mini-moment of time. Rory Gelhart was stooping to pick up the 9mm Ruger pistol that had fallen from his waistband when he had snuffed Alexander Kogan. He also saw that the burly Branko Medvedev had released his hands from around the throat of Hatama Vivekananda, and was letting the body drop to the floor. With hatred burning in his heart, Dillman raised the .380 pistol and squeezed the trigger. The first bullet hit Medvedev between the shoulder blades and made him jerk and half-flap his arms. The second and third projectiles popped him in the back of the neck, zipped out the front of his throat, and pulled a black curtain down over his consciousness. Blood spurted out of his throat from the broken mains of arteries and veins, and he fell across the body of Vivekananda, his legs twitching.

It was then that Dillman spotted Semen Ageev and Mikhail Tavigun, the two KGB backdrop assassins who were coming in from the north. Both Russians had pulled Stechkin machine pistols and were waiting to get close enough to use them.

"To the north!" Dillman yelled at Gelhart. He transferred the .380 SIG-Sauer to his left hand and with his right hand pulled the Ruger autopistol from his belt.

"They're coming from the south too!" Gelhart shouted back. With a 9mm Ruger in his hand, he went into a low crouch and began firing, the explosions of the pistol ringing weirdly throughout the Temple of the Rain.

Dropping down to one knee, Dillman was about to sight in on Semen Ageev when he saw that Suri'an Nushinobey was about to crawl out from underneath the heavy corpse of Alexander Kogan, her head only three feet from him. For a moment her bloody face looked up at him, fear and pleading in her eyes, the *please-let-me-live* more intense than the terror. Dillman didn't have time to take risk one. He brought the underside of the Ruger across the top of her head, cracking her skull. She slumped, her chin striking the floor, and lay still.

Only a few feet to Dillman's right was Franz Holtz, his arms wrapped tightly around his midsection as he tried to get to his feet.

"Flat on your face, you son of a bitch!" Dillman slammed the side of the Ruger across the front of Holtz's face, just hard enough to bring a lot of pain, but not enough to throw him into unconsciousness. With a cry of pain Holtz fell sideways, moaning and wishing he could die.

Dillman raised the Ruger, looked north, snap-aimed, and fired as he heard a Ruger explode behind him.

Sixty-four seconds later, Martin Koss had saved Richard Camellion's life. Yulin Dekanozov, facing south in the direction of the Death Merchant, had been about to throw down on Camellion with his silenced Makarov. Koss had stormed straight down the line and by then reached the Soviet agent. Koss grabbed Dekanozov's right wrist and slammed a fist against the side of the Russian's neck. Dekanozov, although about the same size and weight as Koss, was stronger and more experienced. Staggered by Koss's blow, he twisted around to face Koss, tried to jerk his right arm away, and lashed out with the edge of his left foot. The strike only partially landed on Koss's lower right leg; nonetheless, the blow caused a good deal of pain. But Koss still hung on to Dekanozov's gun arm. In a few more seconds the Russian would have freed his arm and blown up Koss with a 9mm bullet. Koss was saved by Camellion, who, finished with Major Bukashev, didn't have time to turn around and see at whom Rory Gelhart was firing.

Now that the operation had degenerated into gunfire, the Death Merchant didn't waste time. He pulled his Ruger, pushed off the safety, took several big steps, jammed the pistol against the right side of Yulin Dekanozov, and, with pleasure, pulled the trigger. Dekanozov stopped struggling with Koss. His eyes became as round as U.S. fifty-cent pieces, and for only a shave of a second he became rigid. Then he dropped.

So did Martin Koss. Barry Dillman had whacked out Mikhail Tavigun with his second shot, putting a 9mm hollow-point manstopper bullet into the Russian's lower chest. Terminating Semen Ageev had not been as easy. At only fifty feet north of Dillman, Ageev darted to one side and opened up with his Stechkin machine pistol. During that moment, Dillman also moved as a matter of precaution. Ageev's four 9mm projectiles missed Dillman. They didn't miss Martin Koss, who happened to be in the right place at the wrong time. All four projectiles stabbed into the small of Koss' back, one cutting through his spine and going through the cord. Koss blinked, died, and dropped.

The Death Merchant didn't see him fall. He had spun around and was moving west to help Steve Hondergriff, who was struggling with Vasily Tikhon and Zhores Unshlikht. Tikhon, in back of Hondergriff, had one arm around his neck and was trying to get a neckbreaker hold on the CIA street man. He couldn't because Hondergriff was moving his head back and forth and up and down. But the main reason why Tikhon couldn't was that Hondergriff had a first grasp on the KGB man's right wrist with his right hand.

Zhores Unshlikht had first rushed at Hondergriff from the front, and had received a kick in the stomach for his trouble. However, the KGB agent had seen the kick coming and had pulled back. The kick had only partly landed on Unshlikht's midsection, but it had been enough to make him gasp with pain and fall back. He quickly recovered, but not in time to avoid the Death Merchant, whose Ruger autopistol roared. Unshlikht jerked, let out a short cry, and folded, Camellion's 9mm round having gone through his right rib cage.

During that mini-moment Camellion glanced to the south and saw that the two Muslim guards who had been stationed outside the main entrance of the Temple of the Rain were now lying thirty feet inside, one on his back, the other on his face. Between the two men was a pistol. The man facedown had a pistol in his hand. Evidently the two guards had been the targets at which Gelhart had been shooting.

Vasily Tikhon didn't know what to do. He released Hondergriff, stepped to one side, and tried to reach underneath his suitcoat and pull a Heckler & Koch P9S pistol. He might as well have tried to swim with an anvil chained to each arm and leg. Camellion pulled the trigger and the Ruger roared, the slug catching the Russian in the hollow of the throat, the impact rocking him back on his heels before the blood began to spurt.

Mercy! Mercy! Mother Percy! Camellion knew that every second of time had run out and that the only course open to him and his men would be to leave. *If we even have time to wait for Benson and the chopper! What else can we do?* Well, they had accomplished the mission. They had found Franz Holtz, and Camellion assumed that the four PALs were in the attaché case.

"Well, this is another fine mess you've gotten us into!" mocked Steve Hondergriff, jerking his Ruger from underneath his coat. "How in hell are we going to get out of it?"

"All we can do is call Benson and hope he gets here in time," Camellion said. He stared toward the north and saw that only Dillman and Gelhart were alive; they had unzipped their shoulder bags and were shoving magazines of ammo into Spectre submachine guns. Camellion and Hondergriff also saw—and so did Gelhart and Dillman—that a group of men had entered the Temple of the Rain through the west-side entrance. Five of the men were dressed as Indian nationals; others were in business suits. All eight had weapons in their hands. The instant the men spotted Camellion and his three men, 170 feet to the south, they spread out and began to run forward.

"Oh, shit!" muttered Hondergriff, ducking low.

Rory Gelhart dropped to the floor on his stomach and, using the dead body of Alexander Kogan for cover, waited. There was a loud click as Barry Dillman pulled back the cocking knob of his Spectre and got down flat seven feet to the right of Gelhart, with Franz Holtz lying horizontally in front of him.

"Make one sound or one false move and I'll scatter your brain all over this floor!" Dillman warned the East German agent.

The last day and a half had been miserable for Karl Hossinger, Friedrich Seckendorff, and the other East German MfS, as if some mysterious power were deliberately making things difficult for them. It couldn't be any "God," because as any intelligent person knew, there wasn't any God. The turn of events had been only bad luck.

After the helicopter had landed at Dharmdaipur, 157 miles south-east of Jammu, the troubles had started. First, the transmission of one of the cars had developed trouble, and the group had lost half a day in trying to rent another vehicle. They had finally been forced to buy a 1984 American Ford station wagon at a highly inflated price. Fifty miles from Jammu, Herman Krugger had become ill, finally within a few hours doubling over in pain. They had been forced to take him to a hospital where his illness had been diagnosed as acute appendicitis.

Altogether, Hossinger and Seckendorff and their Special Squad had lost almost eighteen hours. Even so, they had still been able to get to Jammu in time to make contact with the MfS agent, who had done a remarkable job of setting up a safe station in only six days; and they had managed to rent two cars and drive to Fatehpur Sikri, the Ghost City. They couldn't rush straight to the temple. They had to act like tourists and not arouse anyone's suspicions. By the time Hossinger and Seckendorff and the other six agents moved through the west entrance of the temple, it was fourteen minutes after three. Too late!

If it had been left up to Hossinger and Seckendorff, they would have told the men to leave and head for the cars. Highly trained professionals, they both knew, the instant they saw the bodies on the floor, to the south, that either the KGB or the CIA had beaten them to Holtz. Yet they both knew they had to try. They had to make an effort to take Holtz away from whoever had him—or had Parveen Babbi tricked them? Had she led them into a trap? Seckendorff, in particular, believed in safety over daring. And here in the temple the odds were against them.

It was how the East German Ministry for State Security operated that forced Karl Hossinger and Friedrich Seckendorff to go on. MfS were always making secret reports against each other. To retreat now, when there were only four men to the south, might be fatal. One of the members of the special squad might write a secret report to Mischa Wolf.

Should that happen, the director's revenge would be swift. Demotion would mean the loss of a roomy apartment and other privileges. Outright dismissal from the MfS was too terrible even to contemplate.

* * *

"Get his shoulder bag," the Death Merchant said to Hondergriff, pushing at the dead Zhores Unshlikht with the tip of his foot. "They used Makarovs. They were KGB. They might have Stechkin or Vitmorkin machine pistols in their bags."

Hondergriff bent down and began pulling at the dark vinyl strap over the shoulder of the corpse. "The jokers to the north aren't DARFA. None of them would be dressed like that. They have to be either more 'pig farmers,' as you call the Russians, or East German agents."

"Krauts. Babbi sold us out," Camellion responded, by then reaching the body of Boris Bukashev. "We assumed that she might. I was hoping that she hadn't."

Camellion picked up the shoulder bag Bukashev had been carrying. He took a few more steps, picked up the attaché case, glanced again to the north, yelled *"Down!"* to Hondergriff, and threw himself flat just as Seckendorff and Hossinger and their men opened fire.

"Watch the main entrance to the south," Camellion said to Hondergriff. "It would be typical of them to send a man or two to come in behind us."

The East Germans had more sense than Semen Ageev and Mikhail Tavigun, the two KGB backups. Instead of charging forward in the open, the Germans made use of the stone pillars to the west, running from column to column as they tried to close in. But after Dillman and Gelhart opened fire and slug-cut the legs out from under one of them, the Germans stayed down.

Hondergriff, pulling back the bolt of his Spectre SMG, said when the lull came, "Now's the time to use the radio and get the chopper here. We can move out the front, go up the east side, and reach the Garden of the Moon. Let's get the hell out of here."

"I can't use the radio in here," Camellion almost had to shout at him when the firing began again. "There's too much danger that the antenna might be hit by a slug. We'll also be able to transmit better outside, in the open. The stones won't be hemming in the signals."

Camellion, who now had his own Spectre ready to fire, didn't get a chance to yell at Dillman and Gelhart and tell them to crawl back to him and Hondergriff.

"Oh, my God!" Hondergriff exclaimed hoarsely. "Paracommandos —coming through the main entrance!"

He might as well have said, *Our number has come up, and it's a black thirteen!*

Prone on the floor, the Death Merchant swiveled his body around and saw that half a dozen commandos were moving cautiously along the sides of the wide entrance. There wasn't any doubt as to their identity. There they were, red berets, Dennison-type combat coats, and FAL assault rifles.

"Don't fire until you have to," Camellion whispered, thinking of Rudyard Kipling's "Charge of the Light Brigade." *Only it's not cannons to the left and the right of us! It's FAL assault rifles!*

He turned and looked north, and saw his possible executioners staring him in the face. Paracommandos were creeping through both entrances to the west, through the single entrance toward the center of the east wall, and through the arched doorway to the north. Camellion and his "mighty" force of three, plus one captive, were completely surrounded. Escape from the building was impossible.

There was only one refuge, the three *kos minars* seventy-five feet west of the east wall, straight across, to the east, from where Camellion and his men were grouped. The nobles and other dignitaries had bathed in the large pool of the Temple of the Rain. The *kos minars* had been reserved for the lowly dancing girls who performed before Akbar, each of whom had to be a virgin and "blessed" in the "holy" waters of a *kos minars*. Each *kos minars*, made of stone and above ground, was three and a half feet tall and eighteen feet in diameter.

"Run for one of the empty bathing pools to the east," Camellion yelled so that Dillman and Gelhart would hear him. By then, the commandos of the 50th Parachute Brigade were storming through both west-side entrances and firing at the East Germans. With their FALs on full automatic, the commandos raked the square pillars, chopping down the Germans before they could even put up a good defense. Karl Hossinger died with blood pouring from a dozen bullet holes. Friedrich Seckendorff went down with his stomach and intestines shot out.

Firing short bursts at the Indians crouched by the sides of the main entrance to the south, the Death Merchant and his men and Franz Holtz raced in desperation toward the closest *kos minars*. The only thing that had saved them from total annihilation was that their sudden action—their jumping up and firing—had caught the commandos to the south off guard. The commandos to the north and the east were too far away to know what was going on while the paras to the west were still approaching the side pillars with caution, still not certain whether they had killed all the Germans on that side.

Camellion and Hondergriff's sudden blast of 9mm Spectre slugs had killed four paratroopers instantly. By the time the other commandos to the east recovered and got into action, the Death Merchant, his three men and their captive were halfway to the first *kos minars* facing the north. But they were still in a storm of silent death. A 7.62mm projectile tore through the shoulder bag—taken from Major Bukashev—that was bumping up and down against Camellion's right hip. There was a loud *ZINGGGgggggg* as the bullet hit the side of an M61 Skorpion submachine gun, the impact making Camellion almost lose his balance. Another bullet missed the rear of his head—horizontally—by only half an inch. Several more projectiles tore through the bottom of his long coat, which was fluttering out behind him.

A slug cut through Barry Dillman's clothes and scraped part of his back where the rear of the two scapula protruded. Another tore off the right heel of his *jabba* boot as his foot was raised. Another came so close, horizontally, to the back of his neck that the metal touched the longer hairs in its passing.

Gelhart, Holtz, and Hondergriff also found themselves in a cloud of flying projectiles. One bullet knocked off Holtz's *nritrya;* another cut across the underneath side of his right wrist, the same bullet, streaking at an angle, almost hitting Rory Gelhart in the right side.

Finally, there was the short and rounded wall of the *kos minars,* and Camellion and the other men were almost throwing themselves over the three-and-a-half-foot-high stones. Inside was their only salvation, at least for the moment.

"AhhhEEEEeeeiiiii!" Hondergriff howled in pain. A FAL bullet had zipped sideways and had cut an inch and a half into his left buttock, leaving behind it a three-inch bloody tunnel before it struck one of the stones in the rounded well of the *kos minars.* Rory Gelhart, already inside the *kos minars,* which was similar to a short-walled, rounded well, grabbed Hondergriff by his left wrist and his left leg, which was half over the wall, and pulled him over and down to safety. Quickly, Hondergriff's pants began to fill with warm blood, making him feel that he had a case of the "runs" and had defecated.

Another score of slugs *zinged, zinged, zinged* from the wall, then nothing but silence, a strange kind of stillness as the paratroopers stopped firing.

"Watch all four sides," said Camellion in a voice that others, including Franz Holtz, considered almost alien. The Death Merchant had unzipped his shoulder bag and was pulling out the Racal-Tacticom hand-held radio. He switched on the transceiver, pulled out the telescoping antenna to its full length of 34.7 inches, and held the set close to his face, at an angle so that only four inches of its antenna protruded above the rounded stones of the *kos minars*.

"This is Eagle-1," Camellion said in a fairly loud voice. "This is Eagle-1. Do you read me, Blackbird. Come in." *(Or we're dead! We might be dead, anyhow, and don't know it yet!)*

"This is Blackbird! You guys ready to pull out?" Chuck Benson's voice was so faint that Camellion could barely hear it.

"Come and get us. We're surrounded in the Temple of the Rain by Indian commandos. That damned Indian whore sold us out to everyone. Come prepared for trouble."

Now Benson's voice was even fainter. "Fuck 'em in the ear. Trouble is our specialty. Hang on, we're on our way. See you guys in a little over 10 minutes."

Major Ghazel Marchchakka stood with Captain Shunta Bliskalmar and Bhabha Jehangir by the side of a Panhard M3 command vehicle, two hundred feet from the southwest corner of the Temple of the Rain. Lieutenant Happuram had just reported by walkie-talkie. The terrorists had taken refuge in one of the virgin baths and seventy-five weapons were trained on them.

Bhabha Jehangir, the DARFA official who had just arrived on the scene, glanced up at the sky, feeling a drop of rain strike his cheek.

"Major, have you ascertained who killed whom inside the temple?"

"Not exactly," answered Marchchakka, lowering his binoculars. "From what the men saw inside, one group met the East German intelligence officer. Another group then surprised them in an ambush. It was then that the third group moved into the building from the west. After the third group was inside, I sent my men in. Whoever survived isn't going anywhere, I can assure you. As you can see, the temple is surrounded."

"What will your next move be?" asked Jehangir. "I suppose you'll now charge them?" For the first time, he noticed that there was a Ramta RBY Mk 1. patrol vehicle and a six-wheeled Alvis Saladin armored car parked in front of the temple. The Saladin was armed with a 1x75mm cannon and a 1x7.62 MG.

Captain Shunta Bliskalmar cleared his throat. Major Marchchakka glanced distastefully at Jehangir. "We could charge the terrorists inside the temple, but we're not going to," he said firmly, thinking of the men he had lost in Delhi on Banda Gupta Road. That mistake had almost cost him his command. "The terrorists are in a position that gives them a clear view of the entire inside. They have a clear field of fire and are using automatic weapons. We would lose a hundred men before we could close in and kill them."

A dissatisfied look dropped over Bhabha Jehangir's dark face. He held out his hand, palm up. Yes, it was beginning to rain.

"Surely, Major Marchchakka, you are not telling me that you intend to let a handful of men stop you and your brigade?"

"Not at all, *Sri* Jehangir," Marchchakka said coolly. "The men will keep the terrorists busy for a short time to make them use their ammo. I'll then have the armored car move in through the front entrance of the temple and blow up a portion of the virgin bath wall. Once the terrorists are exposed to our fire, they will have no choice but to surrender, or commit suicide."

Jehangir nodded slowly. "Yes, that does seem logical, Colonel," he agreed. "Yes, a good plan."

"It's plain common sense," Marchchakka said, his tone slightly sarcastic. "We'll have the terrorists and without losing scores of men. After all, *Sri* Jehangir, DARFA can't question dead men, now, can it?"

Without waiting for Jehangir to answer, Marchchakka turned to Captain Bliskalmar. "Have Lieutenant Happuram open fire. The faster the terrorists use up their ammunition, the faster they will surrender. Let's get out of the rain."

The firing was intense, hundreds of FAL 7.62mm projectiles hitting the rounded north, west, and south sides of the *kos minars.* Hundreds more cut over the head of the Death Merchant and the rest of the men with him and struck the east wall of the temple, the crescendo of ricochets at times a piercing shriek. All Camellion and his men and their captive could do was remain down, hug the floor, and hope that Blackbird arrived on time. Then half of their problem would be solved, the easy half. The other half involved reaching the Garden of the Moon. It was not, however, a "garden." It was a 150-foot square of stones ringed with casuarina trees, directly north of the Temple of the Rain. From the *kos minars,* protecting Camellion and his group, to the center of the Garden of the Moon, the distance was 341 feet, or 4,092 inches. An enemy bullet would come at them with every inch—

unless the fire power of Blackbird created enough confusion to force the paratroopers to be concerned with their own safety.

Barry Dillman raised his head and pushed himself to a sitting position. "Listen! They've stopped firing. I'll bet they're getting ready to rush us, the dumb bastards! We'll cut them to pieces!"

"No, they're not going to charge us," declared Camellion. "They know we could chop down one or two rushes. They're only trying to get us to use as much ammo as possible. Then we'd have to surrender."

"How do you know?" Rory Gelhart fingered the Czech Skorpion he had removed from the shoulder bag that Steve Hondergriff had taken from the corpse of Zhores Unshlikht.

The Death Merchant, a Spectre in one hand, started to move on his knees toward the west side of the rounded *kos minars.* "They tossed too much stuff at us," he said. "That last volley was enough for an army, and they know we're only a handful. Let's accommodate them and make them think we've fallen for the trick."

"Let me have a gun," said Franz Holtz in a low voice, without any trace of an accent. "I have a right to defend myself." He looked from Dillman to Gelhart, then up at Camellion, who had stopped and turned around.

The Death Merchant looked and sounded amused. "We wouldn't give you a pinch of sand if we were in the center of the Great Empty Quarter in Arabia. I'll give you more bad news. You had better hope we don't run out of ammo and have to surrender before the chopper arrives. If we do"——he raised the Spectre SMG and pointed it at Holtz ——"*bang!* You're dead. DARFA will get only your corpse!"

"I was only doing my job for my country!" protested Holtz. "We're all pros. Why take it personal?"

Camellion chuckled. "For 'your country,' huh! How do you reconcile such marvelous patriotism with your double-crossing Mischa Wolf?"

Holtz dismissed Camellion's accusation with a shrug. "What's the difference. You have the PAL. It's in the attaché case." With a handkerchief he wiped his nose on which blood was caked; and there was a long welt across his high forehead.

Rory Gelhart tightened his mouth and his eyes narrowed. Dillman's expression was one of alarm.

"One from four leaves three," muttered Steve Hondergriff, whose hind end felt as if he had been stung by half a dozen hornets.

"Where are the other three PALs?" Camellion demanded in an icy voice. "Or would you prefer to have your head scattered all over the floor?"

"In Chicago," Holtz answered promptly. He knew they had him cold and saw no reason to withhold anything. "I didn't intend to give the Russians all four of the devices at the same time. The other three are in a vault with a storage company—Merton and Jacobi Company in Chicago, on North Halstead Street. There isn't any reason why—"

"Flat on the floor and keep quiet, or I'll stick your mouth in a light socket," the Death Merchant said. "The rest of you fire off half a dozen rounds each, single rounds. Make the paracommandos think we're putting up a fight and have walked into their trap."

"I hope to God you're right," said Dillman, who then shoved his last magazine into the Spectre.

The four of them moved to the north, the south, and the west of the rounded well, Gelhart going with the Death Merchant to the north. It wasn't necessary to watch the east side. Any paratroopers coming from the east would first have to move in from the north or the south.

Slowly they raised themselves and looked over the top of the wall. They couldn't see any Indians in the entrances, but they could discern the barrels of FAL A-Rs protruding from the sides of the fronts of the wide doorways. The Death Merchant and the others rapidly triggered off 9mm rounds from their Spectres, spacing each shot and aiming at various areas of the entrances except the one to the north. It was too far away. Then they dropped and waited for a reply.

An answer they got—FAL assault rifles roared and again hundreds of 7.62mm projectiles ricocheted from the outside stones of the rounded well, the firing so intense that a small cloud of stone dust began to rise into the humid air filled with the fumes of burnt gunpowder. Just before the firing stopped, another sound began to intrude, the faint *flub-flub-flub-flub* of a rotor. Blackbird had almost arrived.

There wasn't any wind or thunder or lightning, the rain, a halfway hard shower, coming straight down. The rain didn't bother Captain Chuck Benson at the controls of the Westland Commando-2 gunship. He was used to flying in all kinds of weather—except a tornado.

Lieutenant Pete Trapp flipped the switch that turned on the 16-Y Ubba chain gun, which fired a 20-millimeter shell. He leaned forward and grasped the turn-and-firing handles. "How do you want to do it, Chuck?"

"There's only one way. We'll rake everything in sight, then sit down on the stones in back of the temple," Benson said lazily. "We did the recon on foot days ago and know where we're going. It'll be a turkey shoot." He spoke into his throat mike. "You ready back there, Bernie?"

"Yeah, let's go in and smear the bastards," came back the reply.

"Hang on. Here we go," Benson said with a laugh.

The gunship—its two Rolls-Royce Ghome turboshaft engines roaring, its five-bladed rotor cutting the rain—roared in. Never had any group of men been trapped so rapidly, the reason being that the paracommandos assumed that the helicopter belonged to the Indian air force.

Benson first roared east, then banked and, at only 175 altitude, flew west so that Bernie Hunter, on the starboard side, could open up with his brace of Browning 50-caliber heavies. For this mission the Browning heavy machine guns contained special ammunition. Every third round was a Rond-D projectile, geared to explode on contact. Every fourth 20-millimeter shell of the electric Ubba five-barreled cannon was a Rond-D.

Hunter, body straps around his waist and shoulders, opened fire with a vengeance, the big Browning heavies filling the sky with thunder. In only seconds, thirteen paracommandos crouched by the left side of the temple's front entrance were blown up. The bodies of four of the men literally exploded from the Rond-D rounds. Browning projectiles wrecked a Ramta RBY Mk. 1. patrol vehicle, but missed an Alvis Saladin armored car that was turning and apparently headed for the main entrance of the temple. More 50-cal projectiles rained over the top of a Panhard M3 command vehicle as Benson banked and took the gunship north. Now more paratroopers were cut down before they could even raise their FAL assault rifles and fire at the killbird butchering them. In their fear, many of the paratroopers ran through the west entrances of the temple to escape the hail of death. Most of those who did were cut down by the Death Merchant and his men. A few escaped by getting down by the west-side square pillars.

In only seconds, Benson was banking and making the run north of the temple and flying over the Garden of the Moon. More Indian paracommandos died, and so did paratroopers on the east side of the Temple of the Rain after the eggbeater turned and was moving up the east side and heading south. Some of the paracommandos attempted to escape by running through the rain across the seventy-five-foot space between the east side of the temple and the west side of the Bi'kuk, the mint of the Ghost City. Some were lucky. They escaped the hail of 50-cal projectiles. Most of the commandos on the east side did not.

This time Benson was very careful in how he banked. It was time for Pete Trapp to take over with the electric chain-gun cannon. Both were worried about the armored car they had seen turning north. Should the Saladin be able to roll through the wide entrance and begin to lob shells at Canover and his men with its 75mm turret cannon, they would not have one chance to live.

It was the Alvis Saladin that "died." The Ubba chain gun could fire ten 20-millimeter rounds per second. In only four seconds, forty projectiles struck the rear right side and the end of the armored car, which by then was halfway through the main entrance. The vehicle exploded with a roar and a large flash of fire and smoke, the intense concussion tossing parts and pieces of the vehicle and its crew to every point of the compass. All that remained was burning junk, black smoke, and parts of bodies and blood mingling with the rain beating down on the stones.

Pete Trapp turned the chain-gun cannon, underneath the nose of the Westland, toward the Panhard M3 command car, which had moved from its original position and was now lumbering west in an effort to escape execution, Major Marchchakka screaming at the terrified driver to hurry, Bhabha Jehangir and Captain Shunta Bliskalmar praying to all three gods of the Hindu trinity. Neither Brahma, nor Vishnu, nor Siva heard their pleas.

BBBBBBBRRRRRRRRRRRRRRRRRRRR! Fifty 20-MM projectiles hit the Panhard, forty-eight going easily through the thin armor plate, twelve exploding with the force of a dozen hand grenades. For the space of a heartbeat there was only flame and smoke as the command car turned itself and its four occupants into hot, twisted metal decorated with bloody parts of arms and legs and other parts of bodies, including internal organs. Major Marchchakka's head flew fifty feet into the air before falling to the stones and bouncing for several feet like a basketball running out of air. When the smoke cleared, the Panhard command vehicle was gone, except for part of the blackened frame and one rear tire that was burning fiercely.

"We'll make one more run, then put down in the Garden of the

Moon," Benson said. All the while Trapp continued to fire short bursts. *BBBBRRRRRRR-BRRRRRRRRRRR-BRRRRRRRRRRR!*

The instant that Bernie Hunter began firing his brace of heavy Browning machine guns, the Death Merchant and his men prepared to make the race for life—north to the Garden of the Moon. To facilitate speed, Camellion had placed the one PAL device in his shoulder bag and the other men had divested themselves of all nonessentials except weapons.

"I don't think I can do it," Steve Hondergriff said with a sigh of finality. "Everytime I move, my ass feels like someone is sticking an ice pick into it."

"You'll do it!" Camellion said sharply. "You'll go over the wall and *run*, or I'll kick your arse all the way there!"

"Be realistic!" Hondergriff said, half in anger. "I'll only hold the rest of you up. There's no sense in all of us getting killed. Leave Holtz here with me and I'll put a slug into him before the Indians get here."

"Canover's right!" Dillman glanced at Hondergriff and jammed the last magazine into a Ruger autoloader. "If you die, you'll die with us."

"Stop being a crybaby and feeling sorry for yourself," snapped the Death Merchant. "Get on your feet and move—or I'll move you and I mean it."

Shaking his head, Hondergriff got to his feet.

Listening to the deafening roar of the chopper's chain gun, they crawled over the wall when the Westland was making its run north on the west side of the temple. As far as Camellion and his men could tell, the inside of the building was free of commandos, although they had to assume that some paratroopers, who had sought to escape the deadly fire of the chopper, were lurking behind stone columns on both sides.

Not a shot was fired as they climbed over the wall and started to move north. Keeping low, they did their best to watch the edges of the square columns to the east and the west, Camellion relieved to see that Hondergriff, although in pain, was managing to keep up with the rest of them. The Death Merchant had assumed that once Hondergriff was in the open, his sense of self-preservation would overpower the pain in his butt—and it had.

They were halfway to the north-side entrance and the chopper was swinging to the west in front of the temple when one of the commandos, who had run inside the temple to escape the chopper, leaned out and tried to fire into the group with his FAL. However, Camellion spotted him before he could trigger the assault rifle and fired on the run, using the Spectre in his right hand. Two 9mm projectiles hit the paratrooper in the chest and he fell back as two commandos to the far west side and one Indian on the east side leaned out from behind pillars and opened fire.

The paracommando on the east side fired blindly and too quickly. His stream of 7.62mm slugs cut by Camellion's right side, sped by Rory Gelhart's left side and Dillman's right arm, then went bye-bye. The paratrooper did not have time to move his FAL and try again. The Death Merchant cut him down with the Stechkin machine pistol in his left hand, two pieces of 9x19-millimeter metal hitting Buru Chagapok in the midsection. His scream sounded like the tortured yell of a puppy that had been kicked.

Franz Holtz was as unlucky as the paracommando. Ten feet behind the Death Merchant and in front of Steve Hondergriff and Barry Dillman, Holtz was in the right place at the right time—to die. Four 7.62mm projectiles popped him in the left lower side and the upper hip, the impact knocking him sideways. The projectiles had cut through vital organs and arteries and the shock had kicked him into instant unconsciousness. He was only minutes from death as his body hit the floor.

Dillman and Hondergriff raked the pillars to the west. One para went down, blood pouring from his mouth and from bullet holes in his chest. The second para pulled back and began to reload his FAL A-R.

Closer and closer loomed the wide north-side entrance, and faster and faster ran the Death Merchant and the others, including Steve Hondergriff, who, wanting to live, hardly felt any pain in his buttock. The four of them were only thirty feet from the north side opening when another commando stepped out from behind an east-side pillar and fired a long burst at hip level. The burst of spitzer-shaped FAL slugs cut at a steep angle into Barry Dillman's back and killed him on the spot, some of the 7.62mms narrowly missing Hondergriff's right side. Both Hondergriff and Gelhart spun around and snap-fired at the sound of the FAL. The paratrooper stopped two of Hondergriff's Vitmorkin with his chest. His stomach got in the way of three of Rory Gelhart's 9mm Spectre slugs. The joker died as quickly as Dillman.

Harsha Pratap, the last paratrooper, was behind the last pillar to the north on the east side. The pillar was only eleven feet from the north-side entrance. The Death Merchant saw Pratap during the same moment that the commando leaned out and squeezed the trigger of his assault rifle. Still on the run, Camellion fired the Spectre and the Stechkin machine pistol a micromoment later. He cried out in pain as one of the 7.62mm pieces of hot metal cut through his pants and raked across his right hip, leaving a bloody two-inch-long gash behind it. Still another slug cut through the fleshy part of his right thigh on the inside, the second slug almost knocking him off his feet. During that flash of a second the Death Merchant knew that neither wound was life-threatening; they were only painful and bloody. Yet he had the satisfaction of knowing that Pratap would never again squeeze another trigger. Camellion's blast of slugs had hit him in the chest and lower throat and he was stretched out on the stones, blood jumping out of his throat, the stream weakening as his heart weakened.

Rory Gelhart had not been as lucky as Camellion. Some of Pratap's slugs had missed him. Three had not. They had hit him in the front, on the left. One had zipped through his stomach. The second and the third had bored through his lower chest. It was the third piece of metal that cut through the brachial artery. Feeling his legs turning to air and his body moving backward, Gelhart couldn't believe what was happening. Then he didn't have to. He became unconscious and was only seconds from the Big Blackness.

This was the most dangerous part, and Benson knew it—putting the bird down. Slugs could always hit the rotor hub or the engine, or strike the tail rotor. For that matter, a blast of bullets might strike the cockpit. He had brought the chopper down so that its nose pointed east and Bernie Hunter could use the starboard Brownings against the entrance in the north wall. The Westland Commando-2 hovered only a foot above the stones of the Garden of the Moon, the engines making a terrific noise.

"How much time are we going to give them?" Pete Trapp wiped sweat from his face. "We're right in the center of the bull's-eye here."

"Five minutes, no more," Benson said. He stared toward the north entrance, his hand steady on the collective control. "Canover is an experienced stone killer. He started his boys this way the moment he heard us making the approach."

Two minutes had passed by the time Richard Camellion and Steve Hondergriff appeared in the north-end opening and Bernie Hunter began waving them to his right so that he could fire a burst of 50-

caliber slugs through the entrance. As soon as they had moved the twenty-one feet to their left and had the north wall of the temple to their backs, Hunter fired a five-second burst through the entrance, moving the brace of big Brownings from left to right. Two of the projectiles struck the para who had been to the west. He had reloaded his FAL and was moving in for final shots, determined to kill the men who had murdered so many of his friends, when he was hit by two big projectiles that tore his heart and lungs from his chest.

Bone weary, Camellion and Hondergriff ran to the chopper and, fighting the terrific downdraft from the big rotor, crawled through the cargo opening on the port side. Neither had a chance to stand as Captain Benson pulled back on the collective and turned the handle of the throttle. The helicopter shot upward and continued to rise and grab gray, wet sky. Benson took the bird upward several hundred feet before he tilted pitch and, while still moving upward at an angle, took the chopper southwest.

Methodically, Bernie Hunter swung the hot Browning MGs inside and closed the starboard doors. He moved across to port, slid the door shut, then unstrapped the first aid kit from the wall. Only after he had the kit in one hand did he turn and grin at the Death Merchant and Steve Hondergriff. Both men were now standing and hanging on to handholds.

"I see the two of you have had a rough afternoon," Hunter cracked, for a moment staring at Camellion and Hondergriff's rain-wet, blood-soaked clothes. "Well, let's see what we can do about those wounds."

He opened the first aid kit.

Hondergriff's voice was uncertain. "How close are we to the Indian-Pak border?"

He had addressed his question to Camellion, but it was Hunter who answered. "Sixteen miles or twenty-five klicks, whichever you prefer," he answered affably. He took out bandages, swabs, and a bottle of alcohol from the metal cabinet. "Then it's 46 miles, or 74 klicks, to Sialkot. This baby will do 153 miles an hour. That's 230 klicks in an hour. Shucks, we'll be there before you guys even have time to get comfortable."

"Those two Muslim guards at the entrance." Hondergriff turned and looked at the Death Merchant. "They shouldn't have been armed. That they were bothers me."

"They weren't Muslims," said Camellion, who started to move toward a bench bolted to the fuselage on the port side. "They were paracommandos. We walked into a trap. But fate saw fit for you and me to walk out of it, or we wouldn't be here!"

"I wonder why," mused Hondergriff.

Camellion didn't answer. He knew why. *The Cosmic Lord of Death is saving us for another time . . . in another place. . . .*

Aftermath

14.00 hours.
Langley, Virginia, U.S.A.
Six days after Richard Camellion's return to the United States.

The Death Merchant sensed that something was very wrong. He had known Courtland Grojean for any number of years and could always tell when the chief of the CIA's covert division was hedging or putting on an act. The Fox was doing his best to act pleased. *And he's not doing a very good job of it. For the moment, let's go along with his little game.*

Camellion, still walking with the aid of a cane because of the wound in his right thigh, leaned forward in the plus wing chair, one hand on top of the cane. "I trust your people retrieved the other three PALs for the storage company's vault in Chicago, or was Holtz lying?"

Grojean, sitting behind his desk, unbuttoned his Martinique blazer and nodded. "Over a week ago," he said. "The three devices were in a shoe box. It was clever of Holtz. Of course, he outsmarted himself in the end. It's a shame you weren't able to bring him back to stand trial."

Camellion knew Grojean was lying. There were always those things that happened in the United States that were carefully kept from the prying media and that nonentity known as "the people." The last thing the United States Government wanted would be a public trial for Franz Holtz. What would "the people" think if they should learn that a foreign agent had penetrated the factory security where nuclear warheads were assembled?

Camellion smiled knowingly, enjoying the way Grojean looked questioningly at him. "Courtland, why don't you stop this charade and tell the truth. I'm too old for fairy tales."

"What do you mean? What's to tell?" Grojean pretended ignorance, but his eyes revealed surprise and extreme caution.

"I know that the Justice Department wouldn't bring Holtz to trial if I had dumped him on your doorstep tied in a red, white, and blue ribbon. I also know you're trying to, as the Russians say, *ochkovtiratel stvo!* When you're attempting to 'throw dust in my face.' It's the Russian idiom for either an insult or a cover-up. In this case, it's both. You're trying a cover-up and you're insulting my intelligence by doing so!"

Grojean folded his arms and gave a polite laugh.

"Death Merchant, I think—"

"Don't call me that!"

"Camellion, I think you're being paranoid. You're dancing with shadows. You're trying to find a four-sided triangle."

"I wish I were," said Camellion, the sureness in his voice making Grojean edgy. "A four-sided triangle is easy to locate. It's nothing more than a three-dimensional pyramid. Quit the stalling. What are you concealing?"

Grojean stared fixedly at the Death Merchant. He and Richard Camellion were not friends. They didn't even like each other! Theirs was an arrangement that was an unusual relationship. Nonetheless, Grojean, now that he was trapped, did not want this to be the first time he would hold something back from the enigma sitting in front of him.

"Very well, Camellion. We didn't think you'd be able to find Holtz, not in India."

The last piece of the puzzle dropped into place in Camellion's computerized mind. *Fudge!*

"Which is another way of saying I wasn't supposed to find Holtz and the PALs! It was a setup, a false operation!"

Grojean shifted his weight in the chair and appeared to be uncomfortable.

"We were wise to Holtz and Erika Hoffman a year before Holtz made his move," Grojean patiently explained. "Don't ask me how we knew. That is definitely ultrasecret—and we knew what he was after. Part of the difficulty was that we didn't know when Holtz would try to steal one or more of the PALs after he had the opportunity. We had to do a lot of triple planning to make sure he would take the PALs we wanted him to grab."

"Fake or altered devices you hoped he would take to Mischa Wolf," the Death Merchant interjected.

"Exactly. However, we were puzzled why Wolf and the MfS wanted the PALs. We still don't know. The real break for us came when we learned that Holtz intended to defect to the Soviet Union. By then, he had grabbed four PALs and fled. It was then that we wanted him to get to the KGB. We knew that Soviet scientists would faithfully copy the PALs we altered. Once they did, the Soviet missile program would be set back several years."

"You should have made it easy for Holtz. Why call me in?"

Grojean sighed and began toying with a stainless steel letter opener. "We had to make it look good to the KGB and the MfS. We knew once you learned he was in India, you'd go after him. We didn't, however, think you'd corner him."

Camellion's eyes met Grojean's levelly. "Did you manage to find out about Holtz's girl friend, or haven't your contacts in India learned anything yet?"

Grojean's granite face gave birth to his version of a smile.

"That broad bothers you, doesn't she?"

"Selfishness always has its reason. I'm positive I never met her. Yet she was familiar in a subliminal way."

"You're on target, Camellion," Grojean said with thin irony. "We're not sure, but we think her name was Suri'an Nushinobey. She was the half-sister of Dev Nargis. We're not sure, though. Not enough data has come back yet."

Satisfied, the Death Merchant nodded. "Your other agents in India, specifically the ones who assisted me. They didn't know it was a cover operation? I know that Stanley and Theimer thought the mission was genuine."

Grojean carefully placed the letter opener next to the green telephone. "You know the answer," he said slyly. "The others couldn't be told the truth. They had to do their best. They had to give everything they had when they helped you."

"They certainly did give everything! They gave their lives, except for Steve Hondergriff. Sure, it happens. They died for a 'noble cause' and all the rest of the croc crap that goes with it."

Grojean, trying to sound pleasant, changed the subject. "A hundred thousand American has been placed in your account in Switzerland. Speaking of Europe . . ."

Camellion was at once on full alert, detecting that certain note in Grojean's low voice. "There's far more to Europe than Switzerland. Spread out all the cards, faceup."

Grojean leaned forward in the manner of a conspirator, even though his private office was soundproof, had two white-sound generators going constantly, was checked twice a day for hidden transmitters, and had special windows. Not only was the double glass bulletproof, the panes contained strips of Raysil as protection against microwave detectors picking up voice vibrations.

"Camellion, what do you know about the Shroud of Turin?"

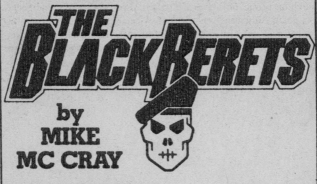

Return to the savage
storm of VIETNAM
in some of today's
best novels.

____	BODY COUNT, William Huggett	11392-X	$3.95
____	CENTRIFUGE, J.C. Pollock	11156-0	3.95
____	CROSSFIRE, J.C. Pollock	11602-3	3.95
____	THE DYING PLACE, David Maurer	12183-3	3.50
____	FRAGMENTS, Jack Fuller,	12687-8	3.50
____	GOING AFTER CACCIATO, Tim O'Brien	32966-3	4.95
____	THE KILLING FIELDS, Christopher Hudson	14459-0	3.50
____	MISSION M.I.A., J.C. Pollock	15819-3	3.50
____	NEVERLIGHT, Donald Pfarrer	36291-1	4.95
____	SAIGON, Anthony Grey	17580-1	4.95

At your local bookstore or use this handy coupon for ordering:

DELL READERS SERVICE—DEPT. B1558B
6 REGENT ST., LIVINGSTON, N.J. 07039

Please send me the above title(s) I am enclosing $ _____ (please add 75¢ per copy to cover postage and handling). Send check or money order—no cash or CODs Please allow 3-4 weeks for shipment

Ms./Mrs./Mr. _____

Address _____

City/State _____ Zip _____